Deadly Undercurrents

Book 2 of Keeper and His Tiger

A Novel by **Aidan Red**

Copyright

To my family and friends that have supported me and have made the challenge of creating and bringing life to my stories so rewarding.

◻-◻-◻-◻-◻

My many thanks to my editors and cover designer.

Content Editing by Trenda London,
http://ItsYourStoryContentEditing.com

Copy Editing by Amy Jackson,
Copy Editing and Proofreading, http://AmyJacksonEditing.com

Cover by Amy Queau,
Q Design Covers and Premades, www.QCoverDesign.com

Tiger's tenacity usually got her into trouble, but nothing like the night she went searching for clues...in the woods...alone...

Contents

Contents
(Continued)

Prologue

Friday, May 6

Billy Mattis stared at her computer monitor in her office at Boster, Lange and Hammersmith Architectural Designs, and the contract she was comparing with the client's design requirements document on the project Carl Boster had assigned her. She was supposed to be checking for discrepancies between the two, but her mind kept drifting back to Frederick Westman's confrontation with the design firm's senior partner, Mike Hammersmith, when he had come in and loudly announced he would no longer do business with Mike or his company. That was the project to renovate the Duckard's Department Store buildings. Westman was supposed to purchase the properties for back taxes, but the properties were never in arrears, there were no back taxes to pay, and he had been unable to purchase the properties.

Mike Hammersmith had lived up to the rumors of his unscrupulousness and mitigated his design firm's potential losses by slipping a healthy default penalty payment clause into his contract with Westman. When time had run out for the project, Westman had barged into Hammersmith's office and all hell broke loose. It was unfortunate, and Billie knew there was nothing she could do but ride out the storm and concentrate on the other, less-glorified projects her boss, Carl Boster, gave her.

Thinking of Hammersmith made her remember Billy telling her about losing his parents in a fiery car wreck and seeing the man walking away carrying a gas can. A shiver ran down her back as she remembered him describing the homeless man they had found in the alleys, admitting to helping cause a car wreck and then setting it on fire to be sure the occupants were dead.

Billy had said the man named Hammersmith was the one that paid the man two thousand dollars to do it. Then, out of deep contrition and seeking to atone his actions, the man had killed himself. At the time, Billie had unexpectedly formed an image in her mind of the contrite man with blood money spilling out of his pockets, torn between the feeling of deep despair and that of having more money than he probably had ever seen.

Then happier thoughts came to mind: those of her and Billy Carson—the "sanitation technician," as he called himself—at the Streetcar Diner. Reconnecting after meeting him fifteen years prior, Billie had been surprised at how familiar he felt and how comfortable she felt being with him, their adult personalities clicking in ways she had never thought possible. She grinned at the thought of their engagement and how it had come about, initially a ruse to protect her when she went with him to volunteer at the soup kitchen in the less-desirable northeast part of town. Billie's friends often mentioned she had a roguish streak in her, matching her redheaded temper, but this time it had really taken the cake; the ruse quickly changed, and against all rational arguments became a reality, and it was obvious to her that he wanted it to be true as much as she did. The horse rancher's daughter had truly fallen for the Streetcar Diner's dishwasher.

She looked at the chain design wrapping around her left wrist, making her smile grow wider. The design was not actually as permanent as a tattoo, but it had become permanent in their hearts, even though he had not actually asked her to marry him. Yet.

Then she thought about Mr. Lange's admonition and Mike Hammersmith's irrational *hatred* for tattoos, of any kind, and anyone that wore them. "Do *not* let Mr. Hammersmith see that," he had said, pointing to her wrist tat. He had been adamant, and after hearing Hammersmith's sudden change when Westman confronted him, Billie had paid attention to Robert's words and stayed clear of Mike, especially on his less-than-good days. And there seemed to be a lot of those.

Her thoughts were a jumbled mess, trying to balance things

in her life that made her fearful with the things that made her happy. But she still had worries, and her thoughts jumped from her first frightening, fear-filled encounter in the homeless village to Billy and his friends helping her learn how to defend herself. Then she thought of Billy's friend, the dark-haired woman she had seen him with, and the doubt she had harbored took her straight to the memory of her abusive ex, Blake. She shuddered. The last time she had seen him, she had had to have security forcefully remove him from her apartment. The bruises were finally gone, but the memories were still vivid. At least being with Billy was helping her to forget.

Leaving the chaos in her mind behind, she forced herself to think about the happy past weeks with Billy, but she quickly remembered those he lived with in the Duckard's basement and their newest dilemma. They had permission to be there, but the owners had unexpectedly hired Kelly and Lloyd Architects out of Chicago and they had applied for real renovation permits. She worried for Billy because he and the others would have to move. She was concerned about what would happen to them and where they would go once the construction began. Billy had only said they would work something out. He was good at looking ahead and solving problems, but she was still worried. There were twenty of them, including the four kids. At least the homeless living in the village on Tenth West and Hadley did not seem affected by the renovation project.

Billie sighed and switched her computer off, anticipating a quiet lunch with her longtime friends Becky and Lori, and an evening out with them and Stacy, if she was of a mind to meet. The four of them had restarted their girls' nights out after she had gotten Blake out of her life, and resumed the occasional lunches at the Streetcar Diner. Today was one of those lunches and evenings out.

She was taking her coat from the rack beside her office door when she heard her name called. She looked up and saw Mr. Hammersmith looking at her through his open office door.

Shit! Not now!

She had been avoiding him since Robert Lange had warned

her, but she knew she could not avoid him this time.

He beckoned and she saw Mr. Lange turn to see her. She folded her jacket over her arm and the tat, slipped her purse strap over her neck, and walked to his office. She was careful to keep her coat over her wrist and saw the disappointment in Mr. Lange's face when she entered.

"Yes, Mr. Hammersmith?" she asked politely, and stopped in the doorway.

"Billie," he said by way of a minimal greeting. "Have you found out anything about the owners of the Duckard property?"

"No, sir. Nothing of value," she said, and glanced at Mr. Lange. "I haven't worked that project in a couple of weeks."

"What was the name you found?" he persisted. "The owners."

"Pas...Pastoric Group," she said. "I don't know what it means and I did not find anything on them from the internet or any city sources."

"But I believe the titles were in some other names," he said.

"Yes, sir," she admitted. "Tri-Funds and CR Associates. My suspicion is they are divisions or subsidiaries of Pastoric, but I couldn't find anything to prove it."

She absently made a flat gesture with her right hand to signify finding nothing. Her coat slipped with her inadvertent movement and she quickly grabbed it, slipping it back over the tat.

Mr. Hammersmith saw the inked chain.

"What's that?" he asked loudly.

"What?" she asked, startled by his sudden change.

"On your wrist. What is it?" he said, pointing.

"It's a partnership chain," she explained, holding her voice calm, vividly remembering Mr. Lange's words.

You should've taken that off. Mr. Lange warned you.

4

I know, but I don't want to take it off. Billy wouldn't want me to.

He wouldn't want you to get fired, either.

"I got engaged last week—"

"No one is allowed to wear tattoos in this company!" he shouted, and struck his desktop.

"That's silly, sir. There's nothing in the policy manual prohibiting them. Many people may have them and may just have them where you can't see them," she said, trying to lighten his mood.

"Well, I see that one and I don't like it," he shouted, louder.

Shit! Really?

"Sir, it's hardly something to get worked up over," she said, trying again.

"I will not have employees that stoop to the ways and morals of the rubbish in the streets! Either you have that removed or I will have you removed!"

Well, damn! I sure hope Billy will understand where this is going.

"That won't be necessary," she said calmly, and squared her shoulders. "I like working here, but I do not have to suffer an irrational tyrant for a boss. I have many friends among the rubbish, as you call them, and they have higher morals and ethical values than some I have had the misfortune to work with."

"Get out, you, you, miscreant! You're fired! I don't ever want to see your face around here again!"

She looked at Mr. Lange and nodded. "It was very nice working with you, sir. Thank you. Please tell Mr. Boster the same for me." She looked at Hammersmith and abruptly recalled the image of the homeless man with blood money spilling out of his pockets. "Maybe this is for the best."

Billie turned, and with a slow, measured pace, walked back to her office to box up her personal items.

5

Damn irrational bastard!

So now what are you going to do? You knew this had to happen!

I did! I wasn't going to take the tat off and Hammersmith wasn't going to like it when he saw it. So I guess I knew it was coming. All right? I admit it!

She inhaled, taking a deep breath, and held it for a moment.

What are the folks going to say?

Nothing. I see no reason to burden them with this minor setback.

Minor setback?

Yeah. I'm okay financially—the lease is paid up and I can make the utilities. I can train and help Billy more now. Something good has to come out of that. Right?

You ought to sue Hammersmith! He has no legal leg to stand on for firing you for a tattoo! You could understand if it was a hateful or suggestive tat, but—

Billie smiled and shook her head at the thought of her wearing a suggestive tat as she collected a letter storage box from the supply closet.

I know, but a discrimination lawsuit will just hurt Carl and Robert. They aren't the bad guys here. I'll just have to think of something else.

Back in her office, Billie started collecting the few personal things she had, like the pictures of her folks, her sister, the desk set with her name *Billie Mattis* engraved on it, and a few other odds and ends.

Hah, I know! Mr. Hammersmith has no idea what he's just done! He's just freed me up to help Billy nail him for his parents' death.

She chuckled.

That's the perfect karma for a man like him.

Thirty-Two

Friday, May 6

Billy closed the dishwasher doors and walked to the bathroom off the kitchen and dry room that Sid and Mary had built for him shortly after he started work at the Streetcar. He hung his white apron on the hook beside the door and walked back through the kitchen, nodding to Sid as he entered the hallway leading to his and Mary's home behind the diner. Billy always felt a little guilty for taking time away from his work to use Sid's computer and take care of "other" business, but Sid always told him he understood. It was necessary.

Every month since he had turned twenty-one, it was necessary.

He slid the chair closer to the desk, switched the computer on, and waited for it to boot. Then, when the initial system activity settled, he selected a network path to the second router and opened an associated browser. The home screen came up, and he input a URL for Pastoric Group with a number of embedded control characters, and a full black screen immediately displayed. Billy smiled, and without a prompt, typed *Circular Reference* followed by three spaces and *1hairBall*.

The screen slowly brightened and filled with random, small floating squares of changing colors that swirled and finally merged into a three-dimensional, three-turn, twisted torus centered on the screen. Again, without a prompt, he entered his Tri-Funds ID and password, *WCH3*, three spaces, and then *3dogFleas*. Another screen coalesced from a mottled background and listed a number of selections.

Opening the first selection in the list, he double-checked the status of the recent corporate taxes paid and read the accountant's summary, assuring himself the past year was clean and the payments for the current year were properly queued for automatic disbursement. Satisfied, he accepted the retainer amounts for both accounting and legal and submitted his approval.

Billy quickly opened the second—a long listing of local charities—and quickly stepped through the list of donations assigned to each. At the end of the list, he keyed the "submit" button and returned to the main menu. Next on the menu were real estate properties, and he stepped through the list, accepting the monthly tax estimates and management fees budgeted for each. But when he reached the city center properties, he noted the new architect's initial billing and approved the amount. He clicked the submit icon.

Billy spent nearly an hour going through all of the items that needed his attention, finally coming to the last topic, trusts. He confirmed the status of each active trust, especially those set up for favored persons' personal income and irrevocable medical insurance policies, then considered the newest on the list, the River Crest Trust. When he had finished double-checking the investment principals and the monthly distributions, and satisfied himself the accounts were viable, properly liquid, and the distribution arrangements were correct, he submitted his acceptance.

He sat back and absently stared at the monitor, thinking about what he should say in his greeting to Mike Hammersmith. His mind kept coming back to a curiosity, and he realized he was missing one piece in the puzzle: he did not know what Mike Hammersmith was planning to do in his plan to renovate the Duckard building.

He scratched his head and knew he needed those details before he could start his next step to intimidate and lure Mike. Billy chuckled to himself. Greg Madison, the Operations Manager at Pastoric, had provided the email addresses Billy had requested, and now he had to wait because of his own folly. He had missed a significant detail and wondered if his absentmindedness was because he was spending so much time with Billie, or if it was the tensions of the situation and his slowly increasing lack of sleep.

With the thought of Billie, he leaned back in his chair and touched each memory he had of her since they met again. *Was it really just three weeks and three days ago?* So much had changed, for him, and he knew a lot had changed for her. The first week after they had met again over the broken bowl of soup, she had followed him to find out where he lived, often into the worst, most dangerous parts of town—especially for an attractive woman alone. He smiled. At least he got her to stop following him until they could talk, one on one.

He remembered her inviting him up to her place and his shock when she asked him to take her with him when he volunteered at the soup kitchen. He had argued with her and finally was swayed by her tenacity and the clothes she put on to dress down and look more like the people she saw at the village. He relented, asking God for patience and strength, and showed her what she would have to do to fit in.

Billy smiled, remembering that was the night, on their way back from the kitchen, on their way into the city center to face Pink, he had recalled the ten-year-old freckle-faced red-haired girl from his childhood holding him in a tight, teary goodbye hug before he and his parents left their ranch on that unexpectedly significant Labor Day evening. That was when he had remembered he had loved her then, and realized that now he loved the grown-up woman she had become. They had hardly spent a day without seeing each other since that night.

Chuckling, shaking his thoughts of their engagement and of a possible future together from his mind, Billy returned to the task at hand, leaned forward, forearms on the desk, and stroked the keyboard. *Maybe Billie can remember what Mike was planning to do with the Duckard's renovation,* he thought as the torus screen returned to the monitor. He logged out with the password *vanish,* and then from the black screen with *illuminate.* When Sid's desktop reappeared, he switched the second router off, verified the network link had disappeared, and then logged his user off, leaving Sid's computer as it was when he had sat down.

◻-◻-◻-◻-◻

Becky and Lori were in a booth at the front window, enjoying the bright midday sunshine and casually studying menus when Billie stepped into the Streetcar Diner and embraced the room-filling murmurs of the lunch crowd. She went straight to their booth, slid in beside Lori, and glanced at the archway with the saloon-style swinging doors into the kitchen.

"Sorry I'm late, but you'll never guess what happened," Billie began just as Angie stopped beside the table.

"Hey, Billie," Angie said, interrupting their budding conversation. "Do you want to hear the specials?"

"Hey, Angie. Sure," Billie said, and listened as Angie rattled them off, while Lori and Becky watched Billie and Angie's familiarity in surprise.

"The chicken fry sounds great! Baked instead of mashed, butter only, fried green beans, small chef salad, Italian, and water," Billie said after hearing the choices.

"Have you been exercising?" Angie asked as she entered her order in the handheld pad. "Your face is looking a little thinner."

"Yeah, thanks," Billie admitted. "A lot of walking and a pretty strenuous workout four or five times a week. I'm so hungry I could eat a horse."

"Well, we don't serve that here, but your routine's working. It's showing. Just don't overdo it. You were pretty trim to start with. Hey, Billy has one just like that," Angie said, and took Billie's left hand to look at the chain. "Exactly, I'd say." Angie smiled knowingly and let her hand go.

"Is he here?" Billie asked, and got up when Angie nodded. "Excuse me a sec," she added to Lori and Becky as she turned to

10

the archway.

Then Angie turned to Lori and Becky. "Have you two decided?"

They each ordered their usual cheeseburgers with fries and a soda, and stared after Billie as Angie left.

-¤-

Billie pushed the swinging doors open and glanced into the kitchen, seeing Billy as he looked up from the dishwasher. He wiped his hands and dropped his towel on the counter and stepped to her. He took his soiled apron off and held it away from her spotless clothes.

"Hey, handsome," Billie said, and caught him in a hug. "How's your day going?"

"Much better now," he said, and kissed her. "You must be here for lunch."

"Yup. Lori, Beck, and me. Did you say no practice tonight?"

"Yeah. I've got to check on some stuff in another part of town tonight."

Billie cocked her head and grimaced. "Tomorrow then. I have our girls' night tonight."

"Okay. Tomorrow. We'll practice in the morning. Is eight too early?"

"Nope." Billie smiled and stole another kiss.

"I'll be by to walk you. Now you'd better get back to your friends before you start a bunch of rumors." He gently turned her to the archway and gave her a push. "I'll see you in the morning."

Billie smiled back over her shoulder. "I think we've already started more than rumors."

-¤-

Billie slid back into her place beside Lori and across from Becky, where they both waited, looking at her.

"Casual conversation and on a first-name basis with the

11

staff?" Becky smiled. "Running off to the kitchen the first chance you get? And she said Billy has the same wrist design? I looked those up and you, girl, are *definitely* off the market."

"I didn't know you've been exercising," Lori said.

Billie laughed at Lori's usual focus on the unimportant issues. "Yes, Lori, I have been. And I guess I am, Beck. I don't know what our future will be, or how long he'll put up with me. But right now, I like where we're at."

Becky smiled and said, "Well, a tat is pretty permanent for just liking where you're at."

"You're *off the market*?" Lori asked, suddenly realizing what Becky had said. "What do those tats mean?"

"It means, Lori," Becky explained, "that our friend Billie is *engaged*."

"Engaged? Like to be married?" Lori stared at Billie.

Billie nodded, grinning softly. "Yup. They do."

"To a dishwasher?" Lori started to argue in a loud whisper. "Think about what you're saying—"

Billie raised her hand and glared at Lori. Angie passed on her way to serve another table and interrupted before Billie's temper made her say what was on her mind. "Your food'll be up in just a sec, Billie. Melony's pulling it together now."

Becky scowled at Lori and shook her head as Angie left again. "Not now, Lori. Can't you see Billie's happy? Stop being so judgmental and let her be. You keep that up and she won't tell us anything." Then she looked at Billie. "So, what happened?" Becky asked, changing the subject. "When you got here you said we wouldn't believe it. What's going on?"

"Oh yeah," Billie said, remembering. "Mr. Hammersmith fired me as I was leaving to come here." Billie took a long sip of her water.

"Fired you?" they said in unison. Then Becky asked, "What on earth did you do?"

She smiled and held up her wrist. "You can't believe how

much this has stirred things up. At least my folks are okay with it. Sort of. Like usual."

"Why did that cause you to get fired?" Lori asked.

"Mr. Hammersmith thinks anyone that wears a tattoo of any kind is a lowlife," she said, "and are not *worthy* to work in his prestigious office. I think everyone there ought to get one and then see what he does."

"What will you do now?" Lori asked, and looked at Becky.

"Nothing right now," Billie admitted, thinking of the many things she was planning to do—none of which she could talk to Lori or Becky about. "I'm okay for a while. The lease on the apartment is paid through the fall and I have funds in the bank, so I think I'll enjoy the spring and see what does happen. I'll talk to Dad this weekend and see if he knows of anything, in case I need a backup plan."

"Wish I could take the spring off," Lori said, and Billie and Becky laughed. Lori was being Lori.

"Hey, Carole," Billie greeted as the attractive, mid-twenties blond waitress set her tray on a folding stand and began distributing their orders.

"Hey, Billie," Carole said pleasantly. "You're looking good today. Angie said you're working out."

When Carole had finished and left, Becky asked, "Are these workouts why you keep missing Monday nights out?"

Billie smiled and picked up her fork and knife. "Yeah. I was hoping you wouldn't mind. It isn't like before, but we do meet four or five evenings a week."

"That means you don't meet on what? Wednesdays and Fridays?" Lori asked. "Do you see him on those nights too, like after our nights out?"

Billie smiled and shook her head. "Not usually. Don't worry so much, Lori. It is really okay."

"That's what you said the last time," Lori said, and took a bite of her cheeseburger.

Becky nodded when Billie looked at her, trying to remember if Lori was right.

"Sorry," Billie said. "Billy isn't possessive like...he was." She could not bring herself to say Blake's name out loud; just thinking about him was enough of a downer. "I just have a lot on my plate, and he's helping me."

Becky smiled. "I can tell he isn't like your ex. You were never happy when he was around."

Thirty-Three

Billie's afternoon was frustratingly quiet, suddenly out of step with her normal routine, not having to go back to work. She had window-shopped along St. Anne and down First Street West, but nothing in the windows seemed to interest her and she wondered why. A month or so ago she would have relished an afternoon off to try on all of the latest fashions or trendy mix-and-matches, but today she looked at the displays and thought about what she had in her closet and how she could put them together to make eye-catching ensembles.

So far, her time with Billy did not let her dress nicely for him, needing to dress down to stay low-key and relatively unnoticed. She really was not complaining, but she did think about days in the future when, maybe, she could dress nice and he would take her out. Maybe even someplace nicer than the Streetcar.

At six thirty, Billie walked the four blocks from her apartment to the Marquee Cocktail Lounge at Main and St. Anne. When she entered and spoke to the door attendant, she saw Stacy and her boyfriend Tom sitting at the high table with Becky and Lori. Becky sat with her back to the corner, casually surveying the male opportunities. Billie absently wondered why she had not seen Becky accept an invitation from any that talked to her or singled her out.

Billie had started to dress up like she usually did for their evenings out—colorful leggings, short skirt, brightly colored fitted blouse, the works—but today her mood was like it had been the week before, preferring the fitted black slacks, black boots, and a colorful pop of another loose-fitting blouse with a matching cap.

Yup, Beck's right. You are definitely off the market, girl.

I know. I think it's the first right *thing I've done in a long time.*

You still could've dressed nicer.

Billie shook her head at the looks that followed her through the crowd.

I know, but I'm not dressing for them anymore. I'll save that for a time when I'm with Billy.

"Hey," Billie said as she settled onto the open stool. "Good to see you, Stace. And you too, Tom."

"Nice to see you," Tom said, and extended his hand across the table. Billie gently shook it once.

"So? How was your quiet afternoon?" Becky asked, and slid the menu pad to her.

"Nice, thank you," Billie said, and scrolled through the drink list. "Almost too quiet. Anyone up for an appetizer?"

"Sure," Lori said, nodding.

Billie shook her head and chuckled. Lori was always up for someone else offering to buy.

"Any preferences?" They all shook their heads and Billie selected a couple of sampler plates and a drink order for herself, and inserted her card.

"Let me see," Stacy said, and reached for Billie's hand. "I want to see this infamous tattoo."

Billie sighed and extended her arm. "I forget that you haven't been involved in the daily episodes of my life's ongoing soap opera." She smiled as Stacy looked at the design.

"It's very nice. A clean design, not too bold, and shouldn't blur too much with age," she absently assessed the tattoo, holding her hand between her and Tom. "Why a tattoo?"

Billie explained, repeating that they originated in the underdeveloped countries of eastern Africa and those in the surrounding areas, and how tats could not be stolen like rings could. She had covered the usual pros and cons of the subject by the time a toned, muscular waiter delivered her drink and the appetizers. When he left, Stacy continued.

"So let me get this straight. You and your new friend Billy are engaged?"

"Yup," Billie said, and scooped a serving onto her small plate. "That's about the size of it."

Stacy sat back and looked from her to Becky, Lori, and to Tom. "That's it? That's all you're going to say about it?"

Billie shook her head. "That's about all there is to tell."

"No, no. What about a date? Have you set a date? Are your folks okay with this? You've only known this guy for what? Less than a month?"

"No date yet," Billie said, and sipped her drink, doing her best to ignore Stacy's probing. "Mom and Dad know we're engaged. And I did meet him fifteen years ago. The rest is for me to deal with." Billie gritted her teeth, hoping Stacy would not keep trying to push her buttons. After dealing with Lori at lunch, Billie knew she only had a tentative hold on her temper.

Stacy sat back and stared at Billie as Becky guided the general conversation back to safer subjects, like weekend plans and the new museum show that she, the museum's assistant curator, was putting together.

"Lori said you lost your job today," Stacy said, finally accepting that Billie was not going to rise to her baiting. "What are you going to do?"

"I'm not sure yet, Stace," Billie said, and glanced at Lori. She knew Lori would spread the word, and decided not to make a big deal out of it. "I told Beck and Lori at lunch that I'm okay financially, so I may just kick back for a little while and see what's out there."

"Last week you said you were working out somewhere," Stacy continued. "Are you still doing that?"

"Yeah," Billie said with a wide smile. "It's intense and invigorating. Helps keep my mind active." She took another sip of her drink, intent on not mentioning how many things were swirling around in her "active" head—all due to her suddenly complicated life with Billy right in the center of it.

They nibbled and chatted, but Billie's mind kept drifting to thoughts of Billy. She figured he was at the kitchen and that the others—maybe Stretch, Hammer, Mace, or Lynx—were watching the areas around the village and the department store. She felt like she was letting them down, being away and enjoying herself when they were facing dangers and unable to relax and enjoy what little they had.

Becky called Billie back into the fold numerous times during the evening before Billie finally admitted she was not being good company.

"I'm sorry, guys," Billie finally said, and slipped her purse strap over her head. "I can't seem to keep my mind on subject. Maybe today was rougher than I thought. I think I need to just go home and crash. I hope you understand."

They nodded and all said they did, and Billie collected her jacket and bid them good night.

She wished she had driven, wanting to go by the department store block, wanting to see what was happening in the alleys and who was watching. But she had not, so she went back to First West and started walking south.

¤-¤-¤-¤-¤

The quieter night sounds surrounded her quickly after she left the Marquee. She listened to every sound that drifted to her. The rattles and clinks of cans and bottles in an alley caught her attention, and looking, she saw someone searching through a dumpster—for what treasures she could not tell. Her own bootheels echoed off the storefronts and the light breeze pierced her light sweater, and together with her nerves, she shivered.

When she turned the corner onto Cheyenne, she unexpectedly saw Billy sitting on the brick planter beside the carded turnstile. She knew she had surprised him as she stepped off the sidewalk and started to walk up the drive toward him.

"I thought you'd still be at the kitchen," she said as he stood and hugged her.

"I asked another fellow to work in my place," Billy said as she swiped her card in the turnstile reader. "My other business ran later than I expected, so it was a good thing I did." He picked up his backpack and followed her in.

When the elevator door closed, he kissed her gently, and held her all the way to the twelfth floor. "I didn't get to see my Tiger enough today."

"She didn't get to see Keeper enough either," Billie said, and led the way to her loft apartment.

Inside, she thumbed the deadbolt and hung his jacket and her sweater on the peg behind the door. She turned to face him, slipped her arms around his neck, and pulled herself up. Feeling his strong embrace, she wrapped her legs around him as he slid one hand under her to support her weight.

Billy slowly carried her to the three-section sofa, sat down, and lay back, his head resting on the cushioned arm, stretching her out on top of him.

"I have so many things to talk to you about," Billie whispered in his ear as she slipped her arms behind his shoulders and pulled herself tight against him.

"You sound like something has happened since I saw you at lunch," he questioned, his arms protectively surrounding her, holding her firmly. "Has something happened?"

Billie sighed and squirmed, gently making herself more comfortable. "Yeah, something has. Hammersmith fired me as I was leaving for lunch today."

"Why?" he asked.

Turning her head to rest her cheek on his shoulder, her forehead against the side of his chin, she smiled, pleased that even though he knew her predisposition for getting into trouble, he had not implied that she had done something to cause being fired.

"My wrist tat," she said, but did not pull her hand free to show it.

"Your wrist tat? How did that—"

"He *hates* tattoos of any kind, and anyone that wears one," Billie said, and then explained the events of the morning. "Robert Lange warned me on Monday. He said Hammersmith was an irrational boss and that he *hated* tattoos."

"I wonder why Mike dislikes tattoos so much?"

"Robert says they remind him of the 'street people,' as he called them, and their deplorable habits, hygiene, and there was something else he couldn't remember. What are you thinking?"

Billy was silent for many minutes, absently caressing her back, occasionally letting his finger follow her bra strap up and down her shoulder. She expected him to be upset, or angry, or...she did not know what she expected. But something. Not silence.

Finally, Billy inhaled and said, "Maybe there's a clue buried in why he is how he is. I have to think about this some. Have you thought about what you're going to do now?"

"Only a little," she said with a sigh. "I felt so odd this afternoon with nowhere to go, no routine to get back to."

"Are you going to be okay?" he asked softly. "Is there anything you need? Anything I can do?"

"I'll be okay, Keeper. As long as I can see you and be with you when things get bad, I'll be okay."

"Are you sure you don't need anything? Sid will give you the same breaks he gives me on meals and—"

"This will give me more time to train and to help you get back at Hammersmith."

Billy slowly shook his head.

"I want to help you nail him for your parents' deaths, and now I have a personal reason to want to get back at him—him and his irrationalness."

"What about your place here? Your rent? Utilities?"

"I'm okay," she said, her legs moving against his as she gently resituated herself. "My lease is paid through the fall. I have savings and investment income. I'm actually good."

"Okay, Tiger. But you let me know if there is anything you need."

"I will, Keeper."

She smiled, eyes closed, reveling in his closeness and thankful for his concerns.

"There is one thing I'd like to know about," she asked. "What's going to happen to you and the others in the basement? The renovation permits were issued on Thursday."

"It's worked out, Tiger," he said cryptically.

"What is?"

"Can I just show you tomorrow? It'll be better than if I tell you."

"You're sure?" she said, and swatted his chest. "I don't mind keeping your secrets, but I hate it when you keep them from me."

"I know," he said, and chuckled, bouncing her gently as he did. "Until I show you tomorrow, just be satisfied to know they all have a new place to live."

"Was that your other business you had to take care of today?"

"Yeah," he said softly.

"Then I know they will be okay. Will those at the village be okay too?"

"The renovation does not affect them directly, so they should be."

"Are you still going to have to watch the department store? After the renovation starts?"

"Yes, we will." He inhaled and she felt his chest lift her. "Until the buildings are occupied and have an official maintenance and security staff, keeping the undesirables out is still my job."

"You never said, but do you have to watch over the other two homeless villages? The one north of the bus station and the one out east on Kiowa?"

"No. We help the men that watch those, but they're not part of our group."

Billie thought about Billy's distinction between the villages, almost like he considered them different tribes, belonging to someone else. She wondered why he did, but she didn't want to think or analyze any more tonight. It was starting to hurt her head.

She shifted herself slightly toward the back of the sofa, letting her legs straddle his one. "If I'm going to have to wait until tomorrow to hear what you won't tell me," she said as she began unbuttoning Billy's shirt, "I need to do something to keep my mind off of the subject. Can you reach the light?"

Thirty-Four

Saturday, May 7

Billy was up, showered, and dressed hours before he woke Billie. While she bathed and dressed for their morning walk, Billy fixed them a light breakfast, and then they walked to the Forest, the wooded, block-sized park between St. Anne and St. Charles, just west of Fifty West. There, as usual, they changed into their frumpy clothes, as Billy called them, and then walked to the department store on Second West and two blocks north. Billy led the way through the narrow cross alleyway where they paused in the main north-south alley at the people-sized steel door. After a few minutes, seeing no one about, Billy took his key from his boot and unlocked the door.

Inside, he relocked the door and put his key back into his boot before he led her down the stairs to the large, familiar basement room where she trained almost every day. He threw the heavy lever on the electrical box and the lights flickered on.

"Tiiggeerr!" Abby, the seven-year-old blond streak screeched as she darted across the room and collided with Billie. "You're here."

Billie chuckled. "Yes. Yes, I am. Where is everyone?" she asked as Billy stopped to talk to Todd.

"We moved, Tiger! We moved!" Abby said loudly as Cathy caught up and pulled Abby off Billie.

"It's just us three this morning, Tiger," Cathy said. "Keeper asked me to come and practice with you if you wanted to."

Billie shook her head and smiled. "I asked what you were going to do with the renovations starting and he said I'd have to wait until today to find out."

"He planned on needing yesterday and today to get us all settled, but we finished earlier than he expected."

"Where?"

"They're called the River Crest Apartments," Cathy said. "Down southwest and just across the river off of Comanche. Crow, actually. They're close enough we can still walk to our jobs. Keeper told us a long time ago that someone he knows was fixing up some old apartments and that if we could measure up, he'd put in a good word for all of us."

"If you could measure up?" Billie asked, trying to grasp the stipulations.

"We had to be good enough," Abby said, dancing on the mat. "And we are."

Cathy chuckled at Abby's antics. "Keeper said that we all had to have a job and keep it for a year. No drugs, no drunken rampages, and no brawls among ourselves. He said there was enough trouble out there." She pointed to the walls and implied the alleys beyond. "We had to look out for each other."

"Wow," Billie said softly with a huge smile. "I know the area. Are they nice apartments?"

"They're very nice," Cathy said. "The landlord is charging us almost nothing for rent and utilities, and Keeper says it will stay that way as long as we keep the area and our apartments clean and orderly. If we get messy, disrespectful of the others, or act like slobs, we're out."

Billie smiled and crouched, suddenly scooping Abby up as she ran past. She spun Abby around and set her down, still spinning. "Are you going to help your mom take care of your new home?"

"Yes, Tiger," Abby said as she twirled and stumbled, toppling onto the mat. "I will. It's real nice and I want to live there a long, long time. It has a yard and trees and everything!"

"Good for you." Then Billie looked at Cathy. "Is everyone together?"

"Everyone moved except Spear. I think Keeper said he went

to another city to be closer to a relative of his. And like you said, with the renovations starting on the department store, the timing is perfect."

"Come on, Tiger," Billy said as he stopped beside a support pillar and shed his boots, shirt, and street pants. "A quick session before we go to the diner and have brunch."

She smiled at Cathy as she stripped down to her sweats. Then she turned and faced Billy, settling into her crouched stance in the center of the mats.

"Okay, Keeper," she said, and smiled. "You're all mine."

"Of course I am," he said, and Billie dropped her gaze to the mat and chuckled.

That was enough of a distraction, and he flipped her onto her back and pinned her. She threw her arms and legs around him and held him tight.

"Tiger, you didn't even try," he complained, and tried to get up. He forced his arms straight and she held on, making him lift her as well.

"I think I like wrestling better," she said, and kissed him.

Billy smiled, remembering she always did like wrestling better, but he did not say anything.

"Okay, guys," Cathy laughed. "I don't think you should practice those moves here."

Billy stood up and Billie clung to him until she could put her feet down and be standing.

Todd chuckled with Cathy and said, "I don't think you can fight that way."

Billie smiled. "I don't want to fight with Billy."

Especially not after last night.

"All right, all right," Billy said, and slipped his arm around her shoulders. "Hammer, will you get a couple of the guys lined up for tomorrow and we can move the mats into that double garage behind the new apartments. We'll leave them rolled up until we need to practice something else."

"Will do," Todd said.

"Thanks. Would you three join us at the Streetcar for brunch?" Billy asked, and Billie smiled at the idea. "Tiger and I need to get into different clothes, but will you meet us there in say, half an hour?"

"We don't..."

"Please?" Billie asked, seeing their concern when they looked at each other. "For all of the help you've given me. A very tiny part of a huge thank you I owe you for everything."

"But you don't owe us anything," Cathy said.

"Yes, I do. We do," Billie insisted.

"It'll be my treat," Billy said, and Billie knew he understood their reluctance.

"Please, Mama," Abby pleaded.

"Please, Cathy. From one friend to another," Billie said, and caught Cathy's hand.

"Okay," Cathy finally said, and nodded. "In half an hour."

¤-¤-¤-¤-¤

"Oh, wow," Abby whispered, holding Billie's hand as Billy pushed the Streetcar's inside glass door open for them. "Look, Mama. Tables. Lots and lots of tables."

Then her eyes caught the booths along the front wall, with the wooden slat racks above them and the shiny chrome tubes holding them up.

"Hey, Billie," Angie greeted warmly, and bent to smile at Abby. "And who do we have here?"

Billie made the introductions and urged Abby to follow Angie. They stopped at a large booth at the back of the dining room, and Angie spread menus on the table. Cathy slid in, pulling Abby behind her, and Todd followed, taking his place nearest to the aisle. Billie and Billy settled on the bench opposite them, watching Abby's awed assessment of the things around her.

"Carole will be right with you."

"Thanks, Angie," Billy said.

Abby slowly surveyed the room and all of the various streetcar appointments mounted on the walls, hanging from the ceiling. She looked up at the wood slatted shelves above them.

"What's all this stuff, Mama?" Abby asked, her voice still hushed, pointing to the overhead shelves, those over the front booths, and different items hung around the dining room.

"Those are things," Billie explained, "that were in real streetcars. Some people called them trollies. They were like buses that followed tracks like a train. Those wooden racks"— she pointed up—"were used by passengers to put suitcases or bags like our backpacks on while they traveled."

"Cooolll," Abby said.

"May I get you something to drink?" Carole asked when she stopped. She quickly spotted Abby. "Hey. We have the same color hair. Do you know what you'd like?"

"Can I have a soda, Mama?" Abby asked.

Before Cathy could answer, Billy asked, "Does Abby like ice cream? How about chocolate?"

Cathy smiled. "Of course. She doesn't get those very often."

"Would you let her have a chocolate shake?" he asked. "Carole makes the best shakes."

Abby's eyes were wide in anticipation.

"Sure. She's never had a shake," Cathy said with a huge smile. "She'd like that."

Carole took everyone else's drink orders and left them to study the menus. Todd and Cathy debated for a few minutes, asked Billy about portion sizes, and then made selections for each of the three of them, deciding on the junior cheeseburger and fries for Abby.

Carole came back and set their drinks on the table, saving

Abby's shake for last. Abby's eyes couldn't get any wider as she stared at the brown shake in a tall, short-stemmed glass with whipped cream and a cherry on top.

"I made it a little thicker than usual," Carole said, and laid a long-handled spoon, a large-diameter straw, and a napkin beside the confection. "I hope you like it, Abby."

"Tell Carole thank you, Abby," Cathy said softly.

"Thank you, Carole," Abby said, barely looking away from the mesmerizing shake. She looked at Cathy. "Can I taste it now?"

Cathy and Todd chuckled. "Yes dear, you can. You don't have to wait," Cathy said.

-¤-

Billy watched Abby slowly and systematically attack her shake, beginning with the cherry and then working her way down through the whipped cream and into the ice cream mixture beneath. Then he looked at Todd.

"Are the others still okay with the same arrangements for watching?" Billy asked.

"Everyone said they should be able to keep to it," Todd said. "It's just a little farther to walk to get there. Do the guys in the village know we're farther away?"

"Most of them do," Billy said. "A few don't like it, but know we didn't have a lot of choice. They know we'll still be watching the department store and coming up to the village, just like we have been. I'm hoping they won't see any change."

"At least," Todd said, "if they need something, they know we're still close at the store."

They stopped talking when Carole brought their food orders, and Abby stared again as Carole slid a large plate past her to Cathy, then slid one in front of her. She watched as Carole placed Todd's order, then Billy's and Billie's. She looked up at Cathy.

"A whole plate just for me?"

28

"That's right, Abby. Just for you," she said, and then asked what she wanted on her cheeseburger: mustard, ketchup, mayonnaise, pickles, and so on.

Abby was in awe as Cathy opened the sandwich and helped her add the condiments—Abby wanted them all—then the lettuce and tomato slice as Cathy set the bun top back in place.

"Would you like for me to cut it in half?" Cathy asked. "So it's easier to hold?"

Abby nodded and watched until Cathy put the knife down and nodded.

"There ya go. Remember to take small bites. We're not in a hurry."

"Okay, Mama," Abby said, and tasted a fry. Then she dipped one in the small puddle of mustard, another one in the ketchup, and one in the mayonnaise, savoring the distinctly different flavors of each.

"Abby's had rather limited exposure to different foods," Cathy said as she started on her own plate. "She loves the deep-fried fish and fries from that place on Blackfoot and Fourth West. But I never get the condiments."

Then, while everyone else ate, she glanced around at the room herself.

"After lunch," Cathy said, and looked at Billie, "I'd like to show you our new place. Do you have time, Tiger?"

Billie glanced at Billy and saw his nod.

"Sure. I'd love to see it."

¤-¤-¤-¤-¤

The afternoon was still young when the five of them crossed the Comanche Street Bridge and turned south on Southbank. The apartments were a block down, and Cathy led them through the white, vine-covered wooden arbor and gate, past the tall hedges, and into the large, grassy yard that she said was a play area for the kids.

At the back of the yard, behind the waist-high shrubbery, were two flanking buildings, each containing six units. Behind those was the wraparound drive and the four multiple-garage units, each with three overhead doors and a people-sized door to one side.

"This is beautiful, Lynx," Billie said as they reached the back of the yard and turned to the first apartment in the right wing.

"Thanks," Cathy said as she opened the door to their place. "We put all of the families with kids on the ground floor, to help with the noise. Cutter and Owl are also on the ground floor." Billie remembered they were the eldest couple in the group. "Everyone else is wherever they happened to choose, leaving three apartments unoccupied."

Abby followed Cathy in and Todd gestured for Billie and then Billy to follow next.

"They're simple two-bedroom layouts," Cathy was saying as she stopped in the living room. "A decent-sized kitchen...What would I know? I haven't been in a kitchen since I used my mom's when I was a little girl. At least it seems adequate and has room for both Abby and me to cook together. There's a nice dining space, just right for the three of us, a main bath, and..." She led the way down the very short hallway. "...two nice sized bedrooms—"

"This one's mine!" Abby announced, and slipped past them and into the room on the right. "It's all mine!" Then her smile softened. "I hope it won't be lonely in here."

"I'm sure you will love having your own space," Billie said encouragingly. "I had my own space when I was growing up. And I liked not having to share with my sister."

Abby smiled. "I didn't know you have a sister. Is she like you?"

"Some, I guess," Billie nodded. "But different." Billie turned to Cathy and followed her back into the living room. "This is a very nice place. I'm happy for you. Obviously the furniture came with it."

"Yeah," Todd said. "I'm sure it isn't top of the line, but it looks like it's durable and should wear well. Keeper says if we have any problems with anything, we just have to call the super's number and it will be taken care of."

"That's about as good as it can get," Billie said, and glanced at Billy. "Is yours like this one?"

Billy nodded. "Very similar. It's just over at the far end of the other building. I can show you when you're done."

"I think that's all I can show you," Cathy said, and looked around. "I'm glad you got to come and see it."

"Me too, Lynx. And I'm pretty sure I'll be back, visiting with one or more of the new residents."

Cathy glanced at Billy and chuckled. "I'm sure you will be, and I'm glad."

"Come on," Billy said. "I'll show off my new digs too. You're all welcome to come."

"I wanna see," Abby said, and hurried out the front door, getting ahead of everyone.

Billie chuckled and Cathy just shrugged. "I sure am glad she minded her manners at the diner."

Thirty-Five

"I can't believe how nice your apartments are," Billie said, breaking their reverie as they walked along Comanche, back toward her place.

"They are nice," Billy said. "It'll take a lot of getting used to. Definitely different than the floor in the basement."

"I'm sure," Billie chuckled. "At least I imagine it will be warmer. I know you had to, but it must've been difficult at times living there."

"Sure. I was able to get secondhand blankets off and on, so it wasn't as bad as it could have been."

"I'm glad."

"But that makes me remember something I was going to ask you."

"Shoot."

"When you were working on Hammersmith's renovation designs, did you ever see what he was actually going to do to the buildings?"

"The biggest part of the estimates was reconstruction," Billie said, thinking back, trying to remember the details of the design requirements document.

"Reconstruction? Don't you mean renovation?"

"No. Renovation was just a small part of the estimates."

Billy looked at her for a long moment. "I'm confused."

"The west building was just renovations," Billie explained. "The east building was going to be redone from the ground up—therefore the biggest share of the costs."

"Wow. Rebuilding is enormously more expensive than refurbishing," Billy said, pondering what Billie was telling him.

"There were some parts that were going to be left alone, but most of it was going to be torn down and rebuilt."

"Was there anything in the design proposal that explained why he wanted to do that?"

Billie shook her head. "No."

Billy rubbed his chin and retreated into his thoughts for a few minutes. "I wonder what's different in the east building."

Billie shrugged and changed the subject. They walked on in quiet conversation.

"From what you said at lunch, I gather you're watching the blocks tonight?"

"Yeah," Billy said. "I'll meet Stretch around dark and stay until around two. Kind of like usual."

"Yeah," Billie admitted. "I've got our girls' night out again tonight, and then I'm off to my folks' place again in the morning. Mother's Day. Can you come with me?"

"Not this time, Tiger," Billy said, and squeezed her shoulder. "I still have a few things to finish up with the moving. I need to get them done before the week starts. Sorry."

"Me too," she said. "I just want you to meet them."

"I want to meet them too," he said. "But this weekend isn't a good time for me."

"Okay." She smiled up at him. "I won't beg."

They turned the corner onto Second West and walked the block north to Cheyenne and her apartment. At the turnstile, he hugged her and kissed her long and tenderly.

"Maybe that'll hold me until I see you again."

"I hope so," she said, and smiled. "I need to go up and get ready for tonight—otherwise I'd suggest something else for you to remember while I'm gone."

He laughed. "I guess I'll just have to remember last night

instead." He stole another kiss and then stepped back. "Drive safe and come back to me."

"I will, Keeper."

Billie went in through the turnstile and waved as he stopped at the curb and waved back. Then, with his backpack over his shoulder, she watched him start walking north on Second.

¤-¤-¤-¤-¤

Billie searched the assortment of tops hanging in her closet, deep in her normal turmoil of trying to choose the right blouse for her evening with Lori and Becky. She had her black slacks laid out on the bed and was considering her brown boots as she looked for a top that might work with them.

She thought about the apartments and the tour Cathy and Todd had given her. She had visited with a few of the others when they had finished looking at Billy's apartment—Ferret and Mouse and their son Richard, Falcon and Sparrow and their son Rusty, and they had caught Cutter and Owl just as she and Billy had started back toward her apartment. Each one of them seemed very happy with their new digs, as Billy called them.

That was a very nice way to spend a Saturday afternoon.

Yes, it was. But I didn't get my private time in the Forest.

Last night probably made up for that.

Obviously could have. Last night was beyond surprising. This is so much different than any relationship I had in high school or since. This feels right. *Billy feels* right—*more than just* right.

But he's still secretive.

Yeah. He'll tell me more when he's ready.

Being secretive should bother you.

I'm curious, but he'll tell me, once he knows he can trust me.

She glanced at her wrist again and chuckled.

I guess that's really it. I trust him completely. In everything, even if he hasn't told me everything yet.

You've fallen in love with him.

I know. Isn't it great? This is so very different than anything I've felt before.

Definitely different than Blake.

Oh, God! Why did I think of him? He was all "gimme, gimme" and turned very abusive, very quickly. Honestly, I could never trust him, anytime.

At least you know what you don't like.

Got that right! Sure am glad I never had sex with him. That would have been a disaster! Letting my guard down and getting into an even more compromising positi—

You know what they call non-consensual se—

I know what it's called! And that was the only way it was going to happen.

Billie exhaled, realizing she had been working herself up. Her breathing was heavy and ragged.

Stop this! Blake's out of my life. I blocked his phone, so I shouldn't have to listen to him again. I have Billy now! Just Billy.

Just Billy? You're sure?

Yes! Somehow he really had *me. I think from the moment he wiped my boot and looked up at me in the diner. I didn't really feel threatened or uncomfortable. I still don't. I feel his confidence, his patience, his compassion, his concern, and after last night, a very deep passion and longing. He wants* me. *Keeper wants his Tiger!*

That's just the sex talking.

Billie shook her head and smiled.

Nooo. It's so much more than that. Like I said, the sex was better than great, but I know there is so much more. I feel it in my heart. I was the one that asked him to let me into his life, to let me help him do the things that were important to him. He didn't come and seek me out. I did that. Surprise, surprise. I did.

I know.

He's the one that chose to live homeless all these years so he could help others in need, protect them and teach them to care for one another. And now, he's taking the time to teach me *how to protect myself, to not be afraid of the uncertainties surrounding me, to stand up for others. He's the one that encouraged the others to share their knowledge to help educate and train me, a nobody, to become my friends and to share the simple joys of each other's company. He hasn't asked me for anything, but instead, he's giving me everything.*

Yes, she admitted, *he does have me, heart and soul. I can't deny it. I look forward to seeing him every day, maybe more than the day before.*

She studied the intricate chain wrapping around her wrist.

It might have been a ruse to keep me safe, but I'm sure our being engaged is not a ruse any longer. I don't want to end it and neither does he. If I haven't fallen in love with him, I don't know what it is that I feel. It sure makes me feel giddy inside, and no one's ever done that to me before.

With a happy sigh, she pulled a bright yellow blouse with splashes of browns from the closet and was laying it with her slacks when her doorbell chimed. She hurried down the stairs and checked the peephole, unlocked the door, and opened it.

"Hey, Lori," she greeted. "What's up?"

"Just on my way to our Saturday night out," she said as she stepped in and Billie locked the door behind her. "You're getting ready?"

"Just going to take a quick shower and then dress," she said, and hurried back up to her bedroom. "I won't be but a minute. Fix yourself a drink. There are fixings in the cabinet beside the fridge."

"Take your time," Lori said, and turned to the kitchen and promise of a free drink.

-◻-

Billie dried herself, fluffed her hair with the towel, and

then wrapped the towel around herself and tucked in the tail in front. She slid the shower room door aside and stepped past the sink and toilet, into her dressing room to pick up her underthings.

She stopped suddenly, seeing Lori stranding at the foot of her bed, holding up a hanger with her worn jeans and bulky sweater on it.

"What are these?" Lori asked in a stern, accusing tone.

"What are you doing, Lori?" Billie asked in a raised voice as she stepped across the short distance and took the hanger. "They're mine! That's what they are!" She hung the hanger back in the closet and grabbed the coat off the bed and hung it back in the closet beside the sweater and jeans. "What are you doing?" she asked again as she closed the closet door. "I don't come to your house and rummage through your clothes and things!" Billie was beginning to lose her grip on her temper.

"I... I...wanted to look at your things..."

"Why? What are you looking for?"

"I...just like how nice your things are," Lori said, and stepped back toward the spiral stairs. "Your clothes are so much nicer than anything I own. I..."

Billie closed her eyes and took a deep breath. Holding it for a moment, she slowly exhaled. "Fine!" Her tone was less threatening and a bit softer. "Just...just ask before you decide to rummage around in my stuff." Billie picked up her underthings from where she had lain them on her bed and turned to the lav. "I'll be out in just a sec."

Billie quickly donned her underwear and stepped back into her dressing room. Lori had not moved from where she stood near the top of the stairs, though she had made a serious dent in the drink she had brought up with her.

"Sorry, Billie," Lori said softly. "I didn't think I was doing anything wrong. We've always talked about your nice things and how much I admire them and how you look. Are you all right?"

"Yeah," Billie said, and sighed. "I'm sorry I snapped at you. I guess everything going on has me on edge. Getting fired, like that happens all the time. Training with Billy and his friends is exhausting. Exhilarating, but exhausting." Billie stopped herself before she started verbalizing all of the things going on that Billy had asked her to keep secret. "But I'll be fine."

Lori took another long sip of her drink and looked at Billie. "Can I ask why you have such old and worn-out clothes in your closet?"

Billie inhaled again and smiled a tight smile. "They're just some old clothes I have hidden away. I'll just say they're special to me..." Billie let her smile grow a little. "...but you won't see me wearing them to the Marquee, or to Whiskey's, or Custer's, or any other place we frequent. I'll promise you that."

"Okay," Lori said as Billie gave her a quick hug and turned to the yellow blouse on the bed.

Billie slipped into the blouse, flipped her hair out, and then put the slacks on. Billie brushed her hair and began blow-drying it. It only took a few minutes for the dryer to work its magic, and Billie turned it off and ran the brush though her hair again.

She turned on her stool, slipped into her socks, and then her low-topped boots.

"Did they belong to someone special?" Lori asked, and Billie thought about how to answer her persistent questions.

"Yes," Billie said instead of explaining, "but I don't want to talk about it."

Billie applied her makeup and her lip gloss and finally stood.

"I think I'm ready. My jacket is downstairs and I'm done up here." She looked at Lori. "Are Stacy and Tom going to be with us tonight?"

Lori shook her head and shrugged one shoulder at the same time. "I don't think so. But you never know."

Thirty-Six

Sunday, May 8
Mother's Day

The morning sun was high in a clear sky with a steady but gentle south wind spreading its warmth across the pastures and corrals. Billie went into the main house through the side door, entered the kitchen, and sat the sack of things her mother had asked her to bring on the island counter. She hollered a "hello" but heard no answer. She checked the living room as she went through, then her dad's den, and the family room.

At the back patio door, noticing the open stable doors, she stepped out and walked across the vibrant green, spring grass yard and the gravel drive in front of the barn. When she reached the open doors, she hollered again and the foreman stuck his head out of the tack room.

"Hey, Billie," he said, and greeted her with a hug. "Yer mom said you were here last week. Sorry I missed you."

"Sorry I missed you too, Jake," she said, and looked around. "Where is everybody?"

"Yer mom, dad, and Sandy took an early ride up to the second lake," he said, and pointed to the open stalls.

"Sandy's here?"

"Yup," he said, and smiled. "Flew in about dark last night and your folks picked her up."

"Hmm. I'm surprised they didn't call or stop by."

Thankfully, last night would have been okay.

Sure am glad they didn't come by Friday night. Might have been a little embarrassing, all naked and tangled up the way we

41

were.

Would've been interesting. At least they would've met Billy.

Stop it!

"Don't know anythin' about that, Billie," he said. "How're you doin' these days?"

"Actually…" She smiled, recomposing her thoughts. "I'm doing really well. Feeling better than I have in a long time."

"Yer lookin' good. I must say somethin's workin' fer ya."

"Thanks."

"Ya want me to saddle up the bay fer ya?"

"No," she said, and shook her head. "I skipped breakfast, so I think I'll go back in and find something to nibble on. Thanks anyway."

"Sure thin," he said as she turned and retraced her steps to the house.

Billie tried to not think about Friday night -as she collected the bread and the jars of jam and peanut butter from the refrigerator. She fixed herself a half a sandwich and a small glass of milk to pass the time and was rinsing her plate when she glanced out the kitchen window and saw the three of them pass the front of the barn and rein the horses inside. She put the plate, butter knife, and her glass in the dishwasher and dried her hands before she stepped outside and started back across the yard.

"Hey, Sandy," she said when Sandy and their mom and dad came out of the stable.

"Hey, Billie," Sandy said brightly, and caught Billie in a tight hug. "I thought we'd be back before you got here."

"Got on the road early. How're you? It's great to see you." Billie turned and hugged her mom. "Happy Mom's Day, Mom."

"Thank you, dear," Maggie said.

"I know it's been a while," Sandy admitted as they started back to the house. "And you know how poor I am about writing or calling."

"Yeah. Jake said you came through the city last night and didn't even call when you were just blocks away." Billie gave her sister a disapproving pout, then laughed. "I was busy anyway."

"Mom said you usually go out with Lori and two of your other friends on Saturday nights," Sandy said, glancing at Maggie as they entered the family room.

"We try to keep a routine going," Billie admitted. "But sometimes it's hard to do. So, how's grad school? Campus life?"

"So far it's been great," Sandy said, and led Billy to her old bedroom. "I want to show you something." Then, over her shoulder, she said, "We'll be back in a minute, Mom."

Billie sat down on the edge of the bed as Sandy dug through a zippered pouch in her carry-on bag, then pulled out an envelope. "Look at this," she said, and handed Billie a picture of her and a chiseled, good-looking man wearing a tie, a button-down shirt, and a V-necked sweater vest.

"And who might this be?" Billie asked.

"His name is Gilbert Fowler," Sandy said. "He's a grad student in neurological medicine. We've been dating since late September."

"And are you still going for pediatrics?" Billie asked.

"Certainly," Sandy said, and slipped the picture back into the envelope.

"Are you and Gilbert serious?"

"I think so—at least as much as two people can be after only seven months," Sandy said, and slipped the envelope back into her bag.

Billie watched her, wondering, *How can you be together seven months and not know how you feel about Gilbert?* "Have you mentioned him to Mom and Dad?" she asked instead.

"No," Sandy said with a sheepish look on her face. "I'm a little scared to."

"I guess the real question," Billie said, redirecting her thoughts, "is whether you and Gilbert have decided it's serious.

43

Has he proposed?"

"Not in so many words," Sandy admitted. "No ring yet. We've talked about having a family, where we might live, depending on where his work might be. In pediatrics, I can go almost anywhere, but Gil won't be as fluid. He'll have to take work where the proper facilities and openings are."

"Well, with everything else that's been happening," Billie said, "you probably ought to give them a heads-up, even if he's just someone you like for now."

"Why?" Sandy asked, suddenly hearing the tone in Billie's voice. "What's been happening?"

"You remember Jack Markins?" she asked, and Sandy nodded. "He's engaged and planning to marry a Katie Biggins this fall. Mom tried to set us up again last week, only to find out he's engaged after Jack and his folks got here."

"That must have been embarrassing," Sandy chuckled.

"If you don't say something and she tries to set you up with someone," Billie said, and cocked her head. "Don't say I didn't warn you."

"She wouldn't," Sandy said at Billie's nod. Then she grabbed Billie's hands. "Oh no, not you too," she said as she noticed Billie's wrist. "Those wrist tats are showing up all over campus." Sandy looked at Billie.

"'Fraid so, sis," Billie said with a wide smile. "No ring either. No date yet. Just the tat."

"Who?" Sandy asked. "Someone I know?"

"Maybe," she answered cryptically. "Billy Carson. You saw him, but I don't know if you really met him. Fifteen years ago at the Streetcar Diner."

"What? Fifteen years ago?" Sandy questioned. "How would I remember someone from fifteen years ago? I have enough trouble with remembering what I did last month, much less people from fifteen years ago."

"Well, I met him again not too long ago and we've been seeing each other," Billie admitted, still smiling, "almost daily."

"Obviously Mom and Dad know," Sandy surmised.

"Yup. They saw the tat last weekend and I talked to them about it. Mom reacted in her normal, challenging manner."

"So? What's he do?"

"This you won't like," Billie said, and watched her sister's expression. "He is a dishwasher at the Streetcar Diner and works with the less fortunate people in the city."

"A dishwasher? Really, Billie?"

Billie shook her head, realizing that that was all Sandy had heard.

"Yes. He's a really great guy and—"

"How much has he taken you for?" Sandy asked sharply.

"What? Nothing, Sandy," Billie snapped, her expression hardening as she stared at her sister. Her voice pitched. "Billy hasn't asked for anything from me. He's happy with his life and so am I!"

"So if he hasn't asked for anything," Sandy pressed, "how much have you given him?"

"Nothing, Sandy! I didn't *buy* his attentions! He isn't after prestige. He isn't after our family's money. He's compassionate for others, caring, and giving of himself and his time."

"Sorry, Billie," Sandy said, "I can't believe that. Believe me, he has a motive."

Billie was breathing heavily, her tone challenging. "You don't think he could just like me because I'm me? Is that it?"

"I don't mean it that way, Billie," Sandy said. "I've just known too many guys that look past us and see our interests in horses as big money. Even if they have to wait until someone dies, they know the family's money is there for the waiting."

"And Gilbert isn't one of those kinds of guys?" Billie asked. "But Billy is? Well, I disagree with you! When I was fired for having a tat, Billy was worried about me, and how I was handling it. After he found out I was okay, he asked what he could do to help me. I've known my share of opportunists

Sandy, I've been hustled, and I've let myself be hustled in order to have a shallow-at-best relationship. Billy and I may not have a future together, but I do know our time together right now is better than any I've ever had in the past. And he hasn't tried anything funny or underhanded."

Sandy eased herself onto the edge of the bed and squeezed Billie's hands. Billie tried to calm her breathing and the pounding in her chest.

"I'm sorry. Maybe you're right, sis," Sandy said softly. "I worry about that all of the time, and I just didn't realize that you worry about that too."

"Yeah, I do," Billie said.

"Wait. You said you got fired for having a tat?"

"Yeah." Billie smiled. "I've thought about filing a discrimination suit against the firm, but the two junior partners are really nice. It's just the senior partner and founder that is irrational. But I'll figure out a way to get back at him, legally."

You're not going to tell her what you're really going to do?

Nope.

"So how are you managing?"

"I have a lot of savings," Billie admitted with a sly smile. "I don't spend much, except occasionally on clothes. I work out a lot and Sid, the owner of the Streetcar Diner, gives me a break on meals. And I have the trust distributions every month."

"Yeah," Sandy said slowly, "about those. Did you get a notice that your distributions would be going up?"

"Yes," Billie said. "Seven percent, I think the notice said. Why?"

"Look at the ranch, Billie," Sandy said. "Mom and Dad aren't doing half the business they used to do. I don't know how stud fees and boarding are going, but things are not as sharp and clean as they used to be."

"I figured the upkeep was because Jake's getting old," Billie said, "but if the income is down, how're Mom and Dad able to make the periodic additional investments? Last year's were sizable."

"Exactly," Sandy said. "In the past I never paid it any mind, but this year, when I was getting stuff ready for taxes, I realized the trust distributions for last year amounted to a decent salary for any average working person."

"My accountant noticed that too," Billie said. "It was actually more than I made at my job with B, L and H. She also told me that last year the trust paid almost all of the taxes on the distributions."

"Really? How's that possible?"

"I asked her to see how fluid the trust is," Billie continued. "You know, if it's well funded for the long haul."

Sandy nodded. "And?"

"She said it's fully funded, mature, and the distributions are from the base annuities within the funds. They were set up before we started high school and they are mature enough now to pay the distributions and the taxes incurred. They're not going away. And the extra investments added periodically just enhance the growth rate. "

"Wow," Sandy whispered, and just looked at Billie.

-¤-

Mother's Day dinner had been an early afternoon affair, and early in the evening, after much reminiscing and Billie and Sandy had taken a long walk around the ranch, they all settled to relax in the family room. Bob built a small fire in the fireplace to take the chill out of the room and offered them each a cordial while they relaxed. Sandy and their mom accepted while Billie went to the bar looking for something else.

"I thought you liked cordials, Billie," Sandy said, noticing Billie's obvious search for something else.

"I did," she admitted, "but since I've been working out, sweets don't set as well as they used to. I've even found I'm not enjoying cookies or sweet rolls in the mornings anymore."

"Does your Billy have something to do with this change?" Maggie asked.

"Yes, he does," Billie admitted, and poured herself a Chablis from the chiller. "We have a one-hour intense exercise regimen almost every evening except when I can't, like the last two Sundays."

"When are we going to meet him?" Bob asked. "I was hoping he might have come with you today."

"Me too," Billie said as she settled back into her chair. "This week he was busy moving six homeless families and three singles into a newly renovated apartment complex. He was helping them get situated this weekend and he couldn't get everything done yesterday."

"Apartments for homeless families?" her mom asked. "Can they afford it?"

"Homeless doesn't mean destitute, Mom," Billie said. "The families in question all have jobs, albeit not high-paying jobs, but real jobs, steady jobs. They had to keep their jobs for a year to qualify, and Billy arranged with the landlord to supplement their rent if the families keep their end of the bargain—you know, keep working, no drugs, help each other, keep the place neat and tidy, inside and out."

"Sounds well thought out," her dad said.

"He tries. He said he wants to find other developers and renovators to do the same," Billie said. "If he can, he'll work with another group of homeless families and see if he can help them get into nice places next year. I think he said he has four other couples he's working with so far."

"I don't believe it," Sandy said, and Billie glared at her. "Sorry, Billie. What I meant," she said when she saw Billie's expression, "was that that's very ambitious. I applaud his efforts. I really do. It's just unusual to hear about someone doing so much."

Bob nodded. "I hope we can meet this Billy of yours before too long, Billie. He sounds like a very compassionate person."

"Thanks, Dad," Billie said, and smiled. "I'll try to pull him away sometime soon. Or maybe we can get together when you're in the city."

After a few minutes watching the fire and reflecting, Sandy looked at Billie. She nodded.

"Hey, Dad," Sandy started. "Billie and I were talking, and I was wondering how the ranch is doing, financially."

"Financially?" Billie and Sandy noticed he glanced at Maggie before he continued. "Well, we're doing okay. Last year we hired Sultan out three times for stud service, five scheduled for this year with four or five maybes, and we have six horses boarded and in training right now. Yeah, I think we're doing okay."

"As good as it was when we were kids?" Billie asked.

"No, not that good," he said. "But the bills are paid and there's still money in the bank."

"We were wondering where you got the money for our extra annuity investments," Sandy said frankly.

"Huh?" Bob looked at her. "What annuities? What investments?"

"Our trust funds," Billie said. "The monthly distributions from those annuities."

"Honey," Maggie said, "we never had money to set up any trust funds. What are you talking about?"

"What are you saying?" Sandy asked. "When we started college, we each started getting automatic deposits from funds set up in our names. The funds are through an investment company in Dallas."

"Honestly," Bob said, "we really don't know what you're talking about."

Thirty-Seven

"I don't, Stretch," Billy said as they climbed the stairs to the eighth and top floor of the warehouse building. "I don't remember anything unusual on any of these floors. Do either of you?"

"Don't look at me," Cat said. "I haven't been in this building in nearly two years. Maybe three."

"Me either," Stretch said. "But we'll take a look at each floor and see what we find. At least they put matching windows in, instead of keeping it dark and making it look like a warehouse. They let in a lot of light. Do you know if they originally planned it as an expansion to the department store?"

"I'm not sure," Billy said as they stepped out on the top floor. "But it would make sense. Duckard's was a very big name at one time."

They walked the central corridor from the south to the north, observing the expanse on either side, divided into three office sections with walls set to align with the support pillars.

"The service elevator is larger than in the department store," Stretch noted. "Maybe it was resized as an afterthought."

"Maybe," Billy said. "But most likely, they figured they could make it smaller if they chose to include the space with the other building. I am surprised the buildings aren't connected somewhere."

"Yeah," Cat agreed. "That would've been nice."

"Nothing on this floor," Billy said when they reached the top of the south stairs. "Let's check seven."

They went down a floor and repeated the walk-through. Then down another, and then another. On the third floor, Cat found an office with a safe mounted to the floor, but it was open and empty—different, but insignificant in their searching. Spotting nothing more, they continued down and searched the second and then the first floor.

At the bottom of the south stairs, situated next to the alley wall, a mirror of the stairs in the department store building, they entered the dark basement and Billy switched on the flashlight he had borrowed from the Streetcar. Stretch and Cat each switched their flashlights on when Billy threw the heavy handle on the breaker panel, and nothing happened: the basement remained dark. They checked the wall switches and were not surprised when no lights came on.

"Was our basement really this dark?" Cat asked rhetorically.

"When we first moved from the village," Stretch said softly, "it was."

"It had about the same amount of trash too," Billy said as they walked through the south two rooms and stopped at the bathrooms, mirroring those in the department store, also backed up to the alley-side wall.

"These bathrooms look larger," Cat said as they moved into the next room north and turned the corner. "They stretch farther this way. Oh, here's a door."

"Give me a hand, Stretch," Billy said as he grabbed a slab from a wooden crate and pulled. "I think I should have paid more attention to this building when the other one was cleaned."

Together they cleared the debris from the half-open doorway and shoved the door panel inward, into the dark room beyond. They shone their lights and followed the beams in.

"Damn," Stretch said softly. "More trash. Why did someone pile this stuff here instead of throwing it out? Surely they had trash service back then."

"It's like they intentionally stuffed trash into this room," Cat said as she half-carried, half-dragged a broken-down refrigerator box out of the room. "The guys in the village sure could use ones like this."

"We'll make sure they get anything we find," Billy said as he carried more empty boxes out, "that will help them."

As the piles of debris in the middle of the room dwindled, Billy stopped and studied the solid concrete walls. "Okay, these two are between us and the rest of the basement, and that wall over there"—he pointed to the south wall—"backs up to the bathrooms. So this one must line up with the outside, alley-side, walls. Probably need to move the rest of the trash out of this room to see if there's anything different about it."

"Look at this, Keeper," Stretch said with a soft chuckle as he shone his light along the alley-side wall, behind the large pile of trash and crate remnants.

"What do you have, Stretch?" Billy asked when he and Cat crowded to see what Stretch had discovered.

"Looks like a steel door," Stretch said, and tried to pull on the debris closest to the wall.

"Sure does," Billy agreed. "But that would go under the alley, if my bearings are right."

"There's no door like this in our basement," Cat said, and grabbed some trash piled against the wall and carried it out into the basement. "You were looking for a difference, and I think you found it."

Billy and Stretch pitched in, and after about a half an hour the three of them had enough trash relocated so the door was unobstructed. Billy tried the handle, but it did not turn. "Of course," he sighed, and shook his head.

"I don't suppose the owner has a key to this mysterious door?" Stretch asked.

"I'll have to ask," Billy said, and stepped back with his hands on his hips. "There's not much more we can do until I check. Do either of you know what time it is?"

"Almost noon," Cat said.

"Okay," Billy said. "How about we clean up, go to the diner, and have a bite of lunch? I owe you for the strenuous activities I have subjected you to this morning."

"Sure," they said together.

"I was wonderin' if you'd offer," Stretch said, and poked Billy's shoulder.

▯-▯-▯-▯-▯

Night settled heavily before Billy walked a block past the kitchen on Crescent and then started back toward city center. It was not his night to work at the kitchen, but Billy left Hammer, Ditto, and Red to watch the village and Stretch and Falcon to watch the department store block while he cruised and listened. Ferret, Mouse, and Sparrow were listening in other areas of town, gathering what they could to help in the battle that was brewing with the drug dealers.

Billy chose his route this night because he was curious about something a kitchen helper had noticed: Knife's anxiousness and snide comments about Keeper and his new lady friend. When Billy checked the kitchen, the normal crowd was there and he recognized many by name, but Knife and his usual gaggle of cronies were not there.

As he walked and listened to the night, most of what occupied his mind was thoughts concerning the locked steel door in the warehouse building and its placement. *Why is it locked? What's inside? Does this room have something to do with Mike's focus on the warehouse building? Why was his plan to raze the building instead of refurbishing it? Is there something inside that you want, Mike? Need? Or are you hiding something?*

Then he wondered about Hammersmith's unnatural reaction to tattoos and those that wore them; to be as adamant as he was, it had to be because he knew someone that had tattoos—someone he seriously disliked, maybe even pulled something over on him.

After lunch, Billy had taken a moment and made another call to Greg Madison, Operations Manager at Pastoric. But being a Sunday, he was not there, and Billy left a message asking Greg to see if there were keys to any of the inside doors in the warehouse building. Billy knew it might take a few days to get a reply, so in the meantime he wrestled with his unfounded speculations and unanswered questions, deciding to bide his time by investigating the infamous Mike Hammersmith and how he got to be who, or what, he was.

Billy dropped south to Calvin a block from the kitchen and slowly started back toward the city center, watching the shadows as he approached the small park between him and Crescent, just west of the kitchen. He listened intently to the soft background curtain of dull white noise that either absorbed or reflected the occasional chatter of voices, the honks and squeals of cars and busses, the staccato footsteps, hard bootheels against the concrete sidewalks—the quiet pulse of the city at night.

When he reached the nearest corner of the park, he paused and silently leaned against a tree trunk, slowly kneeling to obscure his silhouette, and continued to listen. Everything remained unchanged, and after a few minutes he moved diagonally into the park and knelt beside another tree.

Billy was not sure what he was expecting, but something was bothering him and he knew if someone wanted to meet someone quietly, this was one of the best out-of-the-way places to do it. And he had the time to wait.

Darkness settled nearly an hour before he got to the park, and anyone that visited the kitchen would know he did not work tonight. Billy figured they would naturally suppose he was around the city center or out near the village as usual; both assumptions made it easier for him to move about and listen.

Billy was considering a move to another tree when a stretched black limousine turned the corner from the south off Tenth Street East and stopped along the curb on the south side of the park. The lights went out, flashed once, and then stayed out. The obvious signal instantly made him curious, and he watched intently without moving farther. Five minutes or more passed before the curbside back door opened and two large, burly, darkly dressed men stepped out and stood beside the door, one forward and one behind. After another couple of minutes, one of the men leaned close to the door and said something that Billy could not hear, and a third darkly dressed figure stepped out and faced the park.

Billy slowly lowered himself down, moved to keep the tree mostly between him and the limousine, stretched his right leg out away from the tree, and slowly pushed his left arm up along the trunk, altering the shape of his shadowy bulge in case someone should glance his way, or a light across the park happened to illuminate his silhouette from behind. Another few minutes silently slipped by before a tall figure stepped out from behind the tree Billy had considered for his next move.

"Leonard?" one of the men from the limousine asked softly. "You the one they call Leonard, the Knife?"

"Man, you got it wrong," the figure from the park said in a casually lilting, playful voice. "Knife killed that Leonard a long time ago. Only me, Knife is left to talk to."

"I have two deeds that need to be taken care of," the third man from the limousine said, and Billy concentrated on the familiarity of the voice.

"I might can help with those," Knife said.

"I need some help getting Pink into the city center blocks to do a little business there. I understand someone keeps pushing him out when he goes to visit."

"That would be Keeper," Knife said. "He says *that* 'hood belongs to him."

"I want those blocks and I want you to help me get them," the taller man in the middle of the three from the limousine said. "I keep trying to buy them but something always goes wrong."

Billy suddenly recognized Hammersmith and smiled; he had brought some muscle to be sure Knife did not try anything stupid.

"What can Knife do for you, Mr. H?"

"I want you to make sure Pink gets into that area and pedals his dust and powders," Hammersmith said. "I am told you are the best at 'removing' certain obstacles. I want you to do what you have to, to get Pink into the city center."

"Ooh," Knife said. "Yeah. Removin' Keeper's the only way inta the city center."

"Then remove the Keeper!" Hammersmith snarled. "I don't care how you do it. Just do not leave any tracks behind."

"Man, you don't understan'," Knife said. "Keeper ain't an easy one to remove. I might need some help."

The figure in front of the limousine's open door held his arm out with something bulbous in his hand.

"Two thousand cash, now," Hammersmith said, "and another thousand when you finish."

"Three Gs?" Knife whistled softly. "You must want that 'hood real bad."

"When can you do it?" Hammersmith sounded impatient.

"When I do," Knife said, his voice still casual. "This will need a little discussin' and plannin'. Put a number on that envelope, so's I kin call you when it's done."

A small flashlight illuminated and the man wrote something on the envelope. The light went out and the man held out the envelope again. Knife stepped closer and took it.

"I'll be in touch," Knife said as he stepped back and tucked the envelope inside his shirt. "Soon. What was the second deed youz needin' done?"

"When you're through with the Keeper," Hammersmith said, "and you call that number, I'll give you the details. I have an ex business associate that needs talking to, maybe some reminding. He has gotten defiant and needs some disciplining."

Billy figured he knew who Hammersmith was referring to and was not sure he wanted to interfere.

"Knife's pleased to help," Knife said, and chuckled softly as he slowly stepped backwards until he was again behind a tree and mingled with the shadows.

Hammersmith got back into the limousine and slowly his

muscle followed. When the door closed with a soft thump, the limousine pulled away from the curb. Its lights switched on as it turned at the next corner and disappeared south on Ninth East.

Billy waited, certain Knife was watching the limousine leave and would make sure no one was following it. Finally, after a long fifteen minutes, Billy slowly lowered his arm and pulled his leg under him. He needed to move to keep from cramping, but he dared not move too quickly.

When he reached the east corner of the park, Billy slowly stood up in the shadow of the first tree he had used, searched the shadows and darkness, and decided he was still undetected. He backtracked a block, slipped another block south to Baker, and walked back toward the city center.

He suddenly had an idea and decided to stop by the diner before he checked on the village.

Thirty-Eight

Monday, May 9

Wearing new, fitted jeans and dark brown walking boots, a colorful blouse with a flattering cut, and her stylish white, short-waisted jacket, Billie took the steps to the Streetcar two at a time, her long red curls bouncing behind her. Angie smiled and greeted her as Billie pushed the inner doors open and stepped inside.

"Morning, Billie," Angie said, and led her to a booth at the far end of the dining room, closest to the archway into the back rooms. "You look nice. Did you have a nice weekend?"

"Good morning, Angie," Billie said brightly. "And yes, it was a good weekend. My sister came home and is staying with the folks for a few days. I don't get to see her much anymore, so it was a treat."

"Tea?" Angie asked.

"That would be great," Billie replied, and looked down at the menu pad, wondering what she should try that morning.

She had just decided and looked up as Billy slipped onto the bench across from her and caught her hand. Angie stepped up and set her tea cup—with two tea bags and a pot of hot water—on the table, smiling at them.

"Angie," Billie said, "I'm going for the Denver omelet, crisp bacon, and sourdough."

"That exercise program must be working," she said, and entered the order into her handheld. "You're looking good and eating a lot better." Then Angie hurried back to the counter and said something to Julie and Melony.

"Sorry I didn't get back until late," Billie said, and squeezed Billy's hand. "My sister Sandy came in for Mother's Day so we visited late. I almost stayed the night, but I wanted to get back. Did you miss me?"

"What kind of question is that?" he asked. "Of course I missed you. You should have stopped by my place."

"It was almost one when I got in," she said, "but I almost did."

"I didn't get in until after midnight myself," he admitted.

"Are we serving tonight?"

"Yes," he said. "I'm thinking maybe we should start around seven instead of eight."

"Okay with me," she said. "Just because, or is something up?"

"Something's definitely up," he said. "I'll explain on our way to the kitchen tonight."

"Okay. Are you up for dinner? My place? Before we go?"

"How about I take you to Scott's Specialty Hot Dog Cart on First, instead?"

"Billy, I can cook." She was almost offended by his suggestion.

"I know," he said, and smiled at her, "but right now, I think this will be better. Please."

"Will you tell me why?" she asked. "Sometime soon?"

"Yes," he said. "Have I told you how absolutely dazzling you look this morning?"

"Not yet." She smiled and he squeezed her hand.

"You are the prettiest thing I've ever seen." He glanced around the nearly full dining room and pulled her hand as he stood up. "Come here."

When she followed him through the archway's swinging doors into the back rooms, he pulled her to the side and stopped suddenly, facing her. He bent to her and cupped her face in his hands. His gentle kiss held her until she withdrew to take a breath. She blinked and looked up at him, a huge smile filling her face.

"Billie Tiger Mattis," he said softly. "I think you have stolen my heart completely."

"Billy Keeper Carson," she said in return, "I *know* you have stolen mine."

He kissed her again quickly and turned her back toward the archway. "Now go back and eat your breakfast so I can get my work done."

He pushed her gently and she glanced at him over her shoulder as she turned the corner into the dining room.

Damn! I am so glad I came home last night! This is sooo much better than waking up and having to eat breakfast with Sandy and Mom.

◻-◻-◻-◻-◻

Barely noticing the receptionist enough to mumble a greeting, Mike Hammersmith entered the design office mid-morning. As usual, he marched up the left-hand aisle, gruffly said hello to Betty, his middle-aged secretary, took the mail she handed him, and entered his office. He glanced through the mail and was hanging his coat on the coat tree behind his door when Betty came in with his morning coffee.

"Here are the project status sheets…" she said, undeterred by his manner as she set the coffee cup on the coaster on his desk. She handed him an unmarked folder. "…for the current projects. Parks Department meeting at eleven."

He nodded as he took the folder and sat down. Betty pulled his door closed as she left his office.

Mike studied the progress status of each of the projects and double-checked many of the numbers, calling up the associated files on his computer. Finally, he was satisfied with the sheets and opened the parks project folder.

He read the comparison sheets and the contingency clauses and was surprised when the printouts suddenly stopped at the end of a discussion paragraph. He opened the files on his computer and noted the same results.

Confused, he reached over and pressed the intercom button. "Billie. Come in here."

He flipped through the folder again and looked up at the closed door, expecting it to open. He keyed the intercom again. "Billie. Did you hear me? Come to my office."

No response.

Mike pressed Betty's button. "Where's Billie? I need the rest of her comparison sheet for the meeting today."

"Sir? Billie?" Betty asked. "Sir, you fired her Friday. She no longer works here."

"I fired her? She's a good worker. Puts in her time and stays late when needed. Very detail oriented. Why would I fire her?"

Betty hesitated a long moment. "Her tattoo, sir. You fired her because she got engaged and had an engagement tattoo."

"Oh," Mike said, remembering he was angry over Westman losing the Duckard properties. "Well, she shouldn't have gotten one." He disconnected the intercom and turned back to the computer. He absently wondered if Carl would have the comparison, but knew he would not. Carl relied on Billie for all of the detail work.

Suddenly realizing he would have to meet the Parks Department Committee without the comparisons and summaries, Mike felt displeased and his temper began to get a hold of him—again. He put the folder aside and opened his email server account, and waited for the application to load and download the morning's catch.

As the ledger filled with the names of senders and subjects, one caught his eye: "From: Tri-Funds," with no subject.

His curiosity piqued by his recent attempts and searches, Mike quickly clicked the blank subject line and the short email opened.

"Mike. Be careful who you try to
remove and what you try to hide. You have
already removed too many. I'm watching.
W. C. Hawke."

Mike stared at the sender's name, fear and disbelief holding
him captive. His left hand pulled at his tie and collar and the
top button of his button-down shirt; his right squeezed his
computer's mouse, making his cursor on the monitor jiggle
uncontrollably. Cold beads of sweat burst out on his forehead
and on his cheeks, and his throat went dry.

No. No! It can't be. You're dead! I know you're dead!

His eyes flicked around the room as if he feared something,
someone, watching him. The words on the screen said so.

No! You can't be watching! You're DEAD!

He jumped up and stared out of his east-facing window,
seeing nothing, the sweat beginning to soak his collar, tight
around his neck. Frantically, he looked at each wall of his office,
his door, the window again. He began to shake and looked back
at the monitor and the blinking cursor, the name *W. C. Hawke*
now highlighted on the screen.

Suddenly, he could not hold it any longer and his mouth
opened. His bloodcurdling scream filled the Boster, Lange and
Hammersmith Design offices.

-¤-

The few that were working this day in the design offices
were suddenly frozen in shock and fear by Hammersmith's
unexpected, spine-chilling shriek.

Thirty-Nine

It was nearly ten when Billie stopped at the information counter at the *Daily News Beacon*.

Because she felt so depressed after her folks had explained what they knew about how Willum and his parents died, Billy had suggested that she should research the details of the accident to help her put it in the right perspective, so she could come to grips with it and remember the good memories she had of her times with Willum.

So, following Billy's suggestion, there she was at the library straight from breakfast. She quickly discovered their newspaper archives only went back ten years. No better than what she found online, but the lady at the *Beacon* counter directed Billie to the Archived Records Department in the building's basement, and as she descended the wide staircase, she reminisced about the first time she had entered the department store's expansive basement with Billy.

Happily, she noted the archives area was nothing like the department store's empty, almost-dreary basement as she approached the service counter and spoke to the older man behind it.

"Good morning," Billie greeted when he looked up. "I need to research anything you might have on car accidents about seventeen years ago. Probably summer or early fall."

"That's a pretty wide bracket," the man said as he pushed a clipboard toward her. "Do you know where the accident happened? Please fill that form out for us."

She looked at the general inquiry form and started filling in the blanks. "Yes. It was at the Chestnut Creek Bridge on State Highway Forty-seven."

"That might help some," he said, and turned to his monitor. "Hmm, yes. I have three data disks listed that might have something."

He went to a wall of metal cabinets and slowly let his pointing finger drift along the headings above the columns of small, square drawers. He stopped at a specific column and followed his finger down, stopping sixth from the bottom. He thumbed through the contents and finally retrieved three square DVD envelopes. He smiled as he turned to her.

"Try these," he said, and pointed to a row of occupied viewers off the end of the counter. "Use those when one's available." He jotted the numbers from the envelopes onto the form she had filled out and then handed them to her. "There are chairs for waiting and"—he gestured to a door at the opposite side of the room—"coffee, tea, and soft drinks through there."

"Thanks," Billie said, and went to a chair where she could wait for a viewer.

She did not have to wait long before a young man collected a rather large stack of disks from the table beside a viewer and got up. Other users were beginning to gather, so Billie moved quickly when the man vacated his chair.

Thankful the disks each had a linked menu, she quickly searched the first disk but realized there was nothing connected with the Chestnut Creek Bridge. She inserted the second disk and found three accidents associated with the Chestnut Creek and State Highway Forty-seven, but only one mentioned a fire. It also noted a potential roll-over.

The accident was Monday, Labor Day, at approximately 11 p.m. The local fire and rescue arrived at the scene and logged the time. She dove into the copy and learned a nearby resident had reported the accident when they saw the flames. They stated they did not hear the crash.

The report noted the weather was dry and warm, but in the pictures, the ground around the wreckage was damp in places and soggy in others. She assumed that was due to the efforts of quenching the fire. Billie scanned the attached pictures, and one taken from the highway caught her attention. She could see the tire tracks, much like she had envisioned they would look, extending from the highway in a slow left turn as the car had rolled into the ditch. The picture showed the remains of the charred, mangled wreckage.

Oh, Willum. How terrible.

She sighed, her eyes suddenly filled with unshed tears; the images confirmed the wreck was far worse than she had imagined. But they fit with her suppositions and she felt more confident she might have the right files. She read on.

Billie printed hardcopies of the article and the associated pictures as she went, but was surprised when she found a copy of the complete police report on the third disk. She keyed for a print, deciding that she could read the details later in the comfort of her apartment. She glanced at the report, confirming it was for the accident that killed W.C. Hawke, his wife Dotty, and their son William—her Willum.

Tears welled up and overflowed, and her chest felt tight and constricted as the long-repressed memories and feelings flooded back. The invisible rope again tightened around her heart and once again threatened to overwhelm her with grief. Billie wiped her eyes, rubbing them red as she forced herself to retrieve the disks and return them to the man behind the counter.

She left the records room, reliving the deep despair as she walked slowly back to her apartment. Along the way she began to think about Billy's description of the accident that had killed his parents, wondering when it happened, how long had he been without them, how he must have felt when he heard that it had happened. He never talked about them—not even mentioning where the accident had happened. As she closed her apartment door and thumbed the deadbolt, she wondered if his silence was his way of hiding a deeply felt anguish.

¤-¤-¤-¤-¤

"Mr. Westman," Mitchell said when he entered Frederick's office, "two weeks ago last Thursday, we sent two men to visit the Duckard Property and one got picked up by the police."

"Yes," Frederick said, and turned to look at him. "I believe you said there were people in the alleys waiting for them, and one got away when he was approached and the other didn't and was charged with attempted burglary."

"Yes," Mitchell said. "In reality, he hadn't broken into either building and the charges were dropped. I suspect there is a notation in a file somewhere in the police records and he is probably on a watch list."

Frederick nodded and waited as Mitchell stepped in farther and closed the door behind him.

"I had a beer with a friend of mine last night—he's an undercover cop and spends his working time among the street people. He said that a week after our man was picked up, a drug dealer went nosing around and was met and asked to leave the city center area by two other street people, one known on the streets as Keeper and a new one known as Tiger."

"Asked to leave?"

"Yes. My friend explained that some think Mike Hammersmith paid a drug dealer named Pink to move into that area."

"Aaah," Frederick said, and smirked. "Mike is trying to make that area unsuitable in the city's eyes. Damn! He's doing it again."

"Again, sir?"

"He's tried this before," Frederick said, and rubbed his chin. "It didn't work before, and when it doesn't this time he will resort to more physical means to handle the resistance he encounters. Just like the last time..."

"He has? I didn't know. But last night…"

Frederick's thoughts flashed back to an incident where Mike had threatened to pin the death of a competitor on him if he ever tried to expose his business practices to the authorities. Frederick shuddered, realizing the relative quiet of the past seventeen years might be about to change.

"But, last night," Mitchell repeated when he saw that Frederick's thoughts had drifted away. "My friend thinks he also solicited a contract on Keeper."

"He what? A contract?"

"That's the rumor around the east-side kitchen. A street exterminator that calls himself the Knife mentioned it around the soup kitchen yesterday sometime. He wasn't named specifically, but Hammersmith was identified as the buyer in a roundabout way. He's the only one that fits."

"Sounds like he's taking matters into his own hands again," Frederick said softly, not really talking to Mitchell.

"Something this serious…" Mitchell said. "Shouldn't we report it or something?"

"Yes," Frederick said, again softly. "But I don't know how or to who. Anyway, we have only hearsay, and an investigation could hurt a lot of innocent people and raise a lot of unwanted questions."

"Okay. I'll leave that one in your hands," Mitchell said, and turned back to the door. "But sir. There is one other thing."

Frederick looked up.

"He also said that the Knife was laughing, telling one of his cronies that when he finished with Keeper, Mike had another job for him—to pay a visit to one of Mike's colleagues—but my friend didn't know which one."

Frederic knew he had gone pale, his mind instantly recalling the ultimatums he had given Mike, telling him that because he had decided to sneak the paralyzing default payment clause in their contract, neither he nor his firm would ever do business with Hammersmith or his company again. He also remembered telling Mike he would never again do his dirty work for him, nor would he hide any more of Mike's skeletons in his closet.

Now, he was certain, Mike saw him as a threat, knowing what he knew, and Mike would not be above permanently "fixing" that threat.

Forty

Blake Lawrence walked into Whiskey's Bar and Grill and glanced around the room as he stopped at the end of the bar. He saw Lori at a table near a window, eating a late lunch alone. When the bartender asked what he wanted, Blake ordered a tall beer. He turned and leaned against the bar to wait, casually glancing at Lori's image in the long mirror.

The bartender slid his frosty mug across the counter and took Blake's money. Blake nodded, picked up his beer, and wended his way around the numerous tables to Lori's. He pulled a chair out and sat down."

"Hi, good lookin'. Mind if I sit down a minute?"

Lori looked up and stared in surprise, for a moment at a loss for words.

"I was makin' my rounds, doin' a few errands, and saw you eating as I walked by, heading back to the old motel I'm stayin' in."

"What do you want?" Lori finally asked. "What are you doing here?"

"My phone broke," he said, smiling confidently, "and I thought you might let me use yours to make an important call."

He picked her phone up off the table before she could say anything, touched a few icons, and put it up to his ear. Lori shoved her hand out and tried to grab the phone away from him, but he caught her wrist and squeezed. He pushed it down and held it against the table, cocking his head, and glared at Lori in warning.

"Hey, good lookin'" he said into the phone when it was answered. "It's Blake. I was passing through town and knew we needed to talk."

He listened and Lori tried to hear.

"It's Blake, doll. We need...to...talk."

He held the phone away from his ear as the voice on the other end screamed. Suddenly he looked at the phone, surprised and upset. Then he saw Lori's angry expression and smiled.

¤-¤-¤-¤-¤

Flopped across her bed, Billie was numb from coping with the memories her search had reawakened. She wrestled with the details and tried to push the sorrow away, knowing there was no way to reconcile any of it; it was just what it was. She had returned to her apartment and fixed a cup of soup and half a lunchmeat sandwich, then reread the police report and the articles, but there was nothing more there except more pain. Billy's suggestion was well meant, she knew, but facing the details was harder than she had expected.

She finally fell asleep and slept until her mobile phone chimed. Reluctantly, she pulled it out of her pocket, and seeing Lori's picture on the touch screen, rolled over and propped up on her elbows, answering the call.

"Hey, good lookin," the male voice said, startling her. "It's Blake. I was passing through town and knew we had to talk."

"What?" she absently asked in a soft voice, trying to shake the sleep out of her mind.

Who?

"It's Blake, doll. We need to talk."

What the fuck?

She snapped upright and stared at the phone, Lori's picture still on the screen.

Son of a fucking—

"You sonofabitch! You have some nerve!" she shouted when she realized it *was* him and he was using Lori's phone. "Don't call me again!" She broke the connection and wanted to throw something—something big—and throw it hard.

Damn! Damn and damn!

It took all her strength to not throw her phone at the large glass wall.

-◻-

"Well," Blake said as he handed the phone back to Lori, "that didn't go as well as I hoped."

"You crazy bastard!" Lori yelled at him, not caring who in the restaurant heard her. "Now she'll think I agreed to this!"

"Calm down, Lori," Blake said, and smiled as he picked up his beer glass and took a swig. "She'll be all right once she thinks about it."

"What makes you so sure?" Lori asked. "She told us she was glad you were out of her life."

"Well, I'm *not* out of her life and I'm *not* finished with her," Blake said, and set his glass down firmly.

"Well, I'm pretty sure she's finished with you," Lori said, and picked up her purse as she stood. "She must've blocked your number."

He looked up and glared at her. "Don't worry, Lori, she'll talk to me."

"Why's that?" Then Lori put her hands up in front of her. "Forget it. I don't want to know. You made me look bad in front of my friend, and like her, I don't want to hear what you have to say. Not about anything." Lori got up and left the restaurant without looking back.

◻-◻-◻-◻-◻

Billy had taken part of the morning off from the diner

to start his research. To that end, he settled into the viewer chair in the *Chesterfield Herald*'s news article archives. The clerk showed him where the digital files were and he absently went for twenty-five years past, three years before his dad had bought the Duckard properties. He loaded the first disk in the collection and initiated a search for the Hammersmith name.

Warren Hammersmith, Mike's father, was all over the papers with his philanthropic construction projects. He seemed to be a concerned citizen, building both middle-class housing structures and large, more expensive business structures. Billy figured Mike would have been in his thirties then and searched the older records on the disk.

Thirty years back, Billy found a small article that referenced Warren's purchase of the Duckard Department Store properties in town and a statement indicated that Warren's firm had originally designed the twin structures. The article further listed Warren's son Mike as one of the junior architects on the original project.

Billy decided to check on the history of the Duckard's buildings and found they were about forty years old; Mike would have been in his early twenties when the buildings were constructed. They were only used for about eighteen years, before hard times befell the chain and all of their stores closed. Three years after the stores closed, the article mentioned that W.C. Hawke, in a declining market, bought the properties from Warren.

Thinking about the locked door, Billy searched for Mike Hammersmith in the years between the building's construction and when the stores closed. Nothing appeared in the business sections, so Billy turned his search to the society sections, wondering what a young, successful architect would do when he had his father's money to spend.

An article and two pictures of a twenty-something Mike popped up, both of him partying with many young women at a couple of city social events. Ten years after that, another article identified him with a well-heeled socialite named Hannah Quinn. One associated picture was a posed shot of the two of them with Warren and his wife, and the others were of Mike and the woman on a dance floor somewhere, seriously cutting the rug. Mike was certainly living the dream.

Billy printed the pictures and a copy of the article. Searching forward a few months at a time, numerous society articles queued up and Billy selectively printed some. In an article dated two years later, Mike and Hannah announced their engagement.

"Hmm. I wonder what happened. Mike never married," Billy told himself softly.

Billy searched forward for Hannah Quinn, wondering where she was now, but the list of articles with Hannah's name abruptly stopped the year after their engagement, two years before W.C. Hawke had bought the properties. There was nothing after that, and Billy selected the last one.

Startled, Billy read the tribute to Hannah and her life, missing for nearly two weeks and presumed dead at the time of writing. Hannah was thirty-eight and Mike was forty. Billy printed the article and searched back into the assumed last weeks of her life.

He printed a number of the articles when he realized the time. He was going to have to hurry if he was going to meet Billie on time.

Forty-One

Eating a gastronomical delight from Scott's Hot Dog Cart, Billy escorted Billie up First West. He explained what he had overheard in the park near the kitchen and that he had been searching for history on Hammersmith.

"You're shitting me? Right?" Billie said, stopping abruptly in the middle of the crosswalk on Blackfoot, staring at him.

"My, my, Tiger," he said calmly. "There's no need for such language. Especially from a mouth as pretty as yours."

"But you just said—"

"Yes. Mike Hammersmith put a three-thousand-dollar contract on my head." He smiled and gently pushed her to continue crossing the street. "At least it wasn't an open bounty, and I'm pretty sure I know where Knife is likely to try something—just not when. But he could try to do something out in the open."

"But Billy—"

"I will make sure Lynx and Hammer or Cat and Stretch or Mace are with me at all times," he said as they reached the north side of the street, "while we watch and patrol the blocks."

"What about me?" she asked, brow furrowed as she stopped and scowled at him. "And just where do you think I am going to be?"

"We can manage, Billie. This is far too dangerous and I sure don't want you to get hurt," he said, and slipped his arm around her shoulders.

"No, Billy," she said, pushing his arms away as she stepped back. She planted her fists firmly on her hips. "If you're going to face Knife, I'm going to be there to back you up! If you're going

77

to parade around like nothing's happening, I'm going to be there with you! Not Cathy or Mindy or any of them! Me! I'm going to be there! I'm not going to sit back and let someone try to hurt you or worse! End of discussion!"

Billie saw him shake his head and his shoulders droop.

"You haven't had to face anyone for real yet," he said, his voice still calm. "Pink didn't fight back."

"That's just a technicality," she said.

It's more than a technicality.

I know. Just don't start shaking.

This is insane. You're not ready—

No! It isn't! This isn't about me.

"Tiger, I really want you to wait this one out," he said, slowly straightening up and crossing his arms over his chest. "If he tries something with a knife, I know I can handle him, but if he resorts to using a gun...well, he could shoot from a distance and there's no way I can stop him. We don't have time, Tiger."

"Then he'll just have to shoot at me too!" Unflinching, she held his eyes for a long moment. "In the meantime, we'll keep practicing and I'll keep learning. I'll learn all I can in the time we do have."

Billie waited, fists clenched. She could feel his inner conflict as she stared back at him, standing over her, his posture tall and intimidating as he glared down at her.

"We need to get the mats out," she said softly without moving. "Last time we practiced was Thursday and it feels like it's been weeks."

"Damn!" he muttered half aloud, and let his arms drop. "Lynx was complaining about the same thing yesterday." He gently took her arm and turned east toward the bus station. "I'll roll one of them out tomorrow."

◻-◻-◻-◻-◻

Walking back toward city center along the north side of Crescent, Billie started explaining the bad day she had had.

"I got an upsetting phone call this afternoon," Billie said.

Billy did not say anything, waiting for her to continue.

"I told you about the unpleasant, abusive low-life I had for a boyfriend, didn't I?"

"Yes, but no details," he said. "I know you don't have fond memories."

"No, I don't," she admitted. "Being around that sonofa— sorry. My filter's been broken since he woke me up this afternoon. I start swearing every time I start thinking about Blake. Our relationship was not good, not even in the beginning. I was very stupid for letting it even begin. He's a user, and for a while I thought that was okay, that I could live with that. I let him get away with things, his need for me to buy him things he thought he needed—expensive dinners out, you name it. But after a few weeks, I got tired of it and started saying no to his wants. Then that rotten bas—sorry, again." She inhaled and then slowly continued. "He got physical and I didn't know how defend myself against him. In our nearly three months of being together, if that's what you would call it, I only let him up to my apartment twice, and the first time it was all I could do to get him to leave. The second, the last time, security had to take him out. I filed a complaint with the police and he stopped coming around—"

"Until today."

"Yeah. Until today."

"How bad did he treat you?" Billy asked, his voice unusually level and calm. She'd heard him use that tone before, the night he had faced the drug dealers and protected her from the drunk in the village. But he didn't use it as a question that night.

"Welts and bruises," she admitted. "He liked to grab me wherever he thought I would be tender or sensitive. He liked to hit, stomach, chest...face. Luckily, nothing was ever broken." She inhaled a deep breath. "I wish I knew then what I know now about defending myself."

"I wish you never had to defend yourself from anyone," Billy said in the same level tone, but she had seen the change in his manner when she had mentioned Blake hitting her.

"Don't bother yourself about him, Billy," she said. "He isn't worth the effort."

"So he was the call you got today?"

"Yeah," she said, and looked at him. "I blocked his number from my phone, but he used Lori's phone. And I answered it thinking Lori was calling me."

"What did he want?"

"He said to talk," she said. "But he's after more."

"And you?"

"Shit! You're asking *me*? Of all the stupid questions—you know how I feel, Billy." She stomped the pavement and stared at him. "I told him to never call me again and hung up on him." She tightened her lips and glared at him. "But he'll keep trying."

"Stop your cussing, please, and calm down. I'm on your side, remember? What's his name?"

"Sorry. I know you are. Thanks. His name is Blake Lawrence," she said, and forced her shoulders to relax. "The way he acts, he's gotta have a record somewhere. He starts out very smooth and gets his fingers into you before you know it. Then he gets very pushy and ignores anything he doesn't want to hear."

"Does your phone get internet?"

"Yeah, but I have my own wi-fi at the apartment and I use my pad. It's too hard to see things on my phone's small screen."

"Maybe we should check out his background when we get back to your place," Billy said, and pulled her close. "And I can show you what I found out about Hammersmith today."

"Okay." Billie tried to calm her agitation and put Blake out of her mind. But then another concern replaced her anger and she glanced across the street at the dark, wooded park. "Was it in the park across from the kitchen? Where you heard him?"

"Yup. Thank goodness for the trees and shadows."

¤-¤-¤-¤-¤

"We haven't seen Pink around the kitchen lately," Billie said as they walked south from the bus station. They had changed back into their normal clothes and Billy was taking her back to her apartment. "I take it his druggies pay him enough he can have a place of his own and not have to eat at one of the kitchens."

"Probably," Billy said, "but Knife and his cronies don't have to come to the kitchen either. They come to keep the pressure on, to intimidate the rest of the people and keep them afraid. Pink doesn't care. He's in a different line of work."

She looked at him. "One sells some things and the other..."

"Removes some things," Billy finished for her. "Knife fills contracts."

"Yeah. That's what I thought you meant."

"Yeah." His voice was somber.

They walked in silence another block before Billie started again.

"I followed your suggestion and went to the library and then to the newspaper office today," she said, "and tried to find out something about the accident that I told you about."

Billy looked at her, but they were between streetlights and she could not see his face clearly enough to know what his reaction was.

"I stopped at the Chestnut Creek Bridge last week when I

came back from my folks' place, and I tried to visualize how the accident might've happened." She turned back and watched the street. "From the reports, it was worse than I imagined." Her words were barely a whisper as her legs trembled and threatened to fail her.

"Hold onto me," he said softly as he caught her. "I'm sorry this bothers you so much."

"Thanks," she said, trying to regain her poise. "I got to thinking that you never said when or where your parents died. Is it hard for you to talk about?"

"Yeah. Like with you and your friend, I guess."

"I'm sorry, Billy." He nodded. "Is there anything I can research? Anything that will make it easier for you?"

He shook his head. "No. There's nothing more that I need to see. If it would help you, I would look at what you found on your friend's accident. But only if you want me to see it."

"Thanks. I need to digest it first," Billie said with a tight smile. "Then maybe." She stopped and turned to look at him. "Sorry, Billy. Right now I feel like I'm about to explode. With everything that's happened in the last two days, I feel like I'm in some kind of...of...sensory, emotional overload. Tonight, you made me feel like you didn't want me with you anymore. And that scared me." Billie looked at her wrist and then looked at him. "You're important to me too, Billy."

"I'm sorry I made you feel that way. I'm here, whenever you need me."

"Thank you, Billy. You have no idea how much that means to me," she said, and pulled his head down and kissed him.

Forty-Two

Tuesday, May 10

Blake slowly wandered through the aisles between the organized bookshelves in Pages Bookstore. At first he tried to look like he was actually interested in the categories and titles, but after a while he settled into his search, looking at the store clerks and stockers as he went from one aisle to another. He had walked each aisle twice and a couple of them three times, each time passing the unmanned information counter. Finally, he found himself staring at the "Employees Only" sign at the entry into the storage area at the back of the store. About to ignore it, he stopped when a young man carrying a box of Paladin Shadows sci-fi series paperbacks pushed the door open and forced him to step back, out of the way.

"May I help you?" the man asked, and stopped in front of Blake.

Blake blinked in surprise and asked, "Stacy Majors? I'm looking for Stacy."

"She doesn't come in until nine thirty."

"Nine thirty?"

"Yeah," the man said, and then continued on his way.

Blake looked at the clock above the information counter and then turned to the small grouping of chairs in the reading area to one side of the front door. He picked up a copy of the *Herald* and sat down to occupy his next half hour.

-¤-

When Blake saw Stacy walk into the store, through the door from the storage room at the back, his frustration was all already elevated a notch or two above normal. He got up and met her when she stopped behind the information counter.

"Morning, Stace," he said as she shuffled papers beside the computer.

"Oh shit!" she muttered as she looked up and saw him. Her shoulders dropped and she cocked her head to one side. "What?"

"Wow. What kind of a greeting is that?"

"It's not a greeting. What do you want?"

"Information," he said, pointing to the sign over the counter and smiling.

She raised her eyebrows and stared at him with a look that questioned his intelligence.

"Do you guys still get together on Wednesday nights?"

She waited and did not move or change her expression.

"I need to talk to Billie," he said, and leaned forward. "She wouldn't talk to me on the phone, so I figured I'd talk to her there."

"She doesn't want to talk to you. Can't you get that into that nonexistent brain of yours?"

"She'll talk to me," he said confidently. "And your nights out are in public. It can't hurt to talk in public, can it?"

"She's filed one civil complaint against you and she can do it again. She won't put up with you anymore, Blake. Now go somewhere else," Stacy said, and turned back to her stack of papers.

"Stace! I can't let her just throw me out like she did. I need to talk to her. She has to understand."

"Understand what, Blake?" she asked, and stepped back from the counter.

"I have to talk to her," he said softly, his red-faced frustration turning to anger.

"She already knows about your temper and your lack of

self-control," Stacy said, and glanced around in search of the store manager, someone... "She's had enough bruises from you. Leave her alone."

Blake leaned farther forward, forcing Stacy back against the cabinet behind the booth to keep her distance. He snatched up a pencil from the back side of the counter and held it in his fingers in front of him. His eyes flashed and he glared at her. "Tell me. Where?"

"Or what? You going to beat me too?"

"Why Stace, I'd never do that," he said, and curled his fingers into a fist. The pencil snapped and the pieces fell onto the counter.

"Custer's," slipped out before Stacy could catch herself.

¤-¤-¤-¤-¤

"There are two parties interested in the Cedar Hollow properties," June said, and handed the printouts to Frederick. "They both seem to be adequately funded and capable."

Frederick took the sheets and skimmed the content. "Bids?"

"One matched the appraised value and the other a little less," she said, smiling. "Pretty much what we expected."

"It isn't a fire sale, June," he said. "We'll see how high they will go."

"Of course you realize it won't be enough," she said.

"I'm hoping I can work around that," he said, still looking at the figures.

"Collin's Park would—"

"No!" he snapped and then contritely, he looked up at her. "Sorry, June. I'll sell everything else I own before that one."

"Oh, I didn't know it meant that much to you." June looked at him, surprised by his sudden, uncharacteristic fierceness.

"It does," he said, calming himself, reflecting on things

unsaid, and smiled. "Let's see where we can go with Cedar Hollow and then we'll see if I need to consider something else."

"Yes, Mr. Westman," June said, and left the room.

"Donna," he called his secretary through the open door. "A minute, please."

He set June's sheets aside as Donna came in and sat down in the chair at the end of his desk. She held her notepad and stylus ready.

"Donna, I'm going to take a few days and visit two of the projects we have under construction," he said, and noticed her surprise. "Right now I think everyone has things under control and I want to get my hands dirty, feeling the grit of the sites, and talk with the crews."

"Yes, sir. You haven't gone to a site in...What? Two years?" she asked.

"One and a half," he said, and smiled. "Don't you think it's time I did?"

"Probably, sir," Donna said, and smiled in return. "Shall I make arrangements?"

He shook his head. "I've already done that."

"Oh?"

"I have a little bit of personal business to take care of while I'm gone," he said. "So, while I was arranging for that, I added the stops for the projects."

"When are you leaving?"

"Tomorrow, late morning," he said. "You have my number if anything comes up while I'm away."

"May I ask how long you'll be gone?"

"Probably a week," he said. "I'm not sure."

Donna looked at him with dismay. "Probably?"

"My tickets are for a return in a week," he said, catching her look. "But if my personal business needs it, I may extend."

"Yes, sir," she said. "Shall I give you daily updates?"

"Certainly. I'll check my emails every night just like normal."

"Yes, sir. Is there anything else?"

"No, Donna. Not at the moment," he said, and smiled. "I'll keep you informed on how the inspections go."

¤-¤-¤-¤-¤

It's just a prank. It's just a... Mike Hammersmith sat upright in the cushioned recliner chair, staring at his bedroom wall like he had all through the night. Only now, he slowly realized, the window was brighter with its morning light. He blinked, and with shaky hands, slowly pulled himself forward and then pushed himself up onto his wobbly feet. *Damn! It has to be a prank,* he kept telling himself, repeating the thought, trying to convince himself it was not real, like he had tried all through the night. *WC's dead! He can't be sending emails. He just can't be...*

Mike made his way to the bathroom and splashed cold water over his face and head. He took some aspirin and showered, hoping one or the other would take the shakes away. But he knew why he was shaking and he wondered how...

"No. It's just a prank!" he shouted to no one. "Someone has a very sick sense of humor and made a lucky guess!" He stared at his face in the round mirror in the shower. *Lucky? Damn! How's it lucky?*

He stepped out of the shower and stood in a growing puddle as he braced himself and reached for a towel. When he took fresh clothes from the dresser drawer, he saw the empty bottle beside the recliner, remembering how hard he had tried to blot out the images raised by that email—the images of the fire, of WC's wife's screams.... His heart was pounding, threatening to burst in his chest. He had tried very hard to erase the memory of them, but they were still there. *But it can't be from WC. It's impossible. There's no way he survived. It has to be a prank.*

Mike sat down on the foot of his bed, rubbed his pain-filled eyes, and wondered, *If it is a prank, there's only one other person left that knows what happened.*

Forty-Three

Wednesday, May 11

Dressed in a slacks, bright short-sleeved top, and sleeveless leather vest ensemble similar to the one that sent Billy into effusive rapture when she had seen him for lunch the day before, Billie entered the new club for their girls' nights out, Custer's. Becky had picked the place from a pleasant memory of a date night she had had during the winter.

Custer's, named for the U. S. 7th Cavalry's infamous Lieutenant Colonel, who took a stand against the Lakota, the Arapaho, and the Northern Cheyenne, had a twist: its theme favored the Indians and made for a lively open forum whenever their doors were open.

Billie smiled at Stacy and Becky and greeted Lori coolly as she slid into the booth beside Becky.

"You look exhausted," Stacy said as Billie sat down.

"Been working out and I'm tired," Billie said as she pulled the order pad to her.

"Your self-defense class?" Becky asked.

"Yeah. Two sessions today—one this morning, and the other finished about an hour ago. Four against one today," Billie said, and punched a selection into the pad.

"Four against one?" Stacy asked.

"Yes. It took me three tries before I got it," Billie said.

"And how many sessions do you do?" Becky asked.

"Ten, after I get it right," Billie said before she slid her card into the slot. "Each one with a different set of match partners."

"How many did you say you did before you got it right?" Stacy asked.

"Three, I said. Where is that waiter?" Billie said, and started to get up.

Becky caught her arm. "Be patient. Give them a minute," she said softly, so only Billie could hear.

Billie sighed and relaxed a little.

"Are you all right?" Becky asked.

"Of course," Billie said softly, and forced a smile. *All hell's about to break loose and I sure can't tell them what's going on.* "It's just becoming one of those weeks."

"Billie," Stacy said as she leaned closer to hear over the din of the restaurant. "There's something you need to know. Blake. He's back."

"Yeah. I know," Billie said heavily, and nodded. "He used Lori's—"

"I swear he grabbed it before I could stop him!" Lori interrupted, and reached for Billie's hand. "Honest. There's no way I'd *let* him use my phone. But I couldn't get it back before he called you."

Billie sighed and looked back at Stacy.

"He stopped by the store yesterday," Stacy explained. "I told him you didn't want to see him."

"Yesterday?" Billie shook her head. "I told him that when he called and ruined my day on Monday. He still doesn't listen when someone tells—"

"He asked where we were meeting," Stacy added before Billie could finish. "And I let it slip out."

"Are you okay? I mean, really?" Becky asked.

"Yes and no, Beck," Billie said softly, and looked at Stacy, understanding how easily Blake could have made that happen. "Most things are good, but there are a few that really suck!"

"Like Blake?" Stacy asked rhetorically.

"Yeah, like Blake, and right now, I just need a drink."

As if on cue, the waiter stopped at the end of the table and set a goblet full of amber liquid with one cube of ice in front of her. Then he set two shots of Becky's spiced rum beside it, smiled with a nod, and left.

"There's gotta be something you can do about Blake," Stacy said, and glanced at Becky and Lori.

"That would be nice. But first, a toast, ladies," Billie said, and raised the first shot glass up in front of her. "My hope is that each of you find the support of a most wonderful, loving, and dedicated man in your lives, one that cares for you before and more than anything else." She downed the shot when she finished. The others took sips of their drinks.

Billie inhaled deeply as the rum ran down her throat, and with eyes watering, picked up the remaining shot glass. She exhaled and smiled at the group. "You've all been a great pleasure, and I thank you for that." She inhaled the second shot.

She wiped her eyes with her napkin and vigorously set the shot glass down. She saw Becky's and Stacy's startled expressions and turned to see that someone had stopped at the end of the table. Blake stood there, staring at her.

"Oh shit! And now I have to endure people that cannot understand the English language!" Billie said to no one in particular. Then in a louder, cold voice, directed straight at him, "Leave me alone!"

When he tried to sit beside her, she shoved her leg between them and pushed him away. He shifted to Lori and Stacy's side of the booth.

"Not a very nice greeting," Blake said as he pushed his way in beside Stacy, "for an old friend."

"We're *not* friends." Billie fought to hold her temper and resisted the urge to punch him in the face, just because! "Go away!"

God, that would feel better than throwing things.

"I hear you're running around with homeless people these

days," he said as if he had not heard her.

Dumb shit, can't even get that right.

Billie did not answer at first. She just stared at him for a long moment. Finally, she looked at Becky and said, "I know quite a few and I do volunteer at a soup kitchen. If that constitutes 'running around' with them, then I guess I do."

"Aaah," Blake said, leaning across the table to get her attention. "And I suppose your friends don't mind that you're having an affair with a homeless man?"

"You really don't understand the language," Billie said, staring straight at him. She took a longer-than-normal sip of her drink before she looked at Becky again. "An 'affair' would mean that I am cheating on someone I have a pledge with. But since I do have a pledge with someone and I'm only seeing him"—she turned back to Blake—"I am NOT having an affair!" The last she nearly shouted in his face.

"So…" Blake smiled, unperturbed. "…you admit you're seeing a homeless man?"

Hang on! Don't lose it over this no-account, low—

"What an ass!" Billie inhaled a deep breath and held it a moment as she glanced at each of the girls. She pushed herself back against the seat and looked at him. "You've used the term *'homeless'* three times and still don't know what it means. He has his own apartment, and we spend our time in his or mine as we please. Now, go somewhere else! Spill your ignorance at someone else's table! Go find someone that gives a shit what you think!"

"No!" Blake said, "I came here to talk to you! We have a lot to talk—"

"No! We *don't!*" Billie said loudly, and started to slide out of the booth.

Blake was up instantly, blocking her exit. He grabbed her left upper arm with his left hand and squeezed.

You're not going to get away with this. Not this time!

Billie's eyes focused on his, her brow wrinkled in

determination as she hardened her bicep. Her right hand clamped around his wrist and squeezed, her fingers curling, her nails biting into the soft, underside flesh. Forcing herself to ignore the slowly rising pain in her arm, she held his eyes and kept tightening her grip, digging her nails in, squeezing harder. Pleased, she saw the tightly guarded surprise cross his face, slowly turning into a pain-filled grimace. She continued to tighten her grip, holding her steely focus on his eyes, completely unaware of the surprise and disbelief in the others at the table, or the couples at the nearby tables. The normal murmur of restaurant conversations died; everyone that saw the contest watched in awed silence as the battle of wills played out.

Slowly, Blake's grip weakened and his fingers opened, straightening with the growing pain as Billie's nails continued to dig in. His eyes reflected his unexpected anguish as Billie slowly ratcheted her grip tighter.

When his fingers released her arm, Billie pulled his hand away and revealed the white, blood-starved imprint of his thumb and fingers. She held his hand up in front of him, making him stare at his tortured fingers, the blood starting to drip from under her grip.

Then in deeply growled words, each emphasized separately, she said, "Don't...touch...me!"

She slammed his hand down on the table as a large man wearing a Custer's T-shirt stopped behind Blake.

"Is there a problem, ma'am?" he asked, his eyes sliding from the white imprint on her arm to the blood dripping from her clenched fingers.

"Not now," she said in threatening softness, her unblinking eyes firmly locked on Blake's. She slowly released his wrist and said "thanks" to the man in the T-shirt.

The man waited and Blake stared at her as she wiped her hands on her napkin. Complete disbelief filled Blake's expression as his weakened knees dropped him back onto the bench beside Stacy.

"You let me know if he starts anything again, ma'am," the

man in the T-shirt said, and stepped back. "I'll be watching."
Then he turned and went back to stand near the end of the bar.

Billie finished her drink in one long sip, smiled tightly at
the girls. Then she slid out and stood at the end of the booth as
she grabbed her purse and slipped her arm and head through
the strap. "Sorry, but I think I've had about all of a night out I
can take. And shit! Now I have to go and take another shower
to wash the filth off."

She made a gesture of disgust, then turned and started for
the door.

Blake got up and started to follow her. "We still need to
talk."

Ignore him. Just a little bit farther.

He said it again, louder. "We need to talk!"

Don't lose it! You're almost outside.

Becky, Lori, and Stacy grabbed their purses and left their
coats as they slid out of the booth and quickly followed Blake.

Billie reached the door and pushed it open as he shouted,
"Dammit! I'm talking to you!" Then he grabbed for her arm
again.

Tiger's reflexes kicked in the instant he touched her. She
spun around, caught his arm, and wrenched it up behind his
back, twisting it up until his hand was between his shoulder
blades. Her other hand, holding a fistful of hair, slammed his
face into the brick wall beside the still open door.

"I said 'Don't! Touch! Me!'" she shouted, and banged his
head against the wall with each word, pushing his arm higher,
lifting him up onto his toes. "God help me! If you touch me
again I'll break this arm and castrate you on the spot and leave
your whimpering ass for the cops to haul off. Capisce?"

"I'll handle him from here," the large man in the T-shirt
said as he stepped up and grabbed Blake. He looked down
at her and smiled. "I'm sorry for your discomfort and
inconvenience, ma'am, but I sure wish more of our customers
were like you." He handed her a business card. "You come back

as often as you want. Show that to the server and enjoy as many evenings as you want, on us. It has no expiration date and no limit on how many times you can come. I may even think about offering you a job as a bouncer." He nodded again.

She looked at him and slowly let herself smile. "Thanks."

"Go and have that arm looked at," he said as he spun Blake back inside and then pushed him into a room off the end of the bar. As the entry door started to close, she saw Becky, Stacy, and Lori staring at her, mouths agape, and heard the room behind them clapping and cheering, everyone smiling at her.

Forty-Four

Billie's headlights splashed across the front of her apartment building as she turned off Cheyenne and into the drive. She waved as Billy got up from where he was sitting on the brick planter as she waited for the door to the parking garage to open.

"I was getting a little worried," he said as she got out of the SUV and hugged him tight, her cheek firmly against his chest.

"Sorry," she said softly, and slowly tilted her head back, brow furrowed as she looked up at him. "Blake showed up tonight and turned a nice-but-tiring day into a shitty one. I had to have some time to think."

She led them into the lobby and stopped at the counter.

The man behind it looked up. "Can I help you, Miss Mattis?"

"Yes, Thomas. I'd like to get another key to my apartment please," she said, and glanced at Billy. "This is Billy Carson. He'll be coming and going a lot and I want him to have his own key."

"I'll need to get some information from you, and I can have a key tomorrow around lunchtime," Thomas said, and pushed a form to her. He cocked his head and asked, "This isn't the one we—"

"No, Thomas. Billy is definitely not that one."

Thomas nodded and then he looked at Billy. "Sir, are you carrying any weapons?"

"Just a knife," he said, and shrugged.

"May I see it, please?"

Billy smiled at Billie as she listened and turned to watch. He pulled the knife from his pocket and opened the eight-inch blade before he handed it to Thomas, hilt first.

"A bit unusual to have such a large knife, isn't it?" Thomas asked, and looked up at Billy.

"Shucks, Thomas," Billie said as she pulled hers from her purse, flipped the blade open, and held it for Thomas to look at. "I've got two inches on him. His isn't even dangerous."

Thomas's eyes went wide. "Yes, Miss Mattis. If you say so." He handed Billy's knife back.

Billie returned hers to her purse and finished filling out the form.

"You do know," Billie asked as she handed Thomas the completed form, "that the city's streets are not as safe as you'd like to think?"

"Yes, yes, ma'am. I've heard that," Thomas said softly, and took the form.

-☐-

"I'm sorry I made you worry," Billie said as she opened her apartment door and let Billy in. "I seem to be doing that a lot this week. Blake found us tonight at Custer's, and I had to decompress."

Billy waited for her to continue as he hung their jackets on the pegs behind the door. She had stopped behind her three-section sofa and was standing with her back to him, studying the view through her expansive glass wall. She was absently holding her left upper arm with her right hand.

"Blake charged in like he always did, expecting to demand his way with timid Billie, only the problem was he found Tiger in full pounce mode instead." She chuckled softly. "I was so mad when he grabbed my arm the second time, I had him pinned to the building with a bloody face before I knew it. The bouncer even said he'd consider giving me a job." She glanced over her shoulder at Billy as he stepped up to her. She laughed at the absurdity. "Can you imagine a hundred-and-twenty-pound woman bouncer?"

Billy slipped his arms around her shoulders and gently pulled her back against him. He held her tight. "I'm glad you can take care of yourself now. How's your arm?"

"It'll bruise, but his is hurting a lot more and will for a long time. I was so mad I would've broken it if the bouncer hadn't got there when he did. The 'Tiger' almost got loose tonight." She inhaled and rested her head against his chest.

Billy relaxed his hold and grabbed his backpack as he led her to the sofa and sat her down. He took a tube of ointment from the small zippered pouch and began gently rubbing the salve onto her upper arm where she indicated Blake had grabbed her.

Billy had not seen her when she was angry, truly angry, but he figured that as good as she was normally, her anger would make her even more formidable, possibly frightening to face. He wondered if that was the 'Tiger' she was talking about.

"This will relax the muscles and help with any lingering pain," he said, and gently massaged her bicep.

Billie relaxed against the cushioned back of the sofa and smiled at him. "Thanks. That feels good. I'll smell like a gym for hours, but it feels good."

"I heard you had a busy day today," Billy said. "Todd mentioned it when I went by the department store after work."

"Actually, the last two days have been busy," she said. "Todd sparred with me yesterday morning while Cathy was at work, and Russell this morning before he went to work. I sparred with Cathy both afternoons after she got home from work. Today she had ten rounds with four challengers for me, four against one. And after tonight, with the physical and emotional ups and downs, I think I'm officially pooped."

"Ten rounds? He didn't tell me how many." Billy shook his head as he bent down and pulled her boots off. Then he stood up, straddled her legs, lifted her up, and shifted her to lie back against the bolstered arm of the sofa. He sat back down, pulled her legs onto his lap, and began gently rubbing the balls of her feet and her toes.

She sighed softly and closed her eyes.

Now that's worth waiting for...

"God, that feels good. You sure know how to make a girl happy," she said softly, savoring his gentle ministrations.

Billie was asleep before he could make a comment.

Thursday, May 12

Billy removed the security bars and then unlocked the west entry doors to the department store to let the three men wearing suits and two women in business dress in. He closed the doors and relocked them as they arranged themselves in the spacious room and glanced around. Emptied long ago, except for a couple of remaining counters, the room was pleasantly vacant.

"Mr. Donaldson says you've been watching and taking care of the store for nearly sixteen years," the tallest of the men said as he turned to Billy. "You don't look that old."

"Maybe so," Billy said politely. "How is Jim these days? It's been a long time since we have been able to talk."

Billy had dressed in his nicest jeans, his plaid shirt, and his best boots for the meeting, but it was obvious that the man leading this group did not see him as anyone of importance. He certainly did not see him as someone that would be familiar with "the" Mr. Jim Donaldson, owner and head officer in Kelly and Lloyd Architects.

"He's doing very well," the man finally said after a long, appraising look at Billy. "I'm Bob Dawson, and Mr. Donaldson"—he stressed Jim's name formally—"asked me to head up the review of the structures. These folks are Joseph, Dan, Jane, and Lucy."

Billy shook their hands, accepting that they did not know what, or who, he knew, and said the appropriate niceties.

"Where would you like to start?" Billy asked. "This is obviously the ground floor of the store proper. There are store rooms along the back wall" —he pointed to the east wall—"and across the south end of the building with access from the alley between the two buildings. Public access is currently just from the street on the west, but there is a second access blocked off on the north, on Baker Street."

Bob looked at something in the folder he carried and Dan scrolled through something on his digital pad.

"This says," Bob said, reading from the folder, "the second floor is also part of the old store."

"Yes, it was," Billy agreed, and gestured to the inoperative escalator hidden behind a walled façade near the center of the room. "This way." He led the group up the escalator steps.

"I'm surprised it isn't dusty in here," Lucy said as they stepped into the equally empty and spacious second floor.

"It has never been open to the weather," Billy said as they began wandering around the space. "And I've had it cleaned every few years." He noted Bob's curious glance his way.

Billy followed at a polite distance and let them converse among themselves and take their notes, while staying close enough to answer the occasional question they asked. When they returned to the escalator, he asked, "How extensive of a renovation is Jim thinking of?"

"Pretty much every floor," Bob said, and opened his folder. He showed Billy a series of small sketches. "Mr. Donaldson says the owner wants to turn the entire building into a modern apartment complex for the normal middle, working class— regular folks with regular jobs."

"The first and second floors," Lucy added, "will be a combination of entertainment spaces and a dedicated restaurant or cafeteria for the residents, possibly including a small retail shop for those odd items we often forget when we go shopping, or run out of late at night."

"One plan option," Joseph said, "is to connect the two buildings with multiple enclosed bridges or 'skywalks' on various floors."

"That sounds very nice," Billy admitted. "When will construction start?" he asked as he led them to a private stairwell at the back of the building.

"We've had the plans on file for nearly twenty years, so it didn't take long for the city review. We'll amend the plans to incorporate material improvements and updates to meet the code changes, but those won't cause any measurable delays. They approved the plans and issued the construction permits yesterday," Bob said, and looked up and down the stairwell. "So construction can start as soon as we get the appraisal and evaluation finished. Probably in a couple of weeks."

"Nice," Billy said, and turned back to the layout of the store. "These alley-side stairs are one of four sets that connect the floors together from the basement to the top floor, the tenth. The three sets of elevators have not been operated in many years, so the stairs are the only way to look at the rest of the floors."

Bob smiled, getting more comfortable with Billy and his knowledge of the store. "Then we'll use them. Lead on, Billy."

Forty-Five

Mitchell had entered the Westman Associates offices early and was reviewing the information they had collected in the past couple of days on Hammersmith's suspected activities, especially anything their informants had on his relationship with Pink and the Knife. It was a few minutes before seven thirty when Mitchell answered his desk phone.

"Westman Associates. Mitchell speaking," he said in a practiced voice. "May I help you?"

"Mitchell," the voice on the line said. "It's Guy in the city engineer's office."

"Good morning, Guy. What can I do for you?"

"I've been coming in early this week, and this morning I opened our emails and was wondering if you had heard?"

Mitchell caught the odd tone in Guy's voice. "Heard what, Guy?"

He heard Guy take a deep breath. "The city issued renovation permits on the Duckard's Department Store buildings late Tuesday."

"Permits?" Mitchell asked as he sat up straight, certain he had not heard correctly.

"Yup."

"To who?"

"To a construction company out of Des Moines that specializes in renovating commercial properties, and...an architectural firm out of Chicago, a Kelly and Lloyd Architects."

"Damn!" Mitchell said softly. "I doubt Frederick knows

103

about this."

"That's why I figured I should call," Guy said. "Word is that he and Hammersmith were trying to get that job."

"Yeah," Mitchell said. "I better call Frederick. Thanks, Guy. I'll talk to you later."

◻-◻-◻-◻-◻

Billie felt much better this morning, enjoying her walk to the Streetcar. The weather was bright and pleasant, almost without wind, warm enough that she ended up carrying her white jacket. She stopped at the River Crest Apartments, but neither Todd nor Russell could practice with her as she had hoped, so she left her backpack in Billy's apartment and decided to drop in on him and have a cup of tea.

"Morning, Angie," Billie greeted as she stepped into the dining room and Angie met her. "Is Billy available?"

"Sorry, Billie," Angie said. "He came in early like he always does, but a little before seven, he got a phone call. Sid said something came up and Billy needed to take the day off."

"Did he say what came up?"

"Nope. Sid just told Ned he would have to cover for Billy today."

"Shucks," Billie said, and smiled to herself. "I guess I won't have tea with him."

"Billie?" Angie asked as Billie started to turn to leave. "I know this is none of my business."

"What, Angie?"

"You and Billy. It's pretty serious, isn't it?"

"Yes, Angie. I think it is," Billie said, feeling her cheeks warm.

"You know he's never been one to date a lot of women," Angie said, and Billie thought she was unsure of how to say what was on her mind.

"He told me he hasn't dated much," Billie said, and cocked her head slightly. "Why?"

"I want to show you something," Angie said, and led Billie into the back rooms, to Billy's bathroom. She opened a small cupboard beside the medicine cabinet over the sink and took a small envelope off the top shelf. "Billy will kill me if he knew I saw this. I used his bathroom the other day because Julie was in the women's and I saw this cabinet door was open. When I went to close it, this was keeping it open."

Angie opened the flap and took the two-by-three-inch photo out and handed it to Billie. "It says 'Wilhelmina Georgiana Mattis' on the back, but it looks sorta like you."

Billie smiled.

I'm surprised he still has this.

Really? You're surprised that someone that has watched you since you were twelve might still have the picture you gave him?

No. I guess not.

Billie looked at the picture, remembering when she had given it to him. "It's my school picture, Angie, when I was twelve. I gave it to him just over fifteen years ago, when I met him here in the diner. The first time he cleaned my boot."

"The first time?"

"Yeah," she said, still studying the picture. "I had forgotten that I gave him this picture. Totally." She handed it back and Angie put it in the envelope and placed the envelope back on the shelf.

As they stepped out into the back room, Angie smiled at her. "I think you've been special to Billy for a long time. I've always kidded him about not liking women, but I think the truth is he's known all along who he liked."

"He's pretty special to me too. I guess he was back then, and I just forgot how I felt about him when we lost track of each other."

"Well," Angie said as they walked back to the front doors, "from the way he started acting, I don't think he expected to see you when he saw you here in the Streetcar, but it looks like he's very happy to have found you again."

"Thanks," Billie said, and smiled. "It has turned out to be happily unexpected for me as well, but I may be more of a complication."

"It's obvious you're a complication he likes, unexpected or not. When I see him, I'll tell him you came by."

"I'd like that. Thanks, Angie."

-¤-

Thinking about what Billy had told her—her asking him to "watch and see" how she turned out, and that he had checked on her as she grew up, through school and college and probably even her jobs—she was not surprised he still had her picture.

He knows you.

Yeah. Maybe that's why I feel so comfortable around him. He knows me more than anyone else, especially now.

And he puts up with you.

Yeah. There is that, too.

She walked toward city center, noticing the number of people that were out, enjoying an early lunch or running errands or for almost any reason to be outside, to embrace the change, the warmth and sunshine of the beautiful spring day. She thought he might have stopped by the department store or the village and she had decided to check the store first.

When she crossed Second Street in front of the department store, she absently looked up at the building and smiled. To the casual passerby it was an old, unused department store, its usefulness lost long ago. But she knew it fondly, more intimately as the sanctuary that Billy had used to nurture and care for her newest collection of friends.

Billie stopped at the passageway on the south of the building, leaned back against the façade, and casually watched the people on the street. Being dressed better than normal, she knew that if she simply darted into the dim alleyways she would cause people to wonder, so she waited a few minutes. Then, when she felt comfortable with her surroundings, she slipped around the corner, neatly disappearing from one world and stepping into the shadows of another.

At the heavy metal door, she stopped and double-checked the alley. Seeing no one, she unlocked the door and quickly slipped in, relocking it behind her.

She started to go down to the basement, but faint sounds drifted down the stairwell from somewhere above. She was suddenly alert, listening more intently. She had never gone onto the main floor or any of those above, but curiosity got the better of her and she slowly started up the flight of stairs. The sounds became murmurs, then voices of people talking, and she worried that someone might have broken in. But as she started up to the third floor, she heard Billy's voice and instantly relaxed.

She stepped out of the open stairwell into a corridor that stretched completely across the width of the building, listening to the sporadic conversation, hearing it more clearly. She turned at the first intersecting corridor and followed it to a large, central room where Billy was talking with five nicely dressed people. She stopped where the corridor joined with the room and waited.

Almost as soon as she got there, Billy noticed her, and his wide smile and dancing eyes told her she was welcome. He quickly turned and waved for her to join him.

"Gentlemen, ladies," Billy said as Billie stopped beside him. "I'd like to introduce Billie Mattis, a very close friend of mine."

They all greeted Billie and introduced themselves, and when Jane shook her hand, she commented, "More than just 'very close' friends, I presume." She gestured to Billie's wrist. "My son and his wife got something similar before they got married. Congratulations to you both."

Billie smiled.

Don't blush. Don't blush.

"Thank you. We haven't set a date yet," Billy said, "but I'm hoping I won't have to wait too much longer." Then he turned back to their previous conversation. "What else would you like to see? I'm at your service for as long as you need me, with the exception of an engagement Billie and I have this evening."

Bob looked at his watch and then glanced at the others. "What do you think? An early lunch and then come back?"

They nodded and Bob turned to Billy. "How about the two of you joining us for lunch, and then we can look at the roof and basement this afternoon?"

Billy looked at Billie. "Are you open or on your way somewhere?"

Billie shook her head slowly. "I have some errands to run later and I have to meet Cathy at four. Other than that, I'm open."

"Wonderful," Bob said, and closed his folder.

-¤-

Billy led Billie and the architects down two blocks and west one to Nick's Italian Corner. At the door, assailed by the comfortable aromas of fresh baking pizza dough, cheeses, and familiar spices, he greeted Nick's pretty daughter, Miriam, at the hostess station. She counted their number and asked them to wait a moment while she checked on a table, and then she turned and went into the kitchen. A short moment later, a white-haired man in black slacks and a red shirt came out and approached the group.

"Is that Billy?" the man asked with a big smile as he bypassed the well-dressed group and shook Billy's hand. "It is very good to see you my friend. Miriam says you need a larger table. I see seven. I can put you in the front corner with lots of light, if that would suit you?"

"Yes, I think that will do fine," Billy said as Bob nodded.

Billy let the architects follow Nick, and he took Billie's hand and followed them. At the grouping of two tables placed under one tablecloth in the front corner of the dining room, everyone sat down. Billy was helping Billie when Nick stopped and greeted her specifically.

"And who is this, Billy?" he asked while smiling at Billie. "You have never brought a lady friend to visit Nick. And never such a beautiful one."

Billy smiled and introduced Billie as he gently curled a strand of her red hair around his finger and lightly rested his hand on her shoulder. "Billie, this is Nick Florentini, owner of the best Italian restaurant in or near the city center. Maybe the whole city."

Billie returned his pleasantries and then Nick hurried on as Billy settled into a seat between her and Bob.

"Are you and Nick old friends?" Bob asked, having watched the interaction of Billy and Nick. He opened his menu and started reviewing it.

"Only for about twelve years now," Billy said as Miriam stopped and started filling water glasses.

She asked for drink orders and the architects ordered wine, Billie stayed with water, and Billy asked for sparkling water on ice.

-¤-

When they finished eating, the architects each complimented the food and said they would have to remember Nick's place when they came down for project reviews.

Billie asked Bob what the renovations would entail and he proudly dove into an explanation. Bob repeated Lucy's descriptions of the ground- and second-floor arrangement of shops and restaurants and Joseph's plan to connect the two buildings, either at the second floors or on each floor at alternate ends.

"Lucy is responsible for the apartments themselves," Bob said, and gestured to her.

"Ah, yes," Lucy said, and set her wine glass down. "What we are looking at is either eight or ten apartments on each floor.

Suites that actually extend from a wide entry hall along the alley side of the building out to a full windowed front wall with a balcony. The owner's plans called for ten large apartments, but we have considered reducing the size of each and going to twelve per floor. They would still be rather large suites and the change would add sixteen apartments."

"Jane has the roof development," Bob said, and looked her way.

"On the Duckard building which is the taller by two floors, the plans call for a nice-sized,-two level penthouse for the owner's personal use. It's to be situated in the south half of the roof and will rise above the existing roof," Jane explained, "while the rest of the roof will be transformed into a terraced combination of numerous small patios interspersed in a garden setting with trees, shrubs, and hedges."

"It sounds wonderful," Billie said softly. "Is the east building going to be similar?"

"Yes." Bob nodded. "Mirrored, basically, with an easterly view. It has fewer floors so it will be considerably shorter than the department store building and will not have a penthouse."

"I'm sure," Billie said, "the owner will be pleased to know the project is finally moving forward.

¤-¤-¤-¤-¤

Blake slowly stepped down the wide stone steps in front of the city police building, absently taking his wallet and keys out of the letter-sized manila envelope and slipping them into his pockets. He turned and started walking north and barely noticed the sounds of the traffic on Main or the two homeless-looking women that got up from their places on the low stone wall around the police station's front lawn and started walking in the same direction.

He could not believe the bouncer at Custer's had actually called the cops and had him taken in for disturbing the peace.

Hell, he thought, *it was Billie that wouldn't talk to me! What was I supposed to do? Just stand there and let her brush me off?*

He glanced back at the stone building and angrily upended the envelope and pocketed the loose change that spilled out into his hand as he crossed St. Charles. He forcefully stuffed the envelope into a trash bin on the north side of the intersection and continued up the sidewalk, his footsteps heavy with disgust.

Blake stopped at the small sandwich shop on the northwest corner of Main and David, bought a sandwich and a bottled drink, and then continued west, eating as he walked. He stopped at the corner of First Street West and glancing around, noticed two women, both dressed in well-worn coats, sitting on a bench, quietly eating and talking to each other. Put off by their appearance, Blake turned and started walking west again.

Forty-Six

Frederick bought a cup of coffee and sat down at a table in the Michigan State University's Student Union's One Union Square food court. He was early, but mostly he knew his daughter had not been pleased when he had called and told her he was in East Lansing and that he would like to see her. She had been polite, and after a short conversation she had agreed to meet him after her second class.

He sat and watched the coeds passing through the food court and Frederick suddenly felt old, tired. But he knew most of his tiredness came from dealing with Mike Hammersmith's controlling, irrational behavior, and now, everything seemed to be piling on and making him feel even more so.

He looked up and smiled when a very pretty girl stopped beside his table.

"Hello, Collin," he greeted, and stood while she pulled a chair out and sat down. "Can I get you anything?"

"Hello, Dad," she said, and looked at him as she set her stack of books on the table. "Nothing, thanks." She waited as he sat down. "Thanks for not just showing up on my doorstep."

He nodded. "I'm sorry I'm an embarrassment to you," he said, and watched her. "But I'm glad you agreed to see me." He hesitated a minute. "Are you doing okay? Classes going all right?"

"Dad," Collin said, "I know you didn't come here to talk about my grades or classes. You've always just looked them up to know how I'm doing."

"I wasn't meaning your grades," he said, and smiled. "I was wondering if you'd decided whether you want to go on to grad school."

"I've thought about it," she said, and cocked her head. "But Mom always said that would be very iffy—being able to afford it and all."

"You can. I've attached an endowment to your trust," he said softly. "I have one special project that turned out very well and has prospered over the years. I've put the profits from that project into your personal and educational trusts. You should have more than enough to continue if you want."

She stared at him and did not say anything.

"I've also added some project investments to your mother's trust so she'll get the investment returns on a regular basis."

"What's going on?" Collin asked softly. "Why are you doing this? I've only seen you once a year at the most since you left us, some years not at all, and now...?"

"I know you don't understand," he said, and looked at the cup he was toying with on the table, "but it was the best thing I could do."

"You're right, I don't understand," she said, and waited.

"I've always tried to be sure you and your mother had more than enough to live on," he said, "so she wouldn't have to go back to her family for support or to use any of her private funds and investments."

"That was generous of you," Collin said, and watched him.

"I made a very bad business decision when you were little," he admitted, and looked away. "Many years ago, I started a project with a new colleague, and during that project he became very aggressive against a competitor of ours. Actually, he was incensed when the competition would not just bow out and go away. When you were about four, he did something very bad—criminal, in fact—and somehow I got implicated."

"Criminal? What did he do?"

"I won't tell you that, Collin," he said, and looked back at her. "But the worst was that I felt I had to protect you and your mother—"

"By divorcing us? Leaving us? Stepping out of our lives for the past sixteen years?"

"Yes," he said. "It was the only way I could keep the two of you from being implicated as well. I've had to live with knowing what happened, but you and your mother have only had to live with my absence."

Collin shook her head slowly back and forth and then cocked it to one side and asked, "So what's happened now?"

"I didn't have the courage back then to call the police and turn him in, and now, because I didn't, that incident is coming back to haunt me." He smiled weakly and sipped his tepid coffee. "Last week, in a blind fit of very uncharacteristic behavior on my part, I confronted him and told him that neither myself nor my firm would ever work with him again. It felt good to say it to his face—"

"He's going to retaliate, isn't he?"

He nodded slowly. "Yes, I believe he will. He's facing another impediment to his desires in acquiring some land in the city and he's fallen back to handling it the same way he handled the other one. And I know about too many of his skeletons to not be considered a threat."

"So what are you going to do?"

"I thought I'd take a little vacation," he said. "I wanted to see you before I go, and I want to be here for your graduation in, what, two weeks? And then I'll be gone for a while."

"Friday the twenty-seventh. Where are you going?"

He shook his head. "If you don't know, he can't make you tell him."

"He? Who, Dad?"

"Hammersmith. Mike Hammersmith. Once he knows I'm gone, he'll send someone to see what they can find out."

"Does Mom know?"

"No."

"You have to go and tell her."

115

"I...I don't think I can face her."

"You faced me"—she raised her eyebrow—"and she still loves you. You have to tell her."

◻-◻-◻-◻-◻

Billy came from the department store, pleased with the events of the day, and let himself into Billie's apartment. He immediately heard the sounds of her shower drift down from her bedroom bath. He smiled, thinking of her, the glistening, warm water gently running over her beautiful, toned body, the sensual, stimulating memory of her bare skin under his fingers, in the palms of his hands. Lost in his wonderful thoughts, he stopped in the kitchen and got himself a glass of water. He went into the living room and settled in a chair to one side of the large window, set his glass down, and pulled his right boot off. He inserted the apartment key into the pocket in the liner and put the boot back on.

Billy was quietly absorbed in the city scene, thinking about the warehouse building and what effect the changes might have on Hammersmith, what he might do. He chuckled, wishing he could have been a fly on the wall when Mike opened his emails. Lost in thought, he almost did not notice when Billie turned the water off, but after a moment he heard her open the bathroom door and knew she had come out into her bedroom.

"You sure looked beautiful today," he said softly, hoping to not startle her but instead to let her know he was there.

"Oh, thanks. I didn't know you'd come in," she said, and peeked over the open railing to see him in the chair.

He did not look up but said, "I know."

"Come up here, Billy," she said, still watching him. "At least give me a kiss."

"If I come up there I won't be able to stop with a kiss."

He heard her chuckle to herself.

"Well, you'd better start with one."

-¤-

Stretched out on top of him, her head resting on his chest as she listened to his slow heartbeat, his chin lightly touching the top of her head, Billie was thoroughly relaxed, wishing they did not have to serve that night. Then her mind drifted back to Billy when he had come up the stairs and taken his shirt off; that was when she had seen the faint, jagged scar across his stomach. It surprised her, because it had been dark the only other time they had made love, the only other time she had seen him without a shirt, and she had not noticed it.

"Billy?" she asked softly.

"Yeah?"

"Was it a bad fight?"

"A bad fight?" he asked, and raised his head to look down at her. "What fight?"

"The one that gave you your scar," she said, and gently slipped her hand down between them to feel his stomach.

"Aaah, it wasn't a fight," he said softly. "I got that when I was thrown out of Mom and Dad's car and landed in the trees."

"Oh my," she said, and raised up to look at him. "I'm sorry. I didn't know."

"I know," he said, and smiled. "Because of it, I almost bled to death before I found help and Mary could get me to the hospital. It was a long tear and they had a hard time stitching it up—that's why it looks so jagged. At least I had a few stomach muscles and enough strength in my fingers to keep things inside while I made it to the city."

She lay back down and hugged him, happy it was not a fight as she unexpectedly remembered the night they had faced Pink and Billy had slashed Pink's shirt when he lunged. "Does it bother you now?"

"No," he said. "Well, only when you tickle."

"I'm glad," she said, and let herself relax again, forcing her thoughts to happier ones.

She recounted the events of the day: lunch with Billy and the architects, shopping at the recycle shop for a different change of clothes for Billy, her session with Cathy, and the passion Billy showed her when they were together—intimately together. Then she remembered his comment.

"Did you mean it, today?" she asked. "When you said you didn't want to wait much longer to set a date?"

"Yes, I did," he said, and she shivered as his fingers gently caressed her back from her shoulders down to her toned buttocks; his other fingers gently combed through her long hair. "There are only a few things left before I can tell you the rest of the secrets," he added.

"What, besides Knife and Mike Hammersmith?"

"After I take care of Knife, I just need to prove Hammersmith put him up to it."

"And we need to prove he was responsible for killing your parents."

Billy sighed. "I've almost given up on that ever happening, Tiger."

"Don't you dare!" she said without lifting her head, and slapped his chest. "I don't know how yet, but I'm still thinking about it. I'll figure it out."

He kissed the top of her head. "But more important, what I want to know is if you even want to set a date. If you even want to go further than being engaged."

"Are you actually asking me if I will marry you? On purpose asking?" She held her breath and waited.

"I am," Billy said softly. "We are engaged and I do want to marry you, and I know I didn't actually ask when I inked your wrist. But considering your life and upbringing, I'm wondering why on earth you'd even want to consider marrying a man that has lived homeless for the past seventeen years and washes dishes to earn a little pocket money."

"Because I love the man that washes dishes for pocket

money, the man that cares about a group of homeless riffraff and turns them into compassionate, caring people, into families that have earned places to live, and care enough about each other to work rather than panhandle, and who give their friendship to total strangers. And I love the man that cared enough about me to keep his word to a twelve-year-old girl, the man that showed that grown-up girl how to defend herself, how to see past her biases and prejudices and how to grow her friendships in the most unusual places, and the man that patiently tolerates my temper and stubbornness. I know my background is different, a different way of life, but I'm in love with the man Billy Carson and all that he stands for."

He chuckled. "And I thought it was because I gave you a pretty knife and made you buy some normal clothes."

She slapped his chest again.

Tell him.

"Seriously though," he continued. "I think I've been in love with you since we first met."

"I actually realized how I felt when you made me wash the old sketch off my wrist," Billie said. "I felt so lost without it. I felt like I was losing you too."

"I'm here, Tiger," he said. "You're not going to lose me and I don't want to ever lose you."

Billie shivered again, but it was not because she was cold.

Now, tell him.

"I'm not supposed to tell you," Billie said and kissed his chest, "but I saw that you still have the school picture I gave you when I was twelve."

Not that.

He did not say anything, but wrapped his other arm around her and gently held her tight. Billie closed her eyes and savored the warmth his arms conveyed to her.

Now?

"I'm thinking that since I've accepted the fact we are

engaged and have been for a few weeks, and that now you're finally asking me to marry you, I want to say yes."

She felt him sigh and, smiling, realized he had been holding his breath, waiting for her answer.

"Well then, Tiger, you need to think about a date," he said, and rolled them to one side. He bent to her, gently caressed her breast, and kissed her tenderly. "But right now I have to be the bearer of bad news. I need to shower and we have to get dressed and go. We can change into frumpy clothes by the bus station."

Forty-Seven

Friday, May 13

Billie got up a little after daybreak and dressed in her sweats. She rummaged around in the kitchen of Billy's River Crest apartment, put on a water kettle for tea and searched around in his refrigerator and cupboards until she found enough to fix a suitable light breakfast. As she ate, she looked around at the small two-bedroom apartment, just as clean and tidy as it had been the first time Billy had brought her to see it. She smiled at the memory of the previous evening; their passionate intimacy after Billy had finished with the architects at the department store. Then she thought warmly about his asking her to marry him and her agreeing—*Oh God! I'm getting married! I'm really, really getting married!*—her lengthy answer when he had asked her why she would consider marrying a man that had lived homeless for so many years, and then coming back to his place after working at the kitchen.

They had settled into a discussion of what he had found over cups of tea and coffee until after midnight, looking at the articles and pictures he had collected from the *Herald* concerning Hammersmith's younger days. They speculated about Mike's and Hannah Quinn's romance and Hannah's disappearance until they couldn't keep their eyes open any longer and finally surrendered, falling asleep in Billy's bed, comfortably entwined in each other's arms. She absently touched her cheek where Billy had kissed her before he left for work.

After breakfast she met Russell, and with a reduced audience they sparred for most of an hour in the garage behind the apartments. Then she showered and dressed in her street clothes. Billie was back at her place by midmorning. She settled at her dinette over a cup of tea and studied an aerial view image on her digital pad.

Zooming in and moving the image around, she wondered why Frederick Westman, the owner and head of the well-known Westman Associates construction firm, lived in such a small, nondescript tract house. It was nothing impressive—one main structure with an attached two-car garage that looked like every other house in the neighborhood. No outbuildings and a low, wire mesh fence around the back yard.

She tapped the image off and entered a search for his company and his holdings, but the results were the normal business web pages. Billie tried a different search, using a resource engine she used at Boster, Lange and Hammersmith. When she logged in and hit the submit icon, she held her breath, expecting the firm to have canceled her ID and passwords, but was surprised when the engine logged her in and opened her account.

Billie quickly input the search criteria and submitted it. In seconds, information on his company and seven of his projects displayed in a list. She queried the list of projects and noted that for the present year, two were completed and five were nearing completion with expected dates in the late summer. She asked for a list of all his past projects and a reasonably impressive list of twenty-six projects displayed, the earliest dating twenty-three years prior, averaging more than one project a year.

She toggled the pad off, closed its cover, and finished her tea. Billie rinsed the cup, put it in the dishwasher, then picked up her phone and tapped Lori's icon.

"Lori?" she asked when the connection was answered. "I saw you called earlier, but I didn't know if it was really you, or if Blake had borrowed your phone again."

"Sorry, Billie," Lori's voice replied. "I didn't know he was going to call you. He just grabbed my phone up off the table and called. Really, I didn't know. I wanted to explain more at Custer's, but he showed up and everything went to hell."

"Yeah, it certainly did." Billie smiled and put the phone on speaker when Lori's image popped up. "Where are you?"

"I'm in the storeroom at the drugstore," Lori said, and moved the phone around for Billie to see. "I was getting some pricing labels when you called. Can you meet me for lunch at that coffee shop across from the bank by your place?"

"Sure," Billie said. "I'm not seeing Billy until he gets off at five."

"Okay," Lori said. "I'd talk now, but Mr. Swaggard wants these labels filled out and on the shelves as soon as I can get it done."

"See you there," Billie said. "Eleven thirty?"

"Eleven thirty." And Lori broke the connection.

¤-¤-¤-¤-¤

"What was that you did at Custer's Wednesday night?" Lori asked. "You were soooo afraid of Blake when you two were together, and now? Wow."

"I've changed, Lori," Billie said, and took a bite of her pickle spear. "And for the better. I'm not afraid anymore."

"You certainly have changed." Lori smiled.

"And believe it or not, Billy told me to pick a date," she said, and picked up half of her Rueben.

"A date? For what?" Lori asked as she cut her burger in half.

Billie held up her wrist as she took a bite of her sandwich.

"Wait—you're going to marry a dishwasher?"

She shook her head and finished chewing. "I am going to marry the most incredible man I've ever known."

"But he washes dishes for a living," Lori said, shaking her head in confusion.

"So?" Billie took another bite.

"What?" Lori asked, rubbing her thumb and first finger together. "It's called money, girl. How's he going to support you?"

"We'll work that out," she said, and sipped her water. "At least you could be happy for me."

"Okay, okay, I'm happy for you," Lori said, and started eating. "But I'm concerned."

"Thank you. So, what did you want when you called me?"

"Oh," Lori said between mouthfuls. "You mean when I called and you intentionally didn't answer?" She smiled and then turned serious. "Blake's following you around. Stalking might be a better word for it. I don't know what he intends, but you better keep a look out."

"What? You're kidding."

Lori shook her head. "Stacy said he said some pretty bad things the other day, and he either wants something from you or he wants to do something to you. But after Wednesday night—"

"Both, knowing him," Billie said, and Lori stifled a giggle. "Physically, I can handle him."

"Yeah, I saw that. I'm still amazed. Making him turn loose of your arm and then pinning him at the door." Lori smiled and shook her head. "You have most certainly changed, Miss Billie Mattis. Most certainly."

¤-¤-¤-¤-¤

"Cathy said you had a good session this afternoon," Billy said as he stepped into Billie's apartment and tumbled the deadbolt. "I must have just missed you."

"Looks like it," Billie said from the bedroom. "How's Mary doing?"

"She's slowing down," Billy said, and went to the kitchen to get a drink of water. "But she still comes into the diner for breakfast and lunch. Sid says her new medications are helping her rest at night, so she has a lot more energy during the day."

"That's good," Billie said. "How closely did you look at those pictures of Hannah? Did you notice that in one of them it looks like she might've had a tattoo on her upper left arm?"

"Really? No, I missed that," he said, and looked up from the living room toward her voice. "How was your day?"

"I had lunch with Lori," Billie said, and leaned over the rail trying to see where he was. "She told me Blake has started following me around. I figured he would try something. He never was any good at listening or taking a hint."

"From what you said, I thought your hint was pretty clear," he said. "Toss me your phone."

"Sure," she said, and dropped it over the rail. "Who're you going to call?"

Billy caught the phone and smiled back at her. "Go put some clothes on, will ya?" he said as he walked back into the kitchen. "Is it going to be this way every night?"

"Maybe," she said, and he heard her closet door slide open. "You don't like what you see?"

"You know very well *that* is not the issue."

He sat down and entered a number into her contact list and assigned a speed dial icon to it. Then he called the number.

"Detective Nolan?" he said when someone answered. "Billy Carson. I need a favor."

Forty-Eight

Constantly searching the shadows and listening, hearing only the muted sounds of the city and the light wind in the trees, Billy led them along Crescent back toward the city center and the department store. Billie felt his uneasiness and kept her vigil, alert to the sounds and signs of other people that were out and about.

"You think this might be the night?" Billie asked softly.

"Maybe. Neither of us saw him at the kitchen tonight, and most of his cronies were missing," Billy said as they crossed Main Street at Archer, a block east of the department store block. "I think we should check the alleys. He's likely to be waiting where he won't have any witnesses."

They walked in silence and crossed First Street near the southeast corner of the block, and Billie glanced up at the eight-story warehouse building looming above them. As they slipped into the narrow canyon, the passage on the south side of the building, a soft voice stopped them. "Keeper, wait a minute."

A thin shadow rose up from behind a crate and a trash dumpster, barely visible in the darkness.

"Hey, Pidge. What do you have?" Billy whispered as Pigeon stepped closer.

"Hi, Tiger. Knife and Pink are at the north end of the alley between the two buildings," she said. "Stretch, Lynx, and Mace are watching three across Baker to the north. They'll stop them if they try to join up with Knife and Pink."

"Thanks, Pidge," Billy said, and caught Billie's hand. "We'll go up the middle and see what they're going to try. You should watch this end of the alley in case they get past us and head this way or someone tries to come up from behind."

"You'll take care of them," Pigeon said, almost as a question. "You...always do."

"We'll do our best, but tonight's different, Pidge. Knife is out for blood," he said. "Is Cat on the west side?"

"Yeah, she's there. Whose blood?"

"Mine," he said softly, and stepped toward the alley, pulling Billie behind him. "Get Cat, Pidge, and you two watch this end of the alley."

Billy turned Billie to him and pulled her close. He kissed her gently and he felt her melt against him. "Thanks for being my backup, Tiger."

"Always, Keeper. Thanks for letting me."

He took her hand, and as they slowly worked their way up the alley, Billy saw Pink standing in the center of the mouth and Knife leaning against the corner of the department store building to their left. Billy stepped to the left side of Tiger and together they crept closer.

"They should be coming down from Crescent any time now," Pink said, glancing up the street to the east. He stepped back into the mouth of the alley, just enough to be in the building's shadow, out of the streetlight.

When they were about ten feet away, Billy motioned for Tiger to step sideways a couple of steps and he did the same, widening the distance between them. They set their backpacks down and then, knife in hand, Billy balanced on the balls of his feet and lowered slightly into his crouch. Tiger did the same and he saw the glint of her long blade.

"You looking for me?" Billy asked softly.

Pink jumped straight up, spun around, and peered into the darkness trying to locate Billy. Knife slowly stood up and walked toward Pink.

"I wasn't sure you'd show up tonight," Knife said as he stepped past Pink and stopped to Billy's right.

Damn! Billy glanced at Tiger, but it was too late to switch sides.

"Why? Why would you think I wouldn't come and remind you you're not welcome here?" Billy asked calmly, his voice level as Pink slowly drew an eight-inch knife from a belt sheath. Billy stepped forward and saw Tiger mimic him.

"Ah, I see you now," Knife said as his eyes adjusted to the dim light. "And I see you have your lady friend with you." He turned to face Tiger as she moved to lure him farther to one side. "Pink said you two go everywhere together. I think someone called her Tiger." He chuckled. "After tonight, I might have to get to know Tiger real good."

Billy did not rise to Knife's attempted provocation but concentrated on Pink as he started to move toward Billy's knife hand. Billy countered, pressing Pink's timid advance.

"Remember, Pink," Billy said softly, "you almost got cut in half last time you tried this. Has Knife cut you in on his three-G bounty for coming here tonight? Or are you just playing along in the dark, hoping to get a couple of crumbs?"

Pink hesitated. "You gettin' paid for this, Knife?"

"Like Keeper says, Pink," Knife said. "You're going to get a few new customers tonight."

Billy pressed Pink's knife hand a little more as Pink pondered Knife's response. He saw Tiger edge a little closer to Knife as they bantered.

"Well, Keeper," Knife said, his voice lighter, almost pleasant, "I don't want to take up your time, but actually, time is what you don't have any more." His expression sobered as he opened his jacket and pulled a 9 millimeter semiautomatic pistol from his belt. "Let's see now. If I shoot you first, Tiger here will come for me." He turned and leveled the gun at Tiger's head. "But if I shoot her first, then, even if you take Pink, he'll slow you down enough that I can still get you before you get to me. Yeah, I like that idea." Knife smiled and glanced at Billy.

"What?" Pink suddenly turned in disbelief to look at Knife.

When Pink turned, Billy instantly dove on Pink's knife hand.

-¤-

Billie watched Knife pull the pistol from his belt and heard him debating with himself, but when he pointed the gun at her face, panic suddenly filled her. She shook, hearing his calculating words as he analyzed the situation and calmly decide he should make it easy and just kill her first. Then as quickly as the panic came, it left, and she began methodically planning how she could still get him if he did shoot her first.

You gotta make it to him, Tiger. Even if he shoots first, you have to get him before he shoots Keeper.

I don't know if I can get to him if he does. If he makes me angry enough—

You have to, Tiger! Keeper's counting on you!

I know! I know. I have to move before he can fire. I have to be moving first.

She knew she was a lightweight, and wasn't sure if she had the mass or strength to carry herself to him once he fired. She hoped she could still react and follow through. She had to do something or Billy would be dead. She had to try, but she was pretty sure this one was going to kill her.

Don't overthink it. Look for a break and do what he trained you to do.

She took a deep breath, pushed everything else out of her mind, and edged a little closer, listening and watching for a break.

Come on, come on. Show me an opening. Give me something to work with. Anything, no matter how slim. Anything.

She saw the blur out of the corner of her eye as Pink turned his head to look at Knife and Keeper dove on Pink's hand. Before she consciously knew what she was seeing, she lunged in reflex, bringing her knife down as Knife saw Keeper move. Knife's head turned, the pistol fired. Her shoulder hit Knife in the chest and she spun to get on top before he could turn on her. He fell on his side and she landed, her knee hard against his back, her blade pressed tight against the base of his neck. She waited, surprised when he did not turn on her. Tense, ready for him to spring, she slowly realized he was howling, clutching his arm tightly to his chest.

In stunned disbelief, she inhaled and glanced around her. She went rigid with fear when she saw Pink's crumpled body. Then Pink's body moved and Keeper's head popped into view. Sudden relief washed over her as Keeper pushed Pink aside, sat up on his knees, and wiped his knife blade on Pink's sleeve.

"Damn, Tiger," he said as he looked at her with a huge smile. "Remind me to never, ever, piss you off."

"What? Are you okay? What are you going on about?" she asked as Keeper stood up and quickly stepped to her.

He knelt down and slipped his arm around her shoulders, pointing to the gun lying on the pavement with Knife's hand still holding it.

"What? His hand? Oh my God!" She stared at it a long moment, trying to absorb the magnitude of the reality before she looked at Keeper. "I...cut...his hand off?"

He nodded slowly, his expression concerned as he heard the guarded tone in her voice and watched her reaction. "You sure did," he said softly, and tightened his hold on her shoulders. He looked up and saw Stretch, Lynx, and Mace marching Knife's accomplices across the street toward them. "Cat, Pigeon," he called. "Bring some rope."

Mindy and Barbara were quickly beside them, and in minutes had the accomplices bound and sitting against an alley wall.

"Is your phone in your backpack?" Keeper asked as he looked at Knife, still curled up, wailing and clutching his arm.

"Yeah," she said absently.

Keeper retrieved her backpack, then he dug for her phone. When he knelt down beside her again, he touched the speed dial icon.

"Detective Nolan? Keeper. Please come to Baker and the alley between the old Duckard's Department Store buildings. There's one dead, one losing a lot of blood, and three that are very anxious to talk to you. Thanks, I'll be here." He turned to the others. "Cat, Pidge, Stretch, Lynx, Mace. You five can disappear if you want. Tiger and I will wait on Detective Nolan. Thanks for the help."

"Any time Keeper, but we'll be close by. Good work, Tiger," Cathy said as she stood up and quickly led the group down the alley.

"Thank you, Tiger," Billy said, and squeezed her shoulders again. Then he looked at Knife. "I'll bet..." He reached around him and patted the front of his shirt. "...Yup, he still has the envelope."

"What envelope?" Tiger asked, but they were interrupted by the sounds of multiple cars coming. She looked up and saw four squad cars and an ambulance, lights flashing and running silent.

"I think we ought to put these away," he said, and he folded his knife closed and slipped it into his pocket. She followed his example and pocketed hers. "There'll be a beat reporter with them, so it's Keeper and Tiger. They're only supposed to take pictures of the victims."

Billy stepped forward as a stocky man in a long coat stopped a few feet away from Pink's body. With Tiger close at his side, Billy quickly gave the detective the story.

"Knife has an envelope tucked in his shirt. I was watching them Sunday night when Mike Hammersmith gave him two thousand dollars to take me out. One of Hammersmith's men wrote a number on the envelope for him to call after he killed me and to collect another thousand. You should be able to tie him to the killing tonight with what you have here."

"Thanks, Keeper. Who's this?" the detective asked, and nodded to Billie.

"Detective Nolan, this is Tiger. She stopped Knife before he could kill me. Knife killed Pink as he swung around to shoot me, but Pink turned between us at the wrong time. Tiger kept him from taking a second shot."

Detective Nolan looked at the hand still holding the gun and looked at Tiger. "Well, there's no doubt who pulled the trigger and killed Pink." He turned to another police officer. "Sergeant, bring two medium evidence bags over here." Then he knelt down in front of Knife, and when the sergeant returned, he said over Knife's continued wailing, "Take the envelope out of his shirt and put it in the bag. Then collect the gun and his hand."

Tiger curled against Keeper's chest, comforted by his embrace, but she turned her head to watch the detective and the sergeant. Her serious, almost mechanical side wanted to see what happened next.

The sergeant put his latex gloves on and retrieved the envelope over Knife's feeble objections. He placed the envelope in the clear plastic bag, sealed it, and handed it to the detective before he went to the hand lying on the sidewalk.

"Okay, Sergeant, let the EMTs in to take care of Pink and Leonard, the Knife." Nolan looked at the evidence bag, "Looks like there's a phone number on it like you said." He nodded to Billy. "We should've thought to give you a wire—then maybe we could've spared you from tonight."

"Would've been good," Billy admitted. "Do you need us for anything else?"

"No, not tonight, Keeper. I know how to reach you if something comes up. And Tiger must have my number, since you don't have a phone." He looked at Tiger. "Nice to meet you."

"Nice to meet you too, Detective."

Nolan nodded and turned back to the EMTs and the photographer. Tiger smiled and Billy squeezed her hand. After they picked up their backpacks, Billy led her along Baker and around to the front of the department store on Second.

Near the front doors, he stopped and turned her to him, slipped his arms around her shoulders, and held her tight. "It's okay now, Tiger. You did very good tonight."

She pushed herself up and buried her face against his neck, wrapping her arms tightly around him. "Good, in that you're still alive." She slowly shook her head. "I was sure I was going to die before I could help you. I think I'll see that gun in my face for a long, long time. I was so afraid I wouldn't be able to stop him before he shot you, and when…I saw you move…giving me the slightest of chances…I lunged…But the gun went off as I reached him and I just knew I was too late. Then everything became so mechanical. I didn't know what to do when he didn't fight back. I just waited, my heart was like lead in my gut, I couldn't move. Then I saw you push Pink off of you and I just stared, astonished, so relieved. I almost forgot where we were and what we were doing." She hesitated and then said, "I hope I never have to do that again."

"I think you are the bravest, most courageous and wonderful woman I've ever known, Tiger. And I understand, and hope we never, ever have to face anything like this again, either. I didn't do a very good job of protecting you, keeping you out of danger, and I'm very sorry about that."

"We were a team, weren't we?" she asked softly.

"Yes, we certainly *are* a team," he said, and she squeezed him tighter. "I was wrong Monday when I told you to stay home, and I'm glad you insisted. I forgot how obstinate and tenacious you can be, but I'm actually beginning to rely on you."

She curled her fingers and poked his arm. "I know I can be, but you don't have to keep reminding me."

"Just telling it like it is."

"Take me home, Keeper," she said, and looked up at him. "Please. I need you to hold me and tell me I'm okay, that everything is going to be all right."

"I will. It will be. You watch and see," he said, and kissed her long and tenderly.

¤-¤-¤-¤-¤

Stop wallowing!

I'm not wallowing. It scared me.

Billie argued with herself as she sat crosswise on Billy's lap, his arms curled around her as she silently watched the lights of the city through her glass wall. She had been arguing with herself since they got back to her apartment.

Well scared or not, you did what you were taught to do. You asked for an opening—anything, you said—and Billy gave you one. It was what you needed and you did what you were supposed to do.

Yeah. I guess I did.

Billie sighed and took another sip of the Cabernet in the stemless glass she was holding.

"It was over so quick," she said softly, leaning against his chest.

"Always happens that way," Billy answered without moving or changing his hold on her.

"I know you've faced things like this before," she continued. "I saw you in the village when you faced the drug dealers, and when you faced the man that tried to drag me away, and I saw how calm you were with Pink when we met him the first time in the alley. Do you just get used to it after a while?"

Billy chuckled softly. "No, Tiger, you don't. It's scary each and every—"

"You get scared too?"

"Yes. I think I told you that. You never really get used to it, but even though each confrontation is different, you do get to where you know what to expect, what can go wrong, and what you need to make it go right."

"That's why you have switched things up so much in our

training and practicing," she said, and took another sip, "isn't it?"

"Yes, Tiger. So that, like tonight, when you saw an opening, an opportunity, you knew what to do to take advantage of it." He squeezed her tighter. "I know this scared you, and you may wake up dreaming about it, but know for certain that you did everything right, Tiger. Everything. This is what I worried about when you first asked me to help you, to train you. I knew that someday you would have to face something like this."

Billie studied the city lights for another long moment. "I did all right, didn't I?"

"Yes, love. My Tiger was wonderful tonight. Just like she should be."

Billie smiled and looked at him.

"Thanks, Keeper. Take me upstairs. If you're here, and hold me, maybe I can sleep and won't have nightmares."

"Okay, Tiger," Billy said, and slowly helped her up.

Forty-Nine

Saturday, May 14

Billie rolled over and stretched, slowly realizing that Billy wasn't in bed with her. She called him but he did not answer, and then she remembered he had gone to run errands.

He went to be sure Max, Mindy, Cathy, Russell, and Barbara are doing okay. He said he was pleased you slept good.

Oh yeah, I remember. And no nightmares. Did he say he would bring some bagels when he came back?

Yes.

She stretched again, remembering their nonstop night as she forced herself to get up and visit the bathroom. At first she could not sleep, and Billy's tender loving helped her put the thoughts of the confrontation with Knife and Pink aside, and finally, completely consumed, she fell asleep.

She washed, fluffed her messed hair, and went down to the kitchen. She heated some water for a cup of tea, grabbed her digital pad, and flipped the cover open. Once connected to the internet, she resumed her previous search of Hammersmith's properties while her water heated.

She was not sure why she was still researching things concerning the accident that had killed Willum and his parents; being with Billy had helped her accept his death and face it factually, like he was doing with everything else he was teaching her. But, curiosity maybe, she still looked.

Selecting an overhead image of his main home north of the city, she turned at the whistle from the water kettle. With a teabag in her cup, she poured in the water and let it steep for a few minutes as she returned to her pad and studied the image. When the color looked satisfactory, she stirred a dribble of honey into her cup and settled on the tall stool beside the counter. Then, sipping her tea, she looked through the images she had downloaded, each showing a different portion of his property.

Her tea was almost gone and she was focused on a nondescript building in a wooded area at the far back corner of his estate when her door chime rang. Startled, realizing it was not Billy, she hurried up the stairs, unwilling to answer the door completely in the buff, and grabbed a robe from her closet. She slipped it on and tied the waistband as she went to the door and looked through the peephole.

"Hey Lori," she said as she opened the door and let her in. "I didn't know you were going to stop by."

"Sorry," she said, and stopped in the dining area and looked round the living room. "I was in the area and was thinking about lunch. I stopped to see what you were going to do...Did you just get up?"

"Yeah, about a half an hour ago, I think," Billie said, and collected her tea cup and set it in the sink. She smiled, remembering again why she had slept in late.

"You never sleep in this late," Lori said as she went into the living room and sat down in a chair by the window. "Where's Billy?"

"Went out for bagels," she said, and sat down on the sofa and fiddled with the robe, noticing she had grabbed her shorty instead of her longer calf-length one. She stood back up. "Let me go up and put on a different robe."

Lori shook her head. "Look, you don't have to make excuses about..." She hesitated when she glanced up at the railing over the kitchen. "What's your bra doing up there?"

Billie looked up and chuckled. "I wondered where that went," she said, and went up the stairs and retrieved the errant undergarment. She slipped into a longer robe and was chuckling as she came back down and settled again on the sofa. "Sorry, we got a little carried away last night. You were saying?"

Lori just looked at her. "I know you've changed—a lot, actually—but it's just hard to think you're seriously seeing someone and are actually going to get married. He's almost a ghost. I haven't seen him but once, the day he cleaned your boot, and I'm your best and oldest friend. You haven't brought him around. He hasn't been with you when you go out. No one's seen..." She shook her head. "Have your parents even met him yet?"

"We're trying to work that out," Billie admitted. "He's been a little busy lately."

"Washing dishes?" she asked as the apartment door opened and Billy walked in.

He closed the door and asked, "Who's washing dishes?"

Stunned and embarrassed, Lori looked up at Billy as he stopped behind the sofa, taller and trimmer than she remembered, dressed in a bright white and green short-sleeved shirt and slightly faded, narrow-waisted jeans. The muscular tone of his arms and upper body was evident as he smiled at Lori and leaned over the back of the sofa and kissed Billie.

"I didn't know we were expecting company," he said, and then smiled at Lori again. "You must be Lori. Billie's told me a lot about you. Nice to finally meet you."

Lori started to say something, but just smiled and nodded when the words did not come out.

Billy smiled and looked at Billie, eyeing the plunging *V* of her robe and her still ruffled hair. "Lori must have caught you still in bed."

Billie smiled. "Almost. She was wondering what I was going to do for lunch. Do we have any plans?"

Billy sat down on the sofa and pulled Billie's legs up onto his lap. "No, not that I can think of." Billie squirmed as he ran his fingers lightly up and down her shin. "Cathy's not available for your practice session today, said she wants to take Abby to the zoo. They haven't been in a couple of years and Abby is a good age to go now. Max and Mindy are having Russ and Barb over for a cookout, since the weather is good, and we don't have to watch tonight. No, I think we're free today. That is"—he winked at Lori—"unless Billie thinks of something else she'd rather we do."

Billie stared at him, startled. "Don't listen to him, Lori," she said, and swatted his roaming hand as it slipped up under the hem of her robe, caressing her leg up to her knee. Then she looked at Lori, a teasing challenge in her eyes. "You don't mind if Billy comes with us, do you?"

Fifty

Lori went on her way after their lunch, where Billy had carefully avoided her questions and obvious searching for details about his past, and Billie followed him as he led them through the Forest before they went back to her apartment. Billy stopped at a bench, warm in the early afternoon sun, sat down, and she let him pull her onto his lap.

"I think I remember Lori from years ago," he said softly.

"I've known her since grade school," Billie said, and slipped her arm around his neck. "I'm sorry she was so persistent and nosy. She remembered you from the day you first cleaned my boot."

"Yes," he said. "I expected a lot of questions from your friends. I am the new boyfriend and they're just watching out for their friend. They only see me through what you say about me and how quickly I have moved into your life."

Billie smiled. "I'm glad they don't put you off."

"Now Becky? I haven't met her yet, have I?"

"No. Becky and I met in college," Billie explained, "and we became close friends when we found out we were both from around here. Her interest in historical things took her straight to the museum and her assistant curator position."

"And Stacy?" he asked. "You said her father owns a couple of retail shopping complexes?"

"He's the owner and landlord for the Chestnut Ridge strip mall, with seven stores, and the Gull Meadows strip mall, with twelve stores," Billie clarified, and let her head rest against his. "He does pretty good managing what he has and keeping the spaces filled."

"I think I've met him," Billy said softly. "Stan, I believe."

"That would be him," Billie admitted, slowly shaking her head.

"What about Stacy?" he asked again, "You implied that she hasn't been happy with her life and growing up."

"No, she hasn't been. I used to think I understood," she said, "but lately, I just think she feels her dad should've gone after bigger investments, made more money, more...I don't know what. I feel that she just wants more, especially after seeing her with her boyfriend, Tom Bennett, and his affluence."

"Aaah, yes," Billy said, and smiled. "Dave Bennett's boy."

"How do you know Tom's dad?" Billie asked, and raised her head to look at him. "First Stan and now Dave."

"I guess I've just gotten to know a lot of the working people in the city," he said, but she felt like there was more that he was not saying. "Dave has a thriving paving company. He's had his share of problems, widowed six years ago, but for the most part, those issues are behind him. Tom's ambivalence is probably Dave's biggest one at the moment."

"I don't know how you know what you do," Billie chuckled, and glanced around the park, taking in the sight of the gently fluttering leaves and the feel of the soft, warm breeze, "but Becky, Lori, and I were discussing that very thing during one of our recent girls' nights out."

He watched her expression change and she looked at him.

"Do I need to stop going out with Becky and Lori?"

Billy laughed. "No, Tiger. Not unless you want to or decide to. Just please be cautious and continue keeping the few secrets we have between us."

"Certainly," she said, and snuggled into him. "Those belong to us. But there is one thing I'm curious about. The architect the other day..." She hesitated and studied the end of the bench.

Go ahead. You haven't been shy yet.

I know. What have I got to lose, right?

"That architect the other day at lunch mentioned they were going to be renovating the department store buildings using the owner's original designs. A late Mr. Hawke?"

"Yes, he did," Billy said, smiling.

"Is he the same Mr. Hawke that I knew? The one that brought his family out to the ranch on weekends?"

Billy nodded, but his smile did not ease the uneasiness she was suddenly feeling.

"How can he be the owner? If he's dead, I mean."

"He had good plans for the city center," Billy said, "and his investment companies have kept his properties free of all legal and financial encumbrances. Since I came here, I have made sure the properties were physically cared for and kept ready for them when the time was right."

"You have? Then you either knew him, or someone in his companies?"

"Yes, I did," he said.

"Then you must know about the accident and how he died," she said softly.

"Yes." His tone grew somber.

She was silent for a long minute watching him, wondering...

"When I searched and found the accident that he and his family died in, I wondered about the accident that killed your parents." She looked at him and held his eyes. "You said they died in a car wreck like them, and there was a fire like theirs had, but you didn't say where or when it happened."

Billy inhaled and squeezed her waist. "I know you don't realize it yet, but you already know the answer. It's a secret that you won't have to keep for long, but it's the biggest one you'll ever have to keep."

"What? What's a secret?"

"Those were my parents that died at the Chestnut Creek Bridge on that Labor Day night. I can't keep the truth from you any longer, Billie. I've wanted to tell you for so long, but your friend, young William, didn't die in the wreck like everyone thinks. I was thrown out of the car before it was set on fire."

Her eyes slowly went wide; her lips trembled. "What? Why would you say something like—?"

He's lying! He's up to something!

Panic seized her and she jumped up and backed away from him.

Stop it! I have to think. Oh god? What—?

She grimaced and clenched her teeth as she looked away. "What are you trying to do, Billy? This is not funny."

"Billie," he said, and she looked back, seeing that he was still watching her. She stared back at him, confused, certain there was some kind of a game afoot, but he waited and his gentle gaze held her eyes. "Yes, Billie. I'm their son. I'm William. Your William. William Carson Hawke III. And I think that somewhere inside, you've always known who I am."

"How? I don't...You can't be...Dammit, Billy! What are you up to?" She shook her head, her mouth moved, but the words stopped coming out.

Billie stood rigidly in front of him and looked away, her heart pounding harder, more apprehensive with each passing moment.

"Why are you saying this?" *What do you really want? Why are you claiming to be him?* "Oh, God!" She covered her mouth and looked across the park, suddenly wanting to run.

"Billie, wait!" he said firmly, but not a shout. "Please. Please listen to me."

And here I am letting him into my heart, when he's really trying—

She absently folded her arms across her chest and felt the tears slowly begin to dampen her eyes.

Think! Listen to him, Billie. Listen to your heart.

I'm trying, but—

He has always treated you with kindness and caring. Even when you made him angry, he was firm and made you listen to him for your safety, but he was still there when you asked him to meet with you, then to lead you into the worst part of town, to help at the kitchen. Even after you disobeyed him and followed him, endangering yourself. He told you it wasn't safe, but you ignored him and he helped you be as safe as he could. He has tried to support you in every irrational request and obstinate action you have made, teaching you how to believe in yourself again, to learn what you need to survive in his world.

Why did he do that?

You know why! He's as much in love with you as you are with him! The night he had to face Pink, he showed you why! He was afraid for you, afraid something might happen and he would be injured, unable to continue keeping you safe. But he had to face Pink and you would not wait in the shadows for him! You wanted to be beside him. You told him you would not wait in the shadows. And he told you what little he could to help keep you safe in that uncertainty. And last week when he wanted you to stay home because of Knife, you argued because you care. And he changed his teaching to help you be better prepared.

Trembling, Billie looked back at him. He had not moved, patiently waiting for her to listen and decide what she was going to do next. Her heart still pounded with uncertainty.

"Why would I believe you?" she softly asked, and shifted her body to face him, firmly planting her fists on her hips.

"I know this is hard for you to accept, definitely startling, but we've known each other since just before your fifth birthday. Remember?"

Okay, dammit. Let's see if you remember...

"Where was I when we first met?" Without changing her stance, she cocked her head and waited.

"You were fishing on one of your lakes," Billy said with a tender smile. "Our dads found you with your foreman, and you were standing on the end of that little wooden pier with a cane pole and a bobber on a line. I had been there just a little while and you caught a bluegill."

Damn. That's what Mom told me once...

"Did you have a nickname?" she asked, but did not change her posture.

"Not until I met you and you gave me a couple. You used to tease me, called me four-eyes or double-vision. Those were your favorites."

Oh shit! I did.

She swallowed. "Double...but you..." She swallowed again. "Do you remember how I got my scar?"

No one can make up an answer to that one. She set her jaw and hardened her stare, defiantly daring him to come up with a good answer.

Billy pointed to her pant leg. "You almost can't see it now, but we were riding and you were showing off like you always liked to do," he said, smiling at his memory of her antics, "when we came to visit. Your horse slipped on that muddy spot on the trail near the upper lake, fell against a tree, and caught you in between. You broke your left shin. Sandy went after your folks and I sat, holding you just like I was a moment ago, only the other way around so your leg was on top. After that you called me 'Willum,' still teasing me. You never once called me by my correct name."

Oh god, I remember. You had to be there to know—

He tried to protect you even as a boy. And even then, hurting as much as you were, you tried to resist him and his consoling. He held you tightly on his lap, in his arms, keeping you from trying to stand up and deny the reality of the situation until Sandy came back with your fathers. Your temper, anger over getting hurt in front of him, and the worry and fear of others that your parents had taught you kept getting in the way. And now, when your world is better than it has ever been, your temper and fear still argue with everything you see. The fear that everyone is like your exes keeps you from listening, from hearing, from loving.

Unexpectedly, tears filled her eyes and overflowed, streaking her cheeks. She refused to wipe them and let him know she was crying, but softly, she answered, "How can you remember that? You...you—"

You just can't be Willum...You can't. He's been dead for so very long...

Listen!

"I wore glasses and was a little short as a boy, I'll admit," Billy continued, and she saw the smile in his eyes as she finally wiped her eyes with her sleeve. "And I always had a hard time waiting until we came to visit again. Dad and Mom came to see your folks, but I came to see you."

"The glasses..." She slowly dropped her hands and stepped back to the bench, stopping when she stood beside his knees. "Yeah, the glasses. Thick black frames...And you were pretty short. More like me than Sandy."

"Please," he asked as he reached out, took her hands, and gently pulled her back onto his lap. "That last weekend we saw each other, Dad asked me why I was interested in you rather than your sister, being that she was closer to my age, and I asked him why he chose Mom over everyone else. I was yours then and have been ever since, Willa-Willa-Wilhelmina."

In an instant, her anger flared! And before she even thought to stop herself, she clenched her fingers into a fist, swung, and hit him solidly in the chest.

I hate that name!

She remembered kids always teasing and taunting her over that name, and her dad telling her how it had started when she was very young, before kindergarten.

Yeah. He said friends had come to visit when you were barely four and—

I came in crying because they kept teasing me, making jokes about my name, calling me other hideous names and pulling my hair. I told him I was Billie! Not Wilhelmina!

He tried to explain your mother gave you that name after a great aunt—

Yeah, the ugly, dead one in the faded picture in the frame with the domed glass. I remember. Made me feel like Mom thought I should be some quiet, forgotten relic, ashes in an urn, picture in a frame, put away to not cause trouble—

You were a bit of trouble—

Who wouldn't be, being called that! It made me feel like Mom didn't like me, like she preferred quiet, obedient Sandra. Maybe she still does—

You know that's not true—

That's how it makes me feel! And he knows it! He knows he shouldn't ever call me—

Her eyes flashed angrily, staring at him and hearing herself, she realized he did know. He was smiling back at her and her anger slowly abated.

My God! You are Willum!

"Oh, my God!"

Are you sure?

*Oh yeah. He always baited me...called me that...when I was being head-strong, ornery, and—*she smiled—*not listening.*

"My God, you really are Willum..." She wrapped one arm around his neck and the other around his shoulders, hugging him as tight as she could.

"Yes, Billie. I really am," he said as he wrapped his arms around her in return. "After the accident I knew I had to hide until I could figure out who was behind their deaths. I grew out of the glasses and had a growth spurt, and when you saw me in the diner two years later, it was obvious you didn't actually recognize me—taller, thinner, and no glasses. We hit it off because we knew each other, but you didn't see the boy that has liked you since he first saw you fishing."

"I was devastated when you stopped coming to visit," she whispered, and tightened her embrace. "When Dad told me you'd died in an accident, I locked myself in my room for days.

I blamed everyone. I was suddenly alone, with nowhere to go, nowhere to hide from the pain and the emptiness. Eventually, I guess I hid in Dad's horses and then in school. I think that's when Sandy and I stopped being close. I shut her out. I cried over you for years and years and then again when I researched the accident just the other day, reliving everything all over again."

"I'm so sorry, Billie. I was trapped here and couldn't let anyone know I was alive," Billy said, trying to explain. "Not being able to tell you I was all right was almost as hard as losing my folks. Mary made sure I got the medical attention I needed, but knowing my parents' killer was still loose, I knew I couldn't live with her and Sid and expose who I am, so I used my job as a way to stay close and support them the best I could."

Billie slowly sat up to look into his face, to see his smile. "This is so incredible..." she whispered, and touched her forehead to his.

"I know. It's more than I could ever hope for."

She closed her eyes and sighed, letting the moment soak in before she returned to his explanation. "Is Mary actually a relative?"

Billy nodded. "Mary's my mother's sister. Sid's her son, my only cousin." He smiled. "After her husband died, Dad was Mary's silent investment and business partner to get the diner off the ground and to keep it operating."

"And his partnership...?"

"I inherited it—or I should say the investment group holds it for me."

Billie lifted her head and watched his eyes as his hands gently roamed over her back. "And the department store?"

Billy smiled and looked across the street; Billie could tell he was thinking of what he wanted to say and not actually looking at anything. "A company called Pastoric holds a cluster of eight city center blocks and their buildings under Dad's and his heir's name. The Duckard Property is in one of those blocks."

"I've heard of them. Wait, blocks? And their buildings?" She stared at him. "Blocks?"

"Yeah," he said, his voice just a whisper as he looked at her, smiling. "That doesn't count the ten that are not in the city center area."

Oh shit!

She could not think of what to say and just continued to stare at his smile.

"Oh, man. This is harder than asking you to marry me," Billy said. "But do you think you'll be okay being a Hawke instead of just a Carson?"

He inhaled and waited as she put her thoughts together.

"I fell in love with you," Billie began, "and agreed to marry you as an underpaid dishwasher and a recently homeless man, so I guess it's obvious I wasn't after your money or your prestige. I think I'll be okay with it if you are."

He exhaled and smiled. "I am. And I'm not after yours either," he chuckled.

"I know. Was that, the money thing, part of why you waited so long to tell me who you are?"

"Partly. I had to know you could keep my secrets, to let them become our secrets, but I also wanted time to get to know you again and to earn your trust, and maybe even your affections. When I realized I still loved you, I wanted you to love me too, but for who I am, who I've become, and not because I'm my father's son and or because I'm the heir to his businesses and estate. I love you, Tiger. I always have. I felt lost because I was trapped by a situation I couldn't fix, and when I saw you in the diner, my world was turned upside down. I had to see if you could like me again. And when you kept doing things you shouldn't, I was afraid that my correcting you might send you off on one of your tirades, or worse, send you away. But thankfully, you'd grown up a lot yourself."

Billie pulled herself to him with her cheek against his. "Obviously I love you too, Keeper. I have ever since we were

150

kids—at least then as much as a ten-year-old could." Suddenly she sat up and looked at him. "You realize we are going to have to explain this to my folks?"

"Yeah. I've been thinking about that," Billy said, still smiling. "Probably when we go see them and tell them what date you've picked."

Oh shit!

-¤-

They held each other tight for a very long time. He kissed her gently, losing himself in the feel of her lips, her arms around him, and her comforting weight on his lap. He felt her settle into him, gently turning to press herself against him as she responded. After another long embrace, he forced himself back to the now, wishing they weren't on a bench in the Forest as his body threatened to take on a mind of its own.

"Now, I need to change the subject," he said. "Nolan told me this morning that phone number he got from the Knife's envelope was legit and they will pick Hammersmith up—"

Billie squeezed him and squealed. "That's wonderful. We've got something on that bigoted son—"

Billy put his hand over her mouth. "No cussing, Tiger. Yes, it's wonderful. Nolan will charge Mike for hiring a killer, Knife, soliciting a contract to have someone killed, me, and for causing a murder, Pink—not to mention causing personal endangerment to another, you. He will be put away and will not be running any renovation design business." He smiled at Billie and kissed her again. "And Nolan said Knife made it through surgery and will stay in the police ward at the hospital until he's well enough to be moved to the detention center to await a hearing and a trial date. Probably midweek next week."

"A trial date?"

"Whether we like it or not," Billy said, and smiled, "Knife will get a trial—unless, of course, he confesses."

"Well, at least that will get Hammersmith off the streets," Billie said.

"But I still can't pin my parents' death on him."

"We might be closer than you think. I need to do a little more research, but if I take the information I found when I was researching Willum's accident, and put that together with what you've told me about how your parents died, I think I have a pretty good picture of what Hammersmith did and a good idea of how he did it."

"Really?" Billy asked, and smiled.

"When we go back to the apartment," she said, "I have some things to show you about that accident and some of my ideas."

I think you want to talk about more than the accident.

Hush! Quit changing the subject. Of course I do, but I need to show him what I found.

¤-¤-¤-¤-¤

Mike Hammersmith sat in his office, staring at his computer monitor. It was quiet in the offices with everyone gone except for Robert. He tried to think about work, the projects that were overdue or behind schedule. He missed Billie's hand at keeping things moving, but he could not stand seeing that tattoo, much less seeing it on a daily basis.

As soon as he tried to focus on a single task, his mind would jump back and ask if the email was a prank or if there would be another. He fought with himself, one part not wanting to see another and the other part afraid there would be another. And he wondered if Westman might be the one actually sending them.

He slowly keyed for his mail server and watched as the application opened and the list of emails populated the screen. His eyes fixed on another line without a subject.

"From CR Associates," this time. His hand was shaking as he reluctantly keyed for the message.

"Keeper is alive and knows. The dealer
Pink is dead and Leonard, the Knife, is
enjoying the city's hospitality. The property
is still not for sale and is not available. W. C.
Hawke."

Mike was ashen and visibly trembling worse than a man
with severe palsy, but he did not scream. He knew Westman was
the only one left who knew what had really happened that dark
Labor Day night, and he knew how he could fix Westman so he
would not tell.

¤-¤-¤-¤-¤

Blake stopped at the street corner, repositioned the sack and
liquor bottle in his jacket pocket, and noticed the homeless-
looking man sitting on the nearby bench. He glanced back as
he crossed the street, remembering the two homeless-looking
women he'd seen on the same bench a few days before.

He walked west along David, heading back to his room in
the small motel off Ninth West, jotting notes in his small spiral
notepad, documenting what Billie did with her Saturdays.
He saw her, Lori, and a man he had seen her with before, as
they stopped for lunch in a small café on Duberry, and he had
followed her and the man when they left and stopped in the
park between St. Charles and St. Anne.

Halfway through the afternoon, watching Billie and what
seemed to be an argument and making up, Blake noticed a
homeless-looking man and woman under a tree watching him.
It made him uncomfortable and he moved to a different park
bench. But in the moving, he missed seeing Billie and the man
leave the park.

If she has a routine, I can get her alone and we can talk, he told himself as he absently rubbed his wrist. *Even if she is stronger now, she won't dump me a second time.*

Fifty-One

Sunday, May 15

"Do Cathy and the others know who you are?" Billie asked as they walked toward the River Crest Apartments and her afternoon practice session.

"No," Billy said. "They know I take care of the buildings and that I know someone that represents the owner. That's how everyone got 'permission' to live there and keys to the building." He smiled as they turned through the gate and started across the courtyard.

"Tiiggeerr!" Abby squealed as she ran to them and collided with Billie, wrapping her arms around her when they appeared behind the apartments.

"What about me?" Billy asked as he knelt beside them.

"Okay," Abby said, and gave him a big hug, then quickly turned to Billie. "Come on. Mom's waitin.'"

They laughed as he stood up and took Billie's hand. "I guess you've been summoned."

"Good afternoon, Tiger," Cathy said as they entered the multi-stall garage where Billy and the men had unrolled one of the mats. "How are you today?"

"Better, I think," Billie said honestly. "Billy's been helping and trying to keep my mind off of Friday night."

"I have to say," Cathy said, "that as much as I know it bothers you now, you handled that better than I would've ever expected. You two work so well together, it's...it's..." She shook her head when the words failed to come. "I don't know what to call it."

Billie looked at Billy and asked, "Can I?"

He nodded. She smiled and looked back at Cathy. "Billy asked me to set a date."

Cathy quickly congratulated her. In moments, Abby had spread the word and everyone from the apartments came out to extend their congratulations and feelings of encouragement, delaying the practice session with their cheerful exuberance.

After an hour and a half on the mat, revisiting most of the things Billie had learned since they had begun teaching her, Cathy called a stop and bent over with her hands on her knees, panting.

"God, don't you ever run down?" she laughed between deep breaths. "Sometimes you seem possessed, Tiger." Cathy looked at Billy. "If she's like this in bed, you're in trouble."

"Sorry," Billie said, smiling at Billy as she took the towel he handed her and wiped the beads of sweat off her face. "But it was a good workout. Thanks," she said, and Cathy chuckled.

"You're wet through and through," Billy said, looking at Billie's sweat-soaked top and pants.

Billie nodded. "Even my underwear feels soaked. I guess I'm still working the demons out," Billie said as she crossed her legs and sank onto the edge of the mat.

Billy sat down on one side of her and Abby settled on the other when Cathy plopped down ungracefully in front of them.

"Have you thought about where you will live?" Cathy asked as she wiped her arms and then pulled her pant legs up one at a time and began wiping her calves dry.

"We haven't gotten that far," Billie admitted, and then suddenly looked at Billy, remembering a comment the architects had made. "I like my apartment—the view, the seclusion and security. But I like it here, near all of you. I wish we could all have both, you know? We really haven't talked about it, especially with all that's been happening—"

"Yeah. And on top of everything, we heard that Blake Lawrence fella was giving you some trouble," Cathy said without looking at her.

"You heard?"

"Sure," Cathy said, and looked at Billie. "We watch out for our own, Tiger. We listen and talk and try to figure out how to keep us all safe. Ferret, Mouse, and Sparrow are always listening."

"Your own?" Billie asked, still confused. "Me?"

"Yeah, you, silly," Cathy said, and smiled. "Tiger, you've been one of us since you helped Keeper face down Pink, and the first night you helped at the kitchen—when you began helping us."

"That's...that's possibly the nicest thing anyone has said to me in a really, really long time."

"Well, don't let it go to your head," Cathy said, and snapped the towel at her. "You've worked for it." Cathy pushed herself up on her knees and then looked at Billy. "You got somethin' figured out for Blake?"

Billy nodded. "I'll know tomorrow."

"Let us know if it doesn't work." Then she looked at Abby as she stood up. "Come on, Abby. I need to clean up and you can help start getting things ready for dinner." Then to Billie, she added with a chuckle, "I'm still having difficulty realizing I have a real kitchen."

Abby got up and waved to Billie as she followed her mom back to their apartment.

"Are you going to give me one of those someday?" Billy asked softly as he watched Abby dancing behind her mom.

Billie looked at him and then followed his gaze. She smiled. "Maybe."

Monday, May 16

At their usual rap on the diner's front door, Billy unlocked the door and let Angie, Carole, Melony, Julie, Kevin, and Niles in, and Sid reset the alarm after he relocked the door. He went back to the counter, filled six cups and refilled his from the coffee urn, and set them on the counter. Then he stirred two packs of sugar and one of creamer into one and handed it to Angie as she came back into the dining room, pressing the front of her apron with her hands.

"Thanks," Angie said as she stopped at the end of the counter and looked at him. Julie started the second coffee urn and checked everything behind the counter like she did every morning. "What did you do this weekend?"

"Oh, the usual," he said, and sipped his coffee. "Helped apprehend a street assassin, saw a drug dealer die, had the wildest night of my life with the most beautiful woman I've ever known, and I asked Billie to set a wedding date."

"Shit, Billy. I know you didn't—" Angie stopped and stared at him. "You what? You asked Billie to set a date? Are you telling me you really, really asked her to marry you?"

He looked over the rim of his cup and raised his voice. "Sid, Angie needs a sweet roll, warmed. Extra glazing."

"Okay," Sid answered without looking out. "It's almost out of the warmer."

"And she said yes," Billy continued by way of an answer.

"I don't believe it," Julie said as she set her cup down.

"What don't you believe?" Sid asked as he set Angie's roll in the order window. "Here, Angie."

"Billy's getting married," Julie said, glancing at him over her shoulder.

Sid's mouth fell open and he stared at Billy through the opening. The others stopped and stared at him from where they stood.

"Sid, let me know when Mary's up and about," Billy said, and finished his cup. "I'd like to be the one to tell her."

With Sid's nod, Billy got up and took his cup to the sinks, rinsed it out, and set it in the dishwasher rack.

¤-¤-¤-¤-¤

It was mid-morning when Sid stepped into the kitchen and found Billy closing the dishwasher.

"Phone call for you, Billy," he said softly. "A detective named Nolan. Take it in the office."

"Thanks," Billy said, and made his way through the kitchen. He closed the office door, settled into Sid's chair, and picked up the handset. "Billy here."

Billy listened, absently nodding to himself as Detective Nolan spoke, and then finally he repeated, "Ten o'clock at the Bean and Bag Coffee Shop. Got it. Thanks."

Yes, yes. Maybe this will get one worry off Tiger's mind.

He smiled as he tapped the switch hook and held the button for a second. Then he keyed in Billie's sequence.

"Hey, how's my beautiful Tiger?" he greeted. "Are you up yet?"

"Of course," she said. "I'm good. How's your morning?"

"Good. Really good," he said. "Nolan just called and we're all set. Can you call Lori and get her to bring Blake to the Bean and Bag a little before ten tomorrow?"

"It's set up?"

"Nolan said they'll be there waiting."

"Okay," Billie said. "Hope this works. I'll call Lori right now."

"Good. Coming by for lunch?"

"Wouldn't miss it, Keeper."

"See you then, Tiger."

Fifty-Two

"Hey," Billie said, hunched over her digital pad's screen as Billy came in and closed the apartment door behind him. "Have a good afternoon?"

"Uneventful," he said, and stopped beside her.

She looked up and he leaned down and kissed her.

"What're you looking at?" he asked as he set his backpack down beside the counter and looked over her shoulder.

"The images I showed you Saturday and some new ones I found today. There are three possibilities, maybe four," she said, and picked up a small stack of sheets. She moved the image around on the screen, pointed to a detail, and handed him a sheet as he moved her half-full cup of tea out of the way.

"Possibilities?' Billy asked as he took the sheet and straightened up to study the image.

"For where he might have hidden it," she said, as if he should know what she was talking about. "This is my number one choice. It's that secluded shed in a remote wooded area at the back of his principal estate."

"Hidden what? You think he still has something of interest hidden away somewhere?"

"Yeah. From what I can tell, he was a tinkerer. He made things, and if he made something that he used in causing the accident, he might be afraid to throw it away. You know, like someone could link him to it if he threw it away and they found it," she said, and glanced at him with a slowly growing grin.

Billie straightened up and turned on the stool to face him when she saw his confusion.

"You said Saturday you saw a man walking away from the burning car, right?" she asked.

"Yes. He had a gas can and got into the back of a pickup."

"And you said Mace said the man he saw in the alley talked about doing it," she said, thinking out loud. "A pickup? You didn't tell me that."

"Sorry, Tiger. I just remembered."

"So he wasn't alone...He was doing someone's dirty work..." She abruptly stared at Billy. "So the one in the pickup, and I think we know who that was, took care of the road! He had to have a way, a *portable* way to have caused the accident and then to remove whatever evidence there was while the other man set the fire. People would have seen the fire, and it's a well-traveled road, so they wouldn't have had much time."

"And that means...?" Billy cocked his head and sat down on the stool beside her. "Sorry, but I am trying to stay with you."

"Okay, Billy. I was thinking while I was driving home from Mom and Dad's last week, after I saw Sandy and wasn't crying all the way home. It was late, dark, and every time a car approaches I remember two things happen. First you look at the right side of the road so the lights don't blind you, and second, the oncoming car courteously dims its lights."

"Okay...I get that." He laid the sheet on the counter and waited.

"When an oncoming car doesn't dim its lights, there is a short time when you can't see the edge of the road clearly, and even for a few seconds after the car has passed."

"So you think he used car lights to blind them?" he asked, absently nodding as he thought about what she was saying.

"Yes, something like that. But I don't know if car lights would work reliably enough," she said, and glanced at the sheet in her hand. "But if the light was bright enough, like really bright, and mounted on an oncoming car, it might be enough. I was watching the road and slowed down when I got close to the bridge, and today it has a white shoulder stripe to show you where the side of the road is."

"And...you think it might not have back then?"

"I don't know. I came home and checked the online county records and the stripe was added around the time of Willum's—I mean your parents'—accident. I just can't get an exact date for when—before or after."

She stopped and watched him as he rubbed his chin, thinking about her argument.

"So you think Hammersmith might have hidden those lights, assuming he used lights, and anything else he might have needed to hide the road markings? Is that right?"

She slowly nodded. "I know it's a long shot, but do you think Detective Nolan could get warrants and search these places? The satellite images are not sharp enough for me to feel comfortable just picking one."

"He might be able to get one," he said, and smiled. "But if there's something to find, and he picks the wrong place first, whoever's taking care of Hammersmith's places would know the police are suspicious and looking."

"Yeah, and if there is something to hide, it could be moved or destroyed before the police can find it."

"That's assuming there is something to find," Billy said, raising one eyebrow.

Now you sound like the voice in my head. Then Billie asked, ignoring his not-so-subtle jab, "Do you think he would search multiple places all at the same time?"

Billy slowly shook his head. "I think that might be asking a lot. I think he would have to have a very strong case to ask for one warrant. I don't know what he'd need to ask for three or four."

"Well," she said, and picked up the rest of the sheets. "Altogether I have four—three other places on different properties of his." She pointed to each. "They're my choices two, three, and four," she said as she wrote the number on the different sheets.

Billy saw her dejection, put his arms around her shoulders, and pulled her to him.

"You've done a lot of great research, Tiger. Maybe we can talk to Detective Nolan after we finish with Blake tomorrow. Maybe he can tell us what he will need to help us."

"That would be good," she said, and returned his embrace.

"I'm surprised you figured out so much," he said, and smiled to himself. "It actually sounds like it could be how he made it happen. Thanks. Now, come on. Let's get our stuff together. We're serving tonight."

¤-¤-¤-¤-¤

"Did Dad talk to you, Mom?" Collin asked as she sat down at their dining room table and opened her digital pad.

"Yes, honey," Nancy said as she put the supper dishes away. "I was surprised to hear from him. He said he'd seen you at school."

"Do you understand what he was talking about?" Collin continued as she waited to connect with the internet.

"Understand about what?"

"He tried to tell me why he left us," Collin said, and turned to watch her mom.

"Yes, well, that is a very complicated story," Nancy said, and closed the cabinet door.

"He said he made some bad decisions that could've hurt us. Does that make sense?"

"I'm not supposed to know anything about the problem," she said as she sat down across from Collin. "I'm sure he doesn't know that I know what happened."

"He said you didn't know." Collin waited. "Whatever it was, Dad said his ex-colleague was going to do it again."

164

"He did?" Nancy's face went pale. "Did he say who this time?"

"Just that someone was keeping his ex-colleague from buying some property in the city center." Collin watched her mother's growing anxiety. "What's going to happen?"

"Nothing to worry yourself over," Nancy said, and quickly changed the subject and pointed to the pad. "What were you going to look for?"

"You're not going to tell me, are you?"

"No. What else did he talk about?"

Collin stared at her mother but knew she would not say any more.

"He told me he had attached an endowment to my trust so I can consider grad school if I want."

"Really? Have you looked to see what it is?"

"I was calling it up when we started talking," Collin said, and entered the address for her trust organization's website. After a few quick logins, she opened her trust account and started looking down the investment listings. "The investments haven't changed. Oh, he said he added an investment to your account as well."

Collin searched around and finally found a link for Endowments and clicked it. "Here it is."

Nancy watched her and saw her suddenly bend toward the screen.

"What's this? Collin's Park?" She looked at her mother.

"Let me see," Nancy said, and smiled as she came around the table. "Well, I'll be darned." She searched the endowment specs and whistled. "Your daddy just made you an extremely wealthy young lady."

"What? What are you talking about?"

"Look," she said, and pointed to the listings. "He's still listed as the Property and Financial Manager, but he's assigned ownership and all proceeds to you. That property has done very well every year since it was finished—especially last year."

"I...I've never even heard about this one. When did he do it?"

"He finished this one when you were about three," Nancy said. "He always said it was his pride and named it for you, honey. He designed and built that one before he got involved with Hammersmith and things started to fall apart."

"Hammersmith! That's the name he said. He's the one that's going to do something that seemed to scare Dad."

"Yes, he's the one," Nancy said. "I'm so glad your dad was able to keep Collin's Park away from Mike and his underhanded dealings."

"What's Mike going to do?"

Nancy shook her head. "I'll see what I can do to help your dad out, but you need to focus on finals. I certainly don't want you to get distracted now that you're at the finish line."

"You do really still care about Dad, don't you?"

"Yes, I still do."

"Have you been able to see him every now and then?"

"Once a year, sometimes two." Nancy got up and hung her dish towel over the rod under the upper cabinets.

Collin's eyes went wide. "Your birthdays! That's why you're always gone on your birthday. Isn't it?"

"My folks have a cottage that we meet at," Nancy said with a smile. "Don't get me wrong, your dad is not a saint and he admitted, even to you, that he's done some things wrong. But he's never done anything criminal—not like Mike Hammersmith. He still loves us and tries to help us the best way he can. I keep praying this will all go away and we can be together again, someday."

"Wow," Collin said softly.

"I know this doesn't help you in wishing you had a dad around all these years, but he has thought about you. And until Hammersmith gets put away, we're just stuck."

Fifty-Three

The kitchen manager, Randy, was helping the cooks with the soup pots when Tiger and Keeper walked in. He looked up with a grin that stretched from one side of his face to the other.

"Good to see you Keeper, Tiger," he said. "Folks'll be glad to see you tonight."

Billy nodded as they hung their jackets in the side room and stashed their backpacks. He led Billie to the sinks where they washed their hands, dried, and each grabbed a pair of food-handler's gloves. As they reached the serving area, he noticed the number of faces that turned their way and the number of smiles that came with them. He squeezed Billie's hand as she smiled back and took her place behind the trays of fruits and breads. The man that was filling soup bowls handed Billy the ladle and, smiling himself, went to the kitchen to help as a runner.

"Looks like word has gotten around," Billy said softly in a pause between two people in the serving line.

"Word? You mean Friday?"

Billy nodded and turned to say hello to the woman next in line, and after a bit, he realized that people were actually smiling and talking with each other. Something had definitely changed, and he knew it had to be the absence of Knife and his debasing followers.

Billy greeted an elderly woman, and when she stopped in front of Billie, he heard her ask, "Is it true you cut Knife's hand off, Tiger?"

Billie glanced at Billy with her eyebrows raised, and then said, "Well, you know how people like to exaggerate."

The woman nodded and smiled, and Billie turned to Billy and gave him her "you've got to be kidding me" look.

"You've made them happy, Tiger, even if you don't admit to anything. There'll be a dozen more variations of the stories by morning about how you might've done whatever they think you might've done."

"But...?"

"A lot of them are surprised to see us here, and a lot of them are happy because they guessed we would be." He nodded and glanced around the room. "And you can tell which ones didn't think we would be."

-¤-

Billy led them out of the kitchen earlier than normal, only serving for just over two hours. As they walked along Crescent, Billy kept watch around them like he always did, but asked, "Where do you and your friends usually go on Monday nights?"

"I think Becky said they were going to Daisy's, a wine bar," she said, trying to remember.

"Want to change and crash their party?" he asked, and smiled at her. "I've kept you away from your Monday-night gatherings for quite a while."

"You're sure you want to?" she asked, and eyed him suspiciously.

"Just a thought," he said. "I haven't met your friend Stacy or Becky, and I'm sure Lori has spilled the beans."

Billie chuckled. "I'm sure she has, along with her personal slant on whether or not I should be doing what I'm doing."

Billy chuckled, but did not say anything.

They stopped at the building across from the bus station and Billy guarded the door while she changed. When it was his turn, he made it quick and was pleased to see that Billie had waited in the shadows of the Women's entry.

"I called Becky and I think she probably fell off her stool,"

Billie said. "Lori was about to leave and Stacy is still there. I think they'll stick around to see if I'm actually bringing you along for a change."

"Did you tell them I'm coming?"

"Uh-uh," she said, shaking her head. "They'll just have to be curious for a little bit longer."

When they crossed First Street and Billie looked past the east building at the department store, she remembered the architect's comment again and the question she had when Cathy asked where they were going to live.

"Billy?" she asked, and stopped, looking at the building. "Did you say you will actually get ownership of these buildings?"

"Yes. Actually, I already have." He looked at her and waited for her question.

"When Cathy asked the other day where we're going to live," she said, and smiled at him. "I remembered the architect said the new penthouse on the department store building was for the owner's use. Does that mean you?"

"If we want," he said, and gently squeezed her hand. "If we do live there, we have to think about the others and how we stay connected."

"Connected?" she asked.

"They're sort of 'family' too. It's hard to explain, but I've lived just like them and I don't want to become someone different to them after I tell them who I really am."

"Well," she said, "have you thought about letting them live on the top floor and using the River Crest Apartments for the next group we help grow?"

Billy nodded absently. "We'll have to consider that, Tiger," he said, and smiled. "We most certainly will have to consider that."

-¤-

Billie stopped on the sidewalk, under the awning lights in

front of Daisy's, and turned to Billy. "Are you up to this?"

"I'll have to meet your friends sooner or later, Tiger," he said. "And they will be your friends for a long time after we're married."

I sure hope so. I just hope they can accept Billy.

Having doubts?

No! Well, some. I—

"Is that them at the tall table in the corner? I thought I saw Lori."

"Yeah," she said without looking. "Becky likes corners with a view."

"Well then, they need something to 'view.'" He dropped his backpack, bent to her, cupped the back of her head in his hand, and kissed her, slowly and tenderly.

She dropped her backpack and her arms automatically wrapped around his neck. He held her tight, lifting her as he straightened up; she curled one leg around his. It seemed like many minutes had passed before Billie slowly relaxed and blinked, taking a deep breath. He still held her tight and kissed her again before he slowly lowered her back to the pavement and held her until her legs stiffened and gave her support.

"I think we should go in now," he said softly.

She smiled, laying her head against his chest. "I think so, before I forget we're still out in public."

They picked up their backpacks and he slipped his arm around her shoulders, and then they went to the door.

-ᴂ-

When they entered, Billie looked around as if she didn't know where Becky and the girls were sitting, still recovering from the influence of Billy's kiss and embrace. Becky waved when Billie turned toward them, and nodding in response, she pulled Billy behind her as she moved between the tables.

"Hey, guys," Billie said, smiling hugely as she stopped between the two tall stools pulled up to the front side of the table.

"This has to be Billy," Becky said, and extended her hand. "I'm Becky and this is Stacy." She gestured to Stacy sitting beside her.

"Nice to finally meet you," he said, and helped Billie onto the stool beside Stacy. "Hi, Lori," he said as he set their packs beside the stools and sat down between her and Billie.

"Hi," Lori greeted. "Where have you two been?"

"Volunteering," Billy said casually as Billie scanned the ordering pad. "We help at one of the soup kitchens most nights. We got off early and Billie thought it would be nice to join up with you guys."

"You got off early?" Stacy said, glancing at her watch. "When do you usually get off?"

"Usually around eleven thirty," Billy said, and turned to Billie. "Found anything you'd like?"

"You know I like the drier wines, but I really don't want a Chablis," she said, scrolling down the list. "I want something different."

"Try a lightly chilled red," he said.

"What would you suggest?" Billie asked, noticing the girls' intense curiosity.

"Maybe a Pinot or a Pinot blend? Or a Cabernet? Oh, there's one," he said, and stopped her scrolling. "A Shiraz—or they have a nice Shiraz blend. Not overly dry and with a nice bloom. I think you might like the blend."

He never indicated that he knows anything about wines.

He does have a few secrets, doesn't he?

Billie forced herself to hide her surprise.

Like you said, he hasn't told you everything.

Nor have I told him everything.

"Okay," she said, and he pointed to another set of suggestions on the page.

"Get it in a stemless glass and a small bowl of ice," he said, and smiled at her, his face just inches away from hers.

She turned to him and smiled, but resisted kissing him. "Done. What do you want?"

"Just a cola tonight," he said, and turned back to the girls.

"Is Lori right?" Becky asked. "You two are getting married?"

Billy smiled. "When Billie picks a date."

"When?" Stacy asked, still looking like she didn't believe it.

"We need to talk to Billie's folks and see what will work for them," he said. "You know, inviting the rest of Billie's family, Sandy's schedule, making arrangements, dress buying and fittings and those sorts of things. We'll probably try to go out to their place and talk to them this weekend." He smiled, and when Billie chuckled, he changed the subject. "Did you girls have a nice day?"

Stacy closed her mouth and stammered, "Yes, yes. I did. How about you two?" she asked, glancing at Becky and Lori.

"The museum," Becky said, "is always a little slow and stuffy, but the interesting history behind the pieces makes up for it. I spent the day researching some background stuff on the show we're setting up."

Billy nodded and listened to the details as Becky dove into the explanation of her findings. When she hesitated, Lori jumped in and mentioned that Old Man Swaggard finally realized what she had been telling him about on-time deliveries when the week's orders had arrived at the store that day at precisely ten o'clock, as promised.

Stacy did not have much to talk about and seemed more interested in the details concerning Billy and his episode of cleaning floors and spilled food. Billie started to intercept Stacy, but Billy laid his hand on hers and simply told Stacy that it would not be very pleasant if someone did not clean up the occasional messes.

"Where's Tom tonight?" Billie asked, changing the subject again.

"Oh, he's been helping with the books at his dad's business over the weekend and today," Stacy said, "but he said he'll have most of tomorrow off. You know his dad has a paving company?"

"Yes," Billy said. "I know Dave, but I didn't know he had hired office staff to run the store while he handles that parking lot job he's working on this week." He looked back at Stacy and then at Lori with a shrug.

"Maybe he has," Stacy said. "Tom didn't say."

Becky picked up the conversation again as the waiter brought Billie her Shiraz and a bowl of ice, and Billy his cola. When the waiter left, Billy folded one of the cloth napkins, turned the diamond so a corner pointed at Billie, and set the bowl of ice near the opposite point, leaving just enough room near her to set the glass on and catch the water drops before she sipped the wine. Then he had her put the stemless glass in the bowl and settle it into the ice.

"Give that a few minutes and then try it," he said, and they turned their attention back to the girls.

Billie tried the Shiraz blend after a suitable cooling time and smiled. "That is very nice, Billy. Thank you."

"You're welcome," he said, and glanced at the continued curious looks. "I have on numerous occasions had to be the head wine taster for Sid." Then he looked at Billie. "I'm glad you like the suggestion."

"Who's Sid?" Becky asked.

"My boss," Billy said, and saw Billie's eyes dancing. "The Streetcar has a rather extensive selection of the finer wines. It offers its dinner patrons something with a unique flair."

Billie smiled at the disbelieving stares. "Oh, it does indeed," she said, thinking of unique things other than wine.

Fifty-Four

Tuesday, May 17

Billie sat beside Billy at a table away from the Bean and Bag Coffee Shop's front door. She glanced at the clock behind the cashier and the pickup counter.

When they arrived and took their places, Billie watched Billy choose a table, considering where Blake would try to sit. As he moved the long table so its short end was against the wall near the front wall, he asked if she would mind sitting between the table and the wall in the chair closer to the corner, with him between her and the door. She agreed and he positioned two other chairs, one across from him and one at the open end of the table so he would be between them and Billie. Then Billy moved a heavy earthen pot with a low, shrub-like plant into the empty space across from her. Billie felt like he was building a barricade; there were enough obstacles that Blake couldn't get to her unless he tried to go past Billy or over the table.

"Five minutes," Billie said absently, and sipped her tea.

Billie's shoulders twitched slightly and he smiled at her. "Don't worry. If he gets physical, you and I can handle him."

"I know," she said, smiling at him. "I'm not afraid of him anymore, Billy. I'm just hoping this will work and we can make him just go away. He depresses me."

He nodded and she looked around the room at the four other customers casually eating a bagel or reading a book while they drank their coffee. Two men in light-weight long coats, one with his back to them, shared a table just beyond the door, and the other two, one a man and the other a young woman, were at two separate tables closer to the serving counter.

Billy sipped his coffee and set the cup down as Lori entered the front door with Blake right behind her. Lori saw them, waved, and turned to take a seat. Blake nudged her to the chair at the end of the table and then stopped behind the one across from Billy.

"Would you get me a coffee with sugar?" Lori asked as she looked up at Blake.

-¤-

Billy watched Blake's guarded manner as he glanced around the room at the uninteresting people. He nodded as he went to the counter without acknowledging either Billy or Billie and returned with two cups of coffee. He slid one in front of Lori and set the other down, then glanced around the room again before he sat down and looked at Billie's firm stare. "So? What's this all about? I thought you didn't want to talk to me."

"I'm Billy Carson," Billy said, pulling Blake's attention away from her as he casually leaned back in his chair. "I'm the one that asked Lori to see if she could find you and have you come and talk."

Billy watched Blake's posture, assuring himself that he could anticipate any sudden change he might make, anything suddenly aggressive.

"So who are you? I've seen you but I don't know you, and my business is with Billie."

"That's the first part that I want to explain. You no longer have any business with Billie. None. Not anymore." Billy waited a moment before he pulled a folded sheet of paper from his shirt pocket and went on, gesturing to the paper. "I know that you have been following Billie around town. I have times and places where you were seen and what you were doing, including Saturday. What you've been doing is called stalking."

"Hey, wait a minute. You can't—"

"Can't?" Billy interrupted in a questioning voice, but it was not a question. "I have eyes and ears everywhere. I know almost everyone in town and they know me. And you *will* stop stalking my friends—especially Billie. "

"Are you trying to threaten me?" Blake asked with a menacing tone as he leaned forward, setting his arms crossways on the table in front of him. He stared at Billy.

"Of course not, Blake. This is a simple statement of fact," Billy said, leaning forward himself. His voice was pleasant and calm. "Like the fact that I know you have a record in California and the state police there would just *love* to know where you are. I can arrange that for you, if you wish." He gave Blake a blank look. "Or Idaho. It was just a year ago when you decided to leave hurriedly, I believe. There's a young woman—"

"So what?" Blake snapped, and Billy picked up his cup.

He calmly sipped it again, then Billy set the cup down with a slow, audible double tap.

"Just this," Billy said, holding Blake's attention as the two customers near the door stood up, crossed the room silently, and stopped, one on each side of and behind Blake.

Blake looked up, startled, and started to rise when one of the men gently put his hand on Blake's shoulder and said, "Be calm, son. Is your name Blake Lawrence?"

Blake looked at the man's face and Billy wrinkled his nose and nodded. "You really ought to answer the man."

Slowly Blake nodded and said "yes."

The man handed Blake an official-looking tri-folded paper. "This is a cease and desist order, Mr. Lawrence, better known as a restraining order." The officer introduced himself and explained the details of the order. "You are hereby restricted from any physical or verbal contact with one Billie Mattis. You are also restricted from following Miss Mattis, causing Miss Mattis to be followed, or being in the company of Miss Mattis, whether she is alone or in a group. You also may not access or be present in or on any premises in which Miss Mattis is present, including her residence, residences she is visiting, leasing, or owns. This includes any or all lands or grounds associated with those places she occupies. Do you understand these restrictions, Mr. Lawrence?"

Blake slowly nodded.

When the two men stepped away, Blake watched them until Billy spoke again. The lieutenant that served the papers turned and left while Detective Nolan went to the counter and ordered another cup of coffee.

"You would be wise to follow the restrictions of that order, Blake." Billy said, forcing himself to hold his temper. Blake was not worth losing control over. "I won't be preachy, but you really need to change your ways, try to be a better person than you have been. If you don't, you could 'accidently' end up face to face with your demons in a dark alley some night. For a fact, I will tell you that you do not want to meet me in that dark alley, and I'm here to tell you for a fact that I would not want to meet Billie in any dark alley if she was angry with me. The last one that did, the police took away in pieces."

Blake looked at Billie, and he knew Blake suddenly saw her toned arms, her serious demeanor, and that he remembered, absently rubbing his left wrist, her piercing stare, her numbing grip, and how easily she had pinned him to the wall and bloodied his face. Billie cocked her head and his eyes revealed his sudden enlightenment.

"I *will* know if you break any of those restrictions, Blake, and I *will not* ask the police to visit you when I do." Billy was still staring at him when he looked back. Billy waited, letting his words eat into his brain. "That is a promise from me that you can count on."

Blake slowly stood up and glanced back at Billie. He turned to Lori, but Lori looked straight at the wall, ignoring his unspoken question. Then he walked out of the café and Billy watched him until he disappeared around the corner. When he heard Billie exhale, he realized she had been holding her breath.

Lori moved her stare to Billie and slowly found her voice. "Is what Billy says true? You did that too?"

Billie slowly nodded. "I have learned how to defend myself, Lori. And to defend others."

Lori looked at Billy. "You've been teaching her?"

"Yes," he admitted. "Me and a number of our friends."

"We're not vigilantes, Lori," Billie said softly, "but I will defend myself and protect my friends if I can—any of my friends—and I will use force if I have to."

"She's already saved my life, Lori," he said, and smiled softly. "Maybe twice."

Lori inhaled and sighed. "I know I saw what you did at Custer's, but I had no idea that you were that serious when you talked about your training and practice sessions," Lori admitted as she turned her cup in her hands.

"That's okay, Lori," Billie said. "Thanks for bringing Blake here so we could serve him and maybe end this. Billy and his detective friend said that was the necessary first step."

"You're welcome, Billie," Lori said, and smiled.

"Can we talk later—maybe this afternoon or this evening after Billy gets off work?" Billie asked. "Right now I need to talk to Detective Nolan so he and Billy can go back to work."

"This evening then," Lori said, and got up. "I need to get to work too."

Billie looked at Billy. "Are we serving tonight?"

Billy nodded. "I can cancel if you want me to."

"Would you mind, Billy?"

"Not at all," he said, and shook his head.

Billie looked at Lori. "Come by when you get off and we can talk a little before Billy gets home. Then maybe the three of us can grab a burger or something."

"Okay, I'll come by," Lori said, and smiled weakly as she left.

Fifty-Five

"Damn, Keeper," Tiger said as they walked hand in hand back toward her apartment after meeting with Detective Nolan. "I feel like I need to hit something. Really hard."

"I know," he said, and squeezed her hand as she kicked a small rock on the sidewalk. They watched it dance ahead of them.

"I hoped he would have some advice," she continued as they walked.

"He did," Keeper said softly. "He said you did a good job of researching your suspicions, and now we wait until he picks Hammersmith up. Then we'll see what they can get out of him."

"I don't understand why they haven't picked him up yet. Nolan said they have a clear case against him for hiring Knife and Pink's death."

"That was surprising," he said. "It's only been four days—"

"That seems like such a long time," Billie interrupted. "Hammersmith has to know by now Knife failed, and I suspect he's gone into hiding. Nolan's missed his chance to nab him quickly."

"I think you're probably right, Tiger."

Billie squeezed his hand and looked up at him. "Do you have to hurry back to work?"

He shook his head and smiled at her. "I think we'll go and unwind a little. Then maybe I can talk you into lunch at the diner before I go back for the afternoon."

She smiled. "That sounds like a plan. I think I could use a little quiet time with you and some of Sid's cooking for lunch."

As they turned the corner onto Cheyenne, Billie looked at him and added, "At least Hammersmith doesn't know who you really are or that you know what he did."

Billy smiled but did not tell her about the emails.

☐-☐-☐-☐-☐

Mike Hammersmith was studying the park proposal when the phone chimed. He picked up the handset and punched the blinking phone line button.

"Mr. Hammersmith, Joey here," the voice on the other end of the connection said. "Sorry to bother you during the day, but I just heard some news that I think you might want to know about."

"What is it, Joey?" Mike asked, and toyed with a pencil he had lying beside the proposal folder.

"Last week, Thursday night, I was talking to a drug dealer at one of the soup kitchens—a man calling himself Pink. He was a little bit wasted but he mentioned that he was going to help someone called Knife open up the city center blocks on Friday. New customers and all of—"

"So? Get on with it."

"Well, he said the only way to open the blocks up was to remove the one they call Keeper," Joey explained. "But Keeper was at the soup kitchen last night just like he always is."

"He was?" Mike asked, surprised, suddenly remembering the email and that it had said Keeper was still alive. *How would Westman have known that?*

"Yup. I did some askin' when I didn't see Pink or Knife last night. The word around the kitchen is that Knife killed that drug dealer, Pink, and that guy Keeper or someone called Tiger got the Knife."

"I was told the Knife was the best in the city."

"He was. Whichever one got him," Joey continued, "cut him

182

to pieces and left him for the cops to pick up."

Mike's shoulders drooped. "Did anyone say whether Knife died?"

"Seems he's still alive," Joey said. "He's in the police ward at the hospital. No one said how bad off he was."

Mike absently shook his head, knowing they would get Knife to tell all, and he suspected it would be sooner rather than later.

"Any idea who this Keeper is?" Mike asked anxiously, feeling his chest tighten.

"No. I've seen him at the kitchen," Joey said, "but I haven't seen this Tiger yet. And when I asked, no one seems to know where Keeper hangs out."

"Okay," Mike said absently, his thoughts racing. "I'll let you know if I need you to do anything more."

"Okay," Joey said, and disconnected.

Mike glanced back at his computer monitor and thought again about the last email he got, supposedly from W.C. Hawke.

¤-¤-¤-¤-¤

"I don't think Lori understands you," Billy said with a chuckle, "any more now than she did before you tried to explain what you are doing."

"Well, me and my big mouth this morning," Billie said, and shook her head as they walked along Arapaho, enjoying the night and the light breeze. "I felt sorry for her, and then this afternoon I realized I really could not say anything without telling her too much about the village people, or about you and the department store, to why we are always around city center at night."

Billy chuckled. "I was wondering how you were going to get yourself out of this one."

"And you didn't help me at all," she said, and slapped his chest. "Well, except for taking care of Blake earlier. I really owe you for doing that."

"I'll put that on your tab," he said, and smiled. "I just hope he'll follow instructions for once."

"Me too, but he doesn't have a very good track record."

She was pleased at how Billy had reacted to Blake's threat and how he had taken charge when it came to dealing with Blake, asking for the restraining order and arranging for it to be served. And tonight, reassured her feelings for him were right, she was again enjoying his company as they walked along one lighted boulevard after another, taking a slow, casual pace back to the apartment. The light spring breeze was almost cool after the sun went down, but with her sweater and Billy's arm around her shoulders, the walk was much more than just comfortable. It almost felt magical, and she tried to rein in her thoughts of what their future life might be like.

"Have you thought about what you want to do?" Billy asked, bringing her back to the moment.

"Do? What do you mean? I'm doing it." She was fascinated by the dancing splashes of the streetlights through the new leaves as they meandered back toward her apartment.

"I was thinking," Billy said, "with things calming down, you might have something else in mind—besides defending city blocks and accompanying me into dark alleys late at night. I guess I am wondering if you liked the renovation design business? Whether you liked working with Carl and Robert and if you wanted to do that type of work anymore."

"Sure." She thought a minute. "I like the idea of designing renovations, making old things new again. Repurposing them," she said, and looked up at his grin. "But I really want to learn more about the actual designing process, not just the detail checking. To learn what it takes to create the ideas that go into a project and see them happen. Why?"

"Just wondering," he said without looking down. "You weren't really given enough time to make a mark, so I was curious if that was something that interested you. I don't want you to be bored."

"I think Keeper doesn't like me having so much free time on my hands." She smiled and slapped his chest playfully. "But I do hope Keeper lets Tiger work with him on anything and everything he wants to do, even if it isn't guarding city blocks or training a new group of friends."

He squeezed her shoulder. "I just hope Tiger wants to help Keeper as much as he wants her to."

She looked up at him and he stole a kiss.

"You know Tiger belongs to Keeper," she said, turning serious, her expression concerned.

"I do, and Keeper belongs to Tiger," he said. "But Keeper does want to know when we're going to explain to Tiger's parents what we're going to do and who you've decided to marry. Is this weekend going to work?"

"Yeah. I think I know how Mom will react, but I don't want to put it off any longer," she admitted softly, trying to keep her concerns and her giddiness in check. She squeezed his waist. "Sandy went back to school to take her finals, and she should be finished sometime on Thursday. I can call or text her and see if she'll be back for the weekend." She looked up at him, "Sandy has a squeeze, and I don't know if they're doing anything before she comes back again."

"I haven't seen Sandy since you were twelve," he said. "How has she changed?"

"Like the rest of us," Billie laughed. "She's older, prettier, and a little more protective of her little sister. We've always worried about people like Blake getting their fingers into us, trying to get what money we have. Mom and Dad have always been a little paranoid over people thinking horses mean big money, but they don't always. Sorry, Sandy and I got into an argument over you and she brought up the whole opportunist worry again."

"An argument? Over your money?"

"Nothing lasting," she chuckled. "It was over boyfriends and relations, not money. Anyway, it kind of went away when she told me she was afraid to tell Mom and Dad about her man, Gil, for many of the same reasons." Then slowly an unexpected thought crept into her mind and she turned to study his expression. "What do you know about my money? You said you weren't after mine, but...Did you have something to do with our trusts?"

"Me?" He smiled at her. "How could I? I wasn't old enough—"

"You *do* know about them." She stopped and turned to face him.

"Yes, I guess I do." He wrapped his arms around her shoulders and pulled her to him. "When I was old enough to get involved in Dad's company, I found out that he had set up trusts for both of you to help. School, life, whatever you and Sandy needed."

Billie tilted her head back and stared at him. "Why? Why would he do that?"

"I told you," he said, and stole a kiss. "Your family was special to Dad and Mom. They were friends. Unfortunately I can't ask him why, but maybe your folks can shed some light on that when we talk to them."

Wow.

Yeah, wow.

"Well, I hope Sandy can make it back," Billy said as they began walking again, turned the corner, and crossed the street to the apartment building. "It would be nice to see her again."

They went in, and when Billy closed the door behind them and set the dead bolt, she wrapped her arms around his neck, pulled herself up to kiss him, and wrapped her legs around him, pulling his body tight against her. She kept kissing him as he stumbled against the wall and then slowly got his balance. One step at a time, he carried her up the stairs and fell back onto the bed.

-☐-

She lay beside Billy, his arms gently holding her tight against his warm side, her head resting on his shoulder. She felt secure, but as much as she felt their unity, their likeness, their accord and complete surrender to each other, she felt incomplete.

Maybe incomplete *is not the right word,* she thought, *It's more like I'm letting him down. I want to give him something truly meaningful in light of all of the meaningful things he's given me.*

Loving him and caring for him and what he does isn't truly meaningful?

Yes it is, but I need *to give him more.*

Her growing sense of need fought with the warmth Billy had brought into her life, and she knew what she had to do.

I know I can do this.

Fifty-Six

Wednesday, May 18

Sid looked up when Melony said, "Mail's here," through the Streetcar Diner's serving window. He wiped his hands and gestured for Niles to watch the food that was cooking. She met him at the archway and pushed the swinging doors open.

"What have we got today Mel?" Sid asked absently as he took the stack.

"Looks like the usual stuff," Melony said, "except for the box."

Sid turned the small one-rate mailing box and looked at the label.

"Thanks, Mel," he said as he turned back to the kitchen. "Billy, looks like you got something."

Billy, deep in his sink, looked up and nodded. "Just put it in your office with the rest of the mail. I'll look at it when I get a break."

"Okay," Sid said, and walked to the door to the hallway, flipping through the stack of letter-sized envelopes as he went, the box tucked under his arm.

-¤-

Billy pushed the tray into the dishwasher and closed the doors to start the cycle, and finished organizing the next rack of dirty dishes before he wiped his hands and went to Sid's office. He closed the door and picked up the box sitting in the middle of the semi-organized desk. Smiling, Billy saw his name and the Streetcar's address in both the addressee and the return address spots; Greg Madison was thorough.

Visualizing the locked steel door in the basement of the Duckard's warehouse building, Billy pulled the string on the box and flipped the end flap open. He unfolded the wad of bubbled plastic packing material and dropped the three tarnished brass keys into his open hand.

Inside the box, he found a folded half sheet of paper; the printed note read:

"Only these three were found. You have the entry and the roof access keys. Hope these will work for you. Let me know if you need anything more. G.M."

Billy dropped the note in the shredder and pocketed the three keys. He flattened the box and dropped it in the trash, and glancing at the clock, he knew he only had about an hour before Billie arrived for lunch; he'd ask Sid about a key ring later.

¤-¤-¤-¤-¤

Billie took her time and walked to the Streetcar to meet Billy for lunch. She was pleased the weather was still cooperating with warm, gentle breezes and a sky full of cotton-ball clouds for decorations. Angie led her to their table and Billy joined her in minutes. Lunch was pleasant, like it always was when she could eat with Billy, and she reveled in the more relaxed man she was starting to see. She was pleased that her addition in his life made him happy.

"Oh my?" Billy asked as he looked up from his plate. "Your cheeks just turned bright red. What on earth are you thinking about?"

She smiled. "You. And last night and the last few nights we've been together. Sometimes I still can't believe we've actually found each other again."

Yes, finding each other again was a godsend.

You just like the sex.

Yes, that too. But it's a lot more than that and you know it.

"I was thinking next month," she said when he stopped chuckling. "Maybe on the Solstice, to celebrate our 'longest day' together yet."

"Hmm." He smiled at her and put his hand on top of hers. "If this afternoon won't work, then the Solstice would be great. Any word from Sandy?"

"Yeah. She says she'll be back early on Saturday, for a week." Billie winked. "She has to tell Mom and Dad about Gil since they'll be off for two weeks together in Florida after that."

"Aaah."

She smiled as Billy chuckled and gently squeezed her hand.

"So?" he asked as he stacked their dirty dishes and set them near the front edge of their table. "What are you up to this afternoon, while I slave over a hot mop and spilled soups?"

Are you going to tell him?

No. Tonight. I want to be sure first.

"I'll probably visit with Lori at the drugstore on her break, and then maybe see if Cathy is available for another practice session after she gets off work." She looked at him and made a sad face. "And it's Wednesday, girls' night out."

"Where tonight?" he asked, pouted in return, then smiled.

"Whiskey's. Even though I have a 'free-forever-food-and-drink' pass at Custer's, we decided to wait another week or so before we go back. Last week's experience with Blake needs to fade a little more." She chuckled when he nodded in agreement. "So Becky thought going back to Whiskey's would work."

He's not going to like this.

Hush! He has things of his own to do.

When he got up to take the dishes into the back room, she sighed and watched him slip through the swinging doors. He stepped back through the archway as she stood and slipped her purse strap over her head, catching her hand and pulling her into the back room. Her arms found their way around his neck as he bent and kissed her, a wonderful, almost instinctive interaction.

"That's to hold me until I can see you again," he said, and smiled.

She kissed him again, a quick one, and then stepped back. "Go get back to work. I'll see you later," she said, and gave him a gentle shove.

-¤-

Billie walked the six blocks south, caught the diagonal of River, and then turned east on Kiowa. As she got close to Swaggard's Drugstore on the southeast corner at Seventh West, her sense of purpose became more determined.

She pushed the glass front door open, walked past the cashier and the two check-out stations, and headed to the back of the store. Lori was in the small office, sitting with her back to the door, reading a paperback and sipping an iced drink through a straw. Billie knocked on the doorjamb.

"Hey," Lori said, turning in surprise. "What brings you way out here?" Lori glanced at the clock face icon on her computer screen and gestured to the chair beside the door. Billie took it.

"Just out running around after lunch with Billy, but actually, I need to ask you a big favor," she began, and Lori leaned forward, holding her drink on her knees. "May I borrow your car this afternoon?"

"My car?" Lori straightened, surprised, and then shrugged with a smile. "I guess. What're you up to? Not more of what we talked about last night? Or is something wrong with the SUV?"

Billie shook her head. "I want to drive through some residential areas and check out some properties I've been looking at online."

"Properties?" Lori smiled, and Billie knew she had immediately jumped to the wrong conclusion.

You're going to regret this.

Hush!

"For now, I just want to drive by a few and look," Billie said softly, "and my SUV is too...conspicuous. That's why I thought of using your car. It's not..."

"Flagrantly dripping with apparent wealth?" Lori asked sharply.

"Yeah, something like that. I'll even fill it up," Billie said, a gentle plea in her voice.

Lori stared at her a long moment and then slowly smiled. "Sure, you can borrow the car. Just let me know if you find something Billy would like." Lori dug her keys out of her purse.

"I hope that won't be too hard," Billie said, and smiled as she took the keys. *Billy likes to be dry and out of the wind. Doesn't necessarily even have to be warm, if we can snuggle.*

Lori chuckled as Billie stood up.

"I shouldn't be too long," she said, and turned to leave.

"Don't forget to fill it up," she heard Lori say as she took an aisle back to the front of the store.

-¤-

In front of her building, Billie parked in a visitor's space and then went up to her apartment. She collected her second set of printed images, grabbed a bottle of water from the refrigerator, and went up to her bedroom. There, she took her frumpy clothes from her closet, folded them, put them in her backpack, and stuffed the water bottle in one end. The images, she folded and slipped into the zippered pouch beside her knife, leg scabbard, and a small flashlight.

After a quick check around the apartment, she absently laid her SUV keys on the eating counter beside her digital pad and the other printouts.

Going to leave him a note?

I'll be back before he gets off work.

She made another quick glance around the downstairs part of the apartment. Satisfied she had everything she needed, she stepped out and locked the apartment door behind her.

Fifty-Seven

Billy came straight from the Streetcar to Billie's apartment after work. It was nearly six thirty and he was not surprised to see that Billie was already gone. He barely noticed her SUV in her parking spot when he came in, expecting she had already changed and either ridden with one of the girls or had enjoyed the short walk to Whiskey's for drinks and maybe a bite to eat. He knew her routine and did not think anything more of it.

He settled on the sofa with a glass of water and watched the city for a few minutes, thinking about the department store and that the next day after work would be a good time to take Billie, Max, and Mindy and see if the keys from Greg Madison worked in the locked basement door. He glanced at the time and realized he had to get his backpack ready and start across town. No longer living in city center, he needed a few extra minutes to get there.

Billy emptied his glass, set it in the sink, and went up to the bedroom. He took his backpack from the closet and set it on the neat and unruffled bed. He hesitated, unexpectedly bothered as he turned to his clothes on their hangers. He slowly looked back at the bed; Billie was usually a bit indecisive when she chose what she wanted to wear; her unused choices almost always cluttered the bed until she got home.

The lack of clutter held his attention and he glanced back at the closet, noticing her backpack was not on the floor where it should be. Reluctantly, he looked and saw the empty hangers where her frumpy summer clothes normally hung.

A dark, uneasy concern swept over him. *Oh, Tiger. What are you up to tonight?*

He hurried down the stairs to the living room, checked the

kitchen counter for a note, then called the security desk in the lobby, but there were no messages for him. He thanked the man, toggled the hook, and entered the diner's number.

"Sid?" he asked, forcing himself to keep his voice calm and his tone pleasant when the male voice answered. "Sid, it's Billy." He was almost afraid to ask his next question. "Did Billie leave any messages for me?"

"I don't see one. Let me ask the girls." Billy waited impatiently as Sid checked. "No, Billy. No one has heard from her since she was here for lunch."

"Thanks, Sid," Billy said, and placed the handset in its cradle. His hand shook, his confidence shaken for the first time in he could not remember how long. *Billie, Billie, Billie? What are you doing?*

Billy locked the apartment behind him and hurried down through the lobby and out the front door.

-¤-

Billy knocked on Cathy and Todd's door, and hearing someone inside, he impatiently waited, shifting his weight from one foot to the other. After a minute, Abby opened the door. "Biillyy!"

"Hi Abby. Is your mom home?" he asked tersely, and saw Cathy crossing the living room.

"Come in, Billy," Cathy said, and swung the door open farther.

"No, that's all right," he said. "Have you seen Tiger today? She mentioned she might come by."

"No," Cathy said, shaking her head. "We didn't have a session set up and she didn't come by. Is everything okay?"

"I don't know. I feel like something's wrong," he admitted. "It's her night out with her friends, but sometime this afternoon, she left her apartment without her car and took her old clothes with her. She wasn't going to the kitchen tonight, so I can't figure out why she took them."

"Maybe she just put them in her car so she'll have them," Cathy suggested.

"Yeah, maybe," Billy said, and thanked her. As he left and started toward Whiskey's, he knew he was not buying the idea. *We always walk from the apartment to go to the kitchen. We never take her car. Maybe Lori and Becky know.*

Then Billy realized he could have saved himself a lot of worry; instead of calling Sid and going to Cathy's, he should have just called Billie's phone.

¤-¤-¤-¤-¤

Billie looked at the derelict house and outbuildings as she slowly drove by, surveying the details of the rundown structure.

Detached garage, door half open, less than a hundred feet from the road. Choice number four doesn't look like it would hide anything for a week. Sure wouldn't be ignored for seventeen years. Damn!

This was a stupid idea.

Okay, let's go to choice number three.

She followed the dirt road east and then north as she drove to the next property on her list.

Wow. Worse than the last one. Open barn, no doors at all. Only thing going for it is that it is nearly an hour from the city. The blurry images sure didn't do this one justice.

Ready to admit this was stupid yet?

No. It isn't stupid. There are two more.

Back to the west, the next one was also a long way from the city, but...

Okay, okay. Don't say it. With a collapsed roof and no doors, this certainly isn't a candidate. It has to be the last one, but I had to look at the others, just to be sure.

You still haven't proven anything.

She sighed and pulled back onto the road.

Not yet, but we'll see.

The last place, her first choice, was on Hammersmith's main estate. The shed she wanted to see was not visible from either the paved road that passed from east to west on the south side property, nor was it visible from the closest dirt road, the one just to the east. The acreage was almost thirty acres, half again as deep as it was wide, with the house situated near the geometric center on a crest slightly higher than the main road. The shed, in the far northeast corner of the property, was considerably lower on the back side of the hill and completely out of sight.

Billie checked the time on her phone. She had spent over four hours checking all of the properties. It was getting late, but now she was here.

I told you, this isn't a good idea!

It isn't very far. I can go check it out and be back before it gets very dark.

It still isn't a very good idea. You shouldn't be doing this alone!

I'm perfectly capable of looking! It's half an hour back to town and another half an hour to get back out here. If I take an extra few minutes now, maybe I can have something to give Nolan. Just a couple of pictures. I can still be back before Becky and Lori call it a night, and before Billy leaves the kitchen.

There was no traffic on the main road as she drove by the driveway to the house, and she noted the dark gray car and the blue and white pickup truck in front of the garage.

See? Someone is at the house.

It'll be dark enough they won't see me.

Out of sight of the house and the next house along the road, Billie turned onto the dirt road to the east and drove north nearly a quarter of a mile. She pulled to one side of the wide spot just before the road completely petered out into a weedy trail. Nearly hidden from the sky by the huge umbrella of maples and elm trees, the spot was a place where cars simply turned around before the road got too narrow. The trail beyond hinted at summer walks, picnic baskets or fishing gear to possibly a secluded spot on the riverbank another half mile or so farther on.

She got out, looked around, and did not see any recent tire tracks; the place was secluded and had not seen any traffic in a while. She opened the passenger door and took her backpack out.

Billie leaned back against the rear fender and studied the overhead image of the estate, located her position, and identified a likely path she should take to get to the shed. She checked her time again and decided she had about forty-five minutes before dark. It would be enough time to work her way through the woods, staying out of sight while she had light, and then she would return across the more open pasture in the dark. Satisfied with her plan, buoyed by her inflated feeling of purpose, she opened her backpack.

It was too warm to wear her slacks under the worn jeans, so she ducked in front of the open car door and slipped into her jeans as quickly as she could.

You should've brought Billy. He should be here.

But he isn't and I'm going to go look.

Determined, Billy slipped her blouse off and donned the worn, slash-necked, short-waisted jumper, set her light jacket aside, and took the knife and scabbard out of the zippered pouch. She strapped the scabbard to her right calf, and when she was satisfied it was secure and that the inverted knife would not slip out, she straightened her baggy pant leg and stood up. She quickly folded her regular clothes and packed them in the backpack.

Billie took Lori's car key off her fob and with an old shoestring she kept in her backpack, tied it to her ankle, and stuffed her foot into her scruffy boot. She wrapped her hair in a dark gray scarf, put her small flashlight in her pocket, set the backpack in the trunk, and hid the rest of Lori's keys under the front seat. Finishing off her water and tossing the empty plastic bottle on the floorboard, she closed and locked the car door.

Billie took a deep breath and then started her journey west through the brush and trees. Her argumentative rational mind stewed in silence.

¤-¤-¤-¤-¤

"Joey," Herb said as he came into Hammersmith's house from the garage. "When did Mr. Hammersmith leave this message?"

"What message?" Joey asked from the basement. "I didn't hear anything."

"Turn that stupid game off and come up here," Herb said, and punched the replay button.

"Yeah? What's he want?" Joey asked as he came up the stairs with the television remote still in his hand.

"Clothes. A suitcase with some of his clothes in it," Herb said, and pointed to the stairs going up to the bedrooms. "Get a suitcase out of his closet and I'll start emptying drawers."

Together they went to his master bedroom and Joey went to the closet.

"As nice as he keeps things, you'd never believe he's single," Joey said as he selected the larger of the cases. "I could never keep things cleaned up like this."

"Well," Herb said, "having someone clean for him once a week might have something to do with how it looks."

"Yeah, I guess." Joey said as he pulled the suitcase out of the closet. "Did I tell you about Knife and that drug dealer, Pink?"

"Yeah, you mentioned it," Herb said as Joey opened the case. Herb turned to the dresser. "Maybe three or four changes will do him."

"What surprised me is that some at the soup kitchen were

saying Knife lost his hand. Cut clean off, still holding his gat."

"That would mess up your whole day," Herb admitted.

"I'd sure hate to meet up with that Keeper fella, especially in the dark," Joey said, and picked four shirts from the closet.

"The Knife screwed up. He underestimated him," Herb said. "He had the gat and should've shot him first, before he had the chance to get close."

They filled the case, zipped it closed, and put some of the toiletries from the bath in the front pouch.

"Where d'we have to take it?" Joey asked as he lugged the case down the stairs.

"His sister's place," Herb said, and started turning lights off in the main floor rooms. "Twenty miles east, over in Bailey. Put that in the backseat of the car while I get things buttoned up."

Joey nodded, dragged the case through the door to the garage, and punched the garage door open. Herb checked each room, switching off the lights, but as he turned the dining room light off, he glanced out into the dark back pasture and saw the soft flash of a light.

"Hey, Joey," he shouted, and hurried to the open door into the garage. "There's someone out in the pasture." He closed the door and ran out of the garage into the side yard. "We'd better see who's snoopin' around."

Fifty-Eight

Billie stumbled into another tree, brushed a thick bush aside, and stepped over another fallen trunk. The trip through the forested draw had turned into a trek as night fell and the last of the day's light failed. It was full dark, after sundown and before the glow of the rising moon appeared, when Billie, frantically arguing with herself over her audacity and stupidity, finally saw the solid shadow looming ahead of her, barely discernable in the darkness.

There it is! Has to be the shed. Finally!

She tried to be quiet, but it was too dark to really see where to step. *It seems like there's more dead trees than live, standing ones.*

Her journey through the wooded tract was taking far longer than she expected and she cursed again for forgetting how dark it really could be in the country.

After another long few minutes of stumbling and slipping over roots and fallen tree trunks and branches, with the brush constantly snagging and pulling on her clothes, she reached the shadow and touched the rough, weathered boards.

Finally!

Told you this wasn't a good idea.

Yeah, but I'm here. And now I'm going to look around.

She felt the vertical bats spaced about a foot apart and visualized the looks of the board and batten wall as she groped her way past more trees and brush toward the front of the shed.

She felt along the front wall and found the edges of the two doors.

Narrower than I expected, but these are the doors. Hmm, no windows and of course it's locked.

Didn't think they would be open and waiting for you, did you?

Hush!

As tempting as it was, she admitted she did not want to "break and enter," and with no way to pry the hasp and padlock, she was kept honest. She continued around to the west side, and to her relief, her hands found the frame and the smooth panes of a glass window.

Billie glanced around through the few trees at the edge of the wooded area and she could see no one in the dark pasture; only the house on top of the hill looking down at her with a few windows lit. She listened and heard nothing unusual.

It's so dark, you wouldn't know if someone was standing ten feet away.

She shook her head, feeling overly paranoid, pulled the flashlight from her pocket, held it close to the window to keep it from reflecting, and snapped it on.

She shone the light around the inside, slowly looking at each item as the beam passed over it. Old tires, some "Do Not Trespass" signs, tools, boxes of nails and screws on a sagging shelf on the far wall, garden implements of all kinds hung from bowed rafters and wall brackets, some shiny canisters on a rusty metal rack, some rolls that looked like wide gray tape, long boards of a white, reflective material, some— She stopped and aimed the beam back at the shiny canisters.

The light reflected off one, shining on boxes thrown around it on the floor, and then she aimed her beam at the second one. She jumped and snapped the flashlight off when it reflected straight back at her.

She knew it was a lamp and she was seeing the glass lens and the reflector.

Shit! There they are! I don't believe it! They're here. Damn! Damn! Nolan! You wanted solid and I think I've found 'solid.'

She switched the flashlight back on and looked at the rolls and the reflective boards again, confirming what she thought she saw. Elated, she switched her flashlight off and took her phone out of her pocket. She positioned it against the glass and snapped a couple of pictures, then stepped back to cross in front of the shed and start back to the car, turning to take a last look at the shed's dark shadow.

Thank you, thank you. Now, Keeper, we can hold him accountable.

She heard a loud, double *pop* behind her, but before she could turn to look, something unexpectedly slammed her facedown onto the ground.

Stunned, the wind knocked out of her, she suddenly realized her shoulder, neck, and entire left side was on fire! Her chest was hot, she felt nauseous and tried to move. Fiery pain shot through her and down her side, stealing her breath when she tried to push herself up. Her head spun and the ground seemed to move under her. She tried to roll to one side, but the intense, searing pain shot fire through her again. She gasped, unable to catch her breath. Her left arm and leg painfully refused to move and the burning heat under her chest heightened her nausea. She coughed and the contraction tore at her stomach, making her head spin faster. She forced her right hand under herself and felt her chest; her fingers slipped into the gaping, hot tear.

Oh no. Oh, no.

She touched the hot wetness to her tongue and instantly knew it was blood.

Damn! Damn! Lots of blood! Not good! This is so not good! Damn! Billy, I'm sorry.

Fighting off her rising panic, she pulled her phone from her back pocket and touched Lori's icon.

"Lori!" she shouted, her voice heavy, raspy and unfamiliar. "Lori, it's Billie. Find Billy!"

The background noise slowly ebbed and she heard Lori asking her what she said.

"Lori! Find Billy. Tell him...I was right. Choice number one! Got that?"

"Y...yes, number one. What's happened? You were supposed to be back hours ago. Where are you?"

"Tell Billy! Number...number one! Hurry..." she said, feeling her strength quickly draining away. "I've...been shot...! Can't... talk. Can't...get your...car back...Sorry..." she said in gasps. "Tell...Billy, I'm sorry...I...love him..." She disconnected the call, hearing someone yelling, coming down the hill and across the pasture toward her.

Oh God, someone's coming. Billy, Billy. I'm sorry. Please come find me...Please...

She tapped Nolan's icon and slid the phone facedown into the weeds, as close to a nearby tree as she could reach. She faintly heard Detective Nolan answer as the last of her strength disappeared and her world went black.

¤-¤-¤-¤-¤

Detective Nolan poured himself another cup of coffee, added two spoons of sugar, and stirred it with frustration.

"It's too late to get that warrant now," he said to the lieutenant that shared his office. He stared at the swirling black mixture in his cup. "Should've had it before five."

"I know," the lieutenant said as he scrolled through the images on his computer screen. "They shouldn't be backlogged."

Detective Nolan settled back onto his worn-out and taped-together simulated leather chair and set the cup on his coaster. "Get up there first thing in the morning and find out where it is. If they drag their feet too long, Hammersmith will get away. Anything on his partner in crime, Westman?"

"Nothing. We've put out an 'all points' but haven't heard anything," the lieutenant said. "No one's seen him in about ten days."

"That's strange," Nolan said as his mobile phone chimed. He answered it. "Detective Nolan here. How may I help you?" He listened but no one said anything. He asked again, "Can I help you?" Then he heard faint voices slowly getting louder, and he touched the record icon out of habit.

"Damn, Herb," the voice said, and then continued after a short moment. "You don't start shooting to check out someone nosing around." There was a pause. "Damn! You did shoot someone, Herb! You can't go around doin' that."

Nolan looked at his phone and realized the ID was Tiger's number. He touched the Mute icon and put the phone back to his ear as he turned to the lieutenant. "Get me a trace on this cell call. I want to know which tower is picking it up! Now!"

The lieutenant scrambled, fumbling with his phone and computer.

"Shut up, Joey," a second voice said. Nolan assumed it was Herb. "He shouldn't have been here in the first place."

Nolan heard grass or weeds rustling.

"Turn him over," Herb's irritated voice said. There was more rustling and the sound Nolan assumed was Joey turning the person over.

"Damn! It's a woman, Herb," Joey's voice shouted. "She's covered in blood, man!"

Nolan inhaled suddenly, realizing they were talking about Tiger. His hand began to shake. *Damn Tiger! I didn't mean for you to look for something* this *solid!*

"She looks homeless, Joey," Herb said. "No one'll miss her."

"She must've been looking for a place to sleep the night out," Joey surmised. "She would've been gone in the morning, Herb. No muss, no fuss, Herb! No *bo-dy!*" Joey was frantically shouting by the time he finished.

"I said shut up, Joey," Herb said, his irritation rising by the sound of his voice. "Help me get her up to the truck. I know where we can dump her and no one will find her for weeks, maybe months."

Nolan picked up his desk phone and dialed the Streetcar.

"Hello," he said when someone answered. "Is Billy Carson there? Detective Nolan, City Police."

A moment passed then Sid said, "He's been gone since about six. Can I take a message?"

"No. Where does he go after he leaves the diner?" Nolan asked.

Another moment passed and Sid said, "Angie says he's been going over to Billie Mattis' apartment. I don't have the address."

"Thanks," Nolan said, "I do." And he disconnected.

He listened to his mobile and heard the voices fading away, dragging something through the grass. When the sounds were gone, he switched the phone off.

"I'm going to find Billy Carson," Nolan said, glancing at the lieutenant. "Call me as soon as you get a location on that cell tower." Nolan slipped into his shoulder holster and put his jacket on over it.

¤-¤-¤-¤-¤

"Billie! Don't hang up! Billie!" Lori shouted as the mobile phone connection died.

"Lori, what's going on?" Becky asked, hearing the panic in Lori's voice as she stopped beside her on the sidewalk outside of Whiskey's. "What happened?"

"We have to find Billy," Lori said, and looked at Becky. "Billie said she's been shot! We have to go."

Becky ran back inside and grabbed their jackets, and was just coming back out when Lori turned and saw Billy walking toward her.

She ran to him and grabbed his arm. "Oh God, Billie's hurt! She said she's been shot!"

"Hurt? What do you mean, shot?" *No, Billie. No! What have you done?*

"I just got a call from her," Lori said as Becky stopped beside them. "She said she found it. Something about number one. She said to tell you it was her number one. She sounded weak, not like herself, almost couldn't talk, and then hung up. She said to tell you...she's sorry and that she loves you. I tried to call her back, but her phone went straight to voice mail. Billy? What's happened?"

"Come on," he said, and started back toward the apartment.

"Billy! Becky has wheels," Lori shouted when he turned to leave. "This way."

He stopped and followed them to Becky's car, and in minutes, Becky parked in the visitor's parking in front of Billie's apartment building.

He led them in. "I have to look at her notes," Billy said as the elevator started up. "She's been researching some properties."

"Why?" Becky asked as the door slid open and Billy hurried to the apartment.

He explained, barely touching on the details of the accident that had killed her friend and how Billie had been trying to figure out how it might have happened. He quickly went to the kitchen eating counter, grabbed her keys, and picked up the stack of printouts.

"Here it is," he said, and pointed to the out-of-focus image. "Let's go find her."

Fifty-Nine

Billy stepped off the elevator and turned to the parking garage door, suddenly recognizing the man leaning over the counter talking with the security guard.

"Nolan?" Surprised, Billy hurried to the counter.

"Keeper!" he said as he looked up and recognized Billy. "Where's Tiger?"

"Hammersmith's estate," he said, and handed the image printout to him. "She found that *solid* evidence you said you needed, and Lori," he gestured to her, "says she got shot looking for it. We're going to find her."

"Tiger is resourceful, even when she's hurt," Nolan said, and explained the call he had received. "She made sure I'd know what's happened. I'll get my patrolmen and see if we can find her."

He handed the sheet back to Billy and turned to the front door as it abruptly swung open; Todd and Cathy hurried in with Sid close behind. Seeing Billy, they crowded around, clamoring to find out what had happened, where Billie was.

"Detective," Billy said. "Get an ambulance started. We'll see you out here."

Nolan nodded and disappeared through the door as Billy led the group to the parking garage.

Billy climbed into the driver's seat of Billie's SUV and Lori took the front passenger's seat. He started the truck and looked to see where everyone was; Becky, Cathy, and Todd had crowded into the back bench seat and Sid was squeezed crosswise in the cargo area behind them. As quickly as he dared, Billy pulled out and headed north.

"Why did the detective call you Keeper?" Lori asked as they passed through the west edge of town center.

"That's my name on the streets, Lori," he said, forcing himself to concentrate on his driving. "I take care of some people and some properties."

She was quiet for a moment. "And he called Billie 'Tiger.' Is that her street name?"

"Yes," he said. "Like she explained yesterday, she's earned the right to be named Tiger."

They drove on in silence, and Billy's thoughts focused on Billie and he prayed fervently they would get there in time.

¤-¤-¤-¤-¤

"Where are we going, Herb?" Joey asked as they dragged Billie across the recently mowed side yard and onto the drive, dropping her behind the pickup.

Herb lowered the tailgate. "Help me slide her in," he said, and grabbed an arm.

Joey grabbed the other and they lifted her, flopping her onto her back, and Herb folded her legs to one side and closed the tailgate.

"There's a place at the north end of that dirt road, just a mile west, where I can throw her into the Chestnut," Herb said as he went around to the driver's side and opened the truck's door. "You take the suitcase to Mr. Hammersmith. I'll catch up with you at your place as soon as I get her dumped and pinned down so she won't float away anytime soon."

"I don't like it, Herb," Joey said as he opened the car door.

"Well, we can't just leave her here, can we?" Herb looked at Joey. "The sooner I get this done, the sooner I can get out of here. Take Mr. Hammersmith his stuff."

Thursday, May 19

Ow, Dammit! That hurts! Stop hitting me!

The continuous shaking and bumping against the back
of Billie's head slowly aroused her anger and she twitched
suddenly, thinking to stop whatever was hitting her head.
Intense pain swept across her chest and down her side, instantly
stealing her breath, and she remembered!

She gasped for air and slowly opened her eyes, focusing on
the faint stars. She turned her eyes to look at the glow in the
sky and saw the nearly full moon rising. Looking to her other
side, the moon's gentle glow filled the bed and she realized she
was lying on her back in an open pickup, the jostling painfully
bouncing her head. She looked toward the cab and saw the
shadowy back of the driver's head. She thought she remembered
another one, but could not see without twisting her body
around.

Billie felt how her legs were folded into the truck; her right
foot was almost close enough for her to reach. She took a deep
breath, gritted her teeth against the pain she knew would come,
and pushed herself to reach for her leg. Tears filled her eyes as
she pushed a second and a third time, and yet again and again
until she finally caught the pant cuff with the tips of her fingers.

Slowly, she pulled her foot closer and slipped her hand
up her pant leg to the hilt of her knife. After a pain-wracked
eternity of reaching and twisting, normally a quick flick of the
clasp, she finally freed the knife and pulled it out. She gripped
the hilt and slid the knife and her hand under her and waited.
She tried to keep her breathing slow and steady, but the bumps
in the road and the pain drove her to occasional sharp gasps.
She gritted her teeth and silently reprimanded herself; not
daring to let them know she was awake.

The truck finally stopped and Billie saw the shadows of leafy
tree limbs above them and heard the close sound of rushing
water. She forced herself to stay calm and as ready as she could

be in her condition. She had to guess right; she would not get a second chance.

The driver's door opened and Billie watched the driver through squinted eyes as he came to the back and lowered the tailgate. The second door did not open and she continued to focus on the driver, holding her breath as he grabbed her feet and pulled her onto the tailgate. He leaned forward and grabbed her shoulders to pull her up. Pain exploded in her chest and she screamed, shoving the long knife blade up under his breast bone, twisting it until she felt it grate on bone, her hand suddenly hot and wet.

His face filled with silent shock, his eyes bulged in disbelief, and she jerked the knife out, watching him wobble, release his hold, and then fall across her legs. The pain from his weight made her scream again and she fell back, struggling, pushing, kicking with her right leg until he slid off. Panting, tenuously holding onto consciousness, she dragged herself sideways to the lip of the tailgate, but when she tried to sit up she rolled off, falling on top of him. She knew she had screamed again, the pain nearly unbearable. Anger flashed in her eyes and she fought the consuming darkness threatening to overwhelm her. Others could have heard her and could be coming. She had to hurry. She had to try to get to Billy.

Sixty

"Are you sure there's only one road that has access to the river?" Billy asked, trying to keep his blurry focus on the bright spot the headlights made on the road. The moisture in his eyes and the tightness in his chest were unfamiliar. "Nolan said they were going to dump her in the river."

What's wrong with me? I know I'm worried and concerned, but that's no reason to be acting this way.

He wiped his face, trying to clear his eyes. His heart was pounding and it was hard to breathe. It concerned him.

This is different than when Mom and Dad died. They were just suddenly gone! But this is Billie! She's still alive! She can't be gone. She just can't.

He admitted he was *afraid*—afraid of losing her. He had never felt this much fear, not even when he had faced the direst of battles in the darkest of alleys. The mere thought of Tiger lying somewhere, injured...not just injured, but *shot!*—nearly paralyzed him. He worried about who had shot her, what had they done after she had disconnected from Lori, after she had called Nolan. *Dammit, Tiger! How can I take care of you when you pull stunts like this? I ought to wring your pretty little neck.*

With his anger, worry, and fears all balled up together, intertwined, and his emotions jerking him around, first one way and then another, his mind played with him, conjuring up images of victims of foul play that he had seen before. He had never thought about what it felt like to be a victim, to be the loser in a fight. He had vowed he would never think about losing after his parents died, but now, all he could think about was how Tiger must feel, how he might be losing her.

At least she knew she was in trouble. She did at least call

Lori. She was looking for him, but she had to call Lori instead.

I have to get a damned phone, he though absently. *Especially if you're going to keep pulling stunts like this.*

The number of different things that raced through his mind surprised him. He shook his head to focus on Tiger. She was strong, he kept telling himself repeatedly. But he was beyond worried. Everything he was doing, everything he stood for, was paling in importance when he allowed himself to think he might have lost Tiger. His shoulders shook and his vision blurred again when the thought that she might already be dead flitted through his mind.

"My phone's satellite map shows the other roads stop short," Lori said, and unfolded Billie's printout.

"What's the street name?" Billy asked, taking a deep breath, thankful for the interruption from his thoughts.

"Meadowlark," Lori said, and looked out the window, catching sight of the street signs on the south side of the road. "There's Thrush. Meadowlark should be the next one. One more mile."

"This has to be the right one. It has to be," he said, barely out loud, his hands squeezing the steering wheel. He did not notice Lori intently watching him as he slowed, approaching the mile-line.

Lori spotted the sign and he turned onto the dirt-and-gravel road. They bounced up the rutted trace as he hurried them toward the river.

Nearly a half a mile up the road, as they came over a rise, Billy saw the taillights and the reflected glow of a truck's headlights aimed off into the trees. He stopped behind the truck, the SUV's headlights illuminating it and something stretched out on the ground. Lori quickly followed him out with a flashlight in hand, stopping beside Billy as he knelt beside the man.

"Geez!" Lori exclaimed when she realized it was a man. "What happened to him?"

"He's dead," Billy said, rolling the man onto his back, exposing his bloody chest. "Tiger? Tiger?" Billy called, then he turned to Cathy and Todd as they stopped beside him and Lori. "She's alive, Lynx. She's here somewhere."

Sid joined Cathy and Todd and they spread out on the right side of the truck, and Becky stayed close to Billy and Lori as he started around the left.

"Oh, God!" Becky inhaled sharply, seeing the man's blood-covered chest. Her hand instinctively covered her mouth as she caught her breath and fought the urge to expel the remnants of their night out.

"He was trying to kill her, Becky," Billy said. "She had to defend herself. Tiger?"

Billy saw her sitting on the ground, her back leaning against the open driver's door; he hurried and knelt beside her.

"Over here!" he shouted. Then softly to Billie, "Tiger, I'm here. Keeper's here."

She slowly opened her eyes and looked up to him.

"Lori," he said as she knelt beside him. "Call Detective Nolan. Tell him where we are and to get that ambulance here quick." He gave her Nolan's number and turned back to Billie.

"Is she going to be all right?" Becky asked. "I don't think I've ever seen so much blood."

"She's lost some for sure," he said, "and a lot of this is the other guy's, but I'm betting on her. My Tiger is very strong."

Gently, he pulled her blood-soaked head scarf out of her sweater and held her sweater away from her chest. He surveyed the wound; the exit was large, below her collarbone and above her left breast. He noticed the wet stain just above her waist on her left side. "Get me a cloth," he hollered, and heard Todd answer.

"Bad...huh?" Billie whispered. "Hurts...like hell."

"I bet it does," he said, and tried to smile. "I'm no doctor, but I think it could've been a lot worse. But you have lost a lot of blood."

"I...couldn't get in," she said, and turned her head to look into the truck. "I needed...to tell you...it's going to be...okay. I found it."

"I know. Lori told me you found it," he said, and gently took the knife out of her hand, folded it closed, and stuffed it into his jeans pocket.

He sat down beside her, leaned back against the door, and looked at Becky. "Help me with her legs," he said as he slipped one arm behind Billie and the other under her, lifting her gently onto his lap.

Becky knelt in front of them, caught Billie's boots, and slowly swung her legs so Billie sat across his lap and leaned against him as he held her close, her head on his shoulder, her hands in her lap. He could feel his tears beginning to slide down his cheeks again. Only this time it was partially in relief.

Todd stopped and handed him a wadded cloth he had found in the SUV. "Sorry, Keeper. It's all I could find."

"Thanks," Billy said, and stuffed the cloth inside her sweater and held it against the wound.

"Detective Nolan said they're only a couple of minutes away," Lori said as she came back and knelt beside Becky.

-¤-

When Billy saw the flashing lights come over the rise in the road, he leaned forward and curled his legs under himself. He pushed up on his knees and Becky and Lori quickly steadied him as he stood up with Billie cradled in his arms. He started walking toward the ambulance as it turned around and backed in beside the SUV. A patrol car stopped in the grass on the other side, and Detective Nolan and a patrolman got out and hurried to Billy.

"She's alive, Nolan," Billy said, and smiled. "It looks like Tiger took that one out when he tried to take her and dump her in the river. She said she tried to get into the truck but couldn't make it up." He shook his head slowly. "She was going to try to drive herself back to town."

The EMTs unfolded a gurney and helped Billy lower her onto it.

Suddenly Billie grabbed his arm, realizing he wasn't holding her anymore.

Billy leaned down and kissed her. "They're going to take you to the hospital now. I'll be right behind you and see you when you get there. Trust me, Tiger. I'll be right behind you."

When they closed the ambulance doors and it started driving back up the road, Billy turned to the SUV, opened the driver's door, and told everyone to get in.

Detective Nolan stepped up to him and asked softly, "Keeper, I know it's been a tough night, but might I ask when you got a driver's license?"

"Hmm." Billy inhaled, thought a minute, and glanced at the SUV. "Maybe I need to think about that sometime."

"Let one of the girls drive," he said, and smiled. "I wouldn't want to blemish your service to the department or your fine record with a violation."

"Thanks," Billy said, and extended his hand. "I'll see you sometime later today, I presume?"

"After I get all of this taken care of," he said, "and take a look around Hammersmith's house before we lock it up, I'll be in to talk to you and see how Tiger's doing."

"You know where we'll be. Don't forget to check that shed in the northeast corner of his property," Billy said, and turned to the SUV. "Lori, why don't you drive us back. Seems in all of the confusion, I forgot to pick up my wallet and license."

¤-¤-¤-¤-¤

Joey turned off the highway onto the gravel driveway. Mike Hammersmith came out of the old farmhouse and stood beside the drive as Joey stopped the car.

"Where's Herb?" Mike asked, peering in the passenger

window as Joey opened the rear door and pulled the suitcase out.

Joey stepped close and answered softly. "Some homeless person was nosing around looking for a place to stay the night, and Herb shot her."

"What? He shot a homeless woman?"

"Yeah," Joey said, and pushed the suitcase into his hand. "For no reason. He could have shooed her away and she'd been gone, but he shot her before he knew who or what she was."

"Damn! Where is he now?"

"He was going to dump the body and then meet me at my place."

Mike squeezed the suitcase handle and paced in the dark beside the driveway.

"Good. Go there," Mike said.

"What're you going to do?" Joey asked, and glanced back at the car.

"The police came to the office looking for me today," Mike said.

"About the Knife?"

"Yes. And Pink," he admitted. "Somehow they made a connection, and I can't stick around."

"You got someplace to go?"

"Yes," Mike said. "Go back home where I can reach you and Herb if I need to."

Sixty-One

Billy slowly paced, walking again up the length of the ecru hallway with a wide burgundy chair-back-height stripe, absently sipping the tepid coffee from his paper cup. It was just after three a.m. when he reached the double doors to surgery, turned, and slowly walked back to the waiting room and glanced in. Becky and Lori had been troopers through the night and in the face of everything, and once they had settled in the waiting room and the tensions of the night finally drained them, they had both fallen asleep, curled up in two of the occasional high-backed chairs. Sid had gone back to the diner to check on Mary and to be certain Angie got everything turned off and the place locked up. Todd fell asleep sitting in a corner low-backed chair with his chin hard against his chest, and Cathy sat beside him, watching Billy walk the hallway.

"Can I get you anything," Billy asked when he saw her watching, "while I'm up?"

Cathy smiled. "You should sit down and get off your feet. You've been pacing ever since they took her in."

"Can't relax, Cathy," he said, and smiled at her. "You know how it is."

"Yeah," she said, nodding in understanding. "We all do. I'm sure the doctors are doing everything they can."

"I'm sure they are," he agreed. "Thanks for being there tonight. You sure I can't get you something? Coffee? Water? Anything?"

Cathy shook her head and Billy started back up the hallway.

When his circuit brought him back to the waiting room, he saw a middle-aged couple exiting the elevator and he started walking toward them; instantly recognizing them as Billie's parents,

The woman, Billie's mother, was talking rapidly to her husband as they entered the waiting area. She turned to the nurse's station, and seeing no one, she quickly scanned the room.

"There's Lori and her other friend. Come on," she commanded, and led her husband across the waiting area.

Billy followed as Billie's mother stopped in front of Lori, bent to her, and gently shook her shoulder.

"Lori? Lori, it's us," she said. "What's the news? All they would say downstairs was she was still in surgery. Is it normal to take this long?"

Billy stopped beside Billie's dad as Lori shook herself awake and realized who was asking her questions.

"Oh, hi, Mrs. Mattis," Lori stammered, and glanced at Billie's dad and saw Billy. She shook her head. "Yeah. I think she's still in surgery. Is that right, Billy?"

Billy nodded. "There hasn't been any word since they took her in. She's been in surgery for over two hours now." He extended his hand to her. "I'm Billy Carson, a close friend of Billie's."

"Is there a doctor I can talk to? Who's in charge here?" Maggie asked, her voice getting louder with each breath.

"The nurse will be back in a few—" Billy started to say.

"I want to talk to someone! Now!"

"Maggie! Calm down," Billie's dad said firmly. "I'll find out what I can as soon as the nurse comes back. For now, maybe Billy can tell us something."

Maggie inhaled and visibly forced herself to wait. Then she looked at Billy. "She's talked about you. What was she doing? How could you let this happen? How—"

"Maggie, stop!" Billie's dad said, and turned to look at Billy. "I'm sorry. Maggie is a little stressed right now. We know it was not your fault. Do you know what happened?"

"Yes," Billy said, and gestured to a chair beside Maggie. "Sit down and I'll try to explain."

"I'm Bob, by the way," he said as he sat down, "Billie's dad, and this is Maggie, her mom."

"Sorry to meet you under such trying circumstances," Billy said as he pulled another chair closer. "I'm glad that Lori was able to reach you."

Billy looked back at Maggie's intense stare and wondered what was going on in her mind.

"Billy was the one that knew where to find her," Lori added before Billy could begin. "He drove and took the rest of us in Billie's Rover."

"I'm glad you knew where," Bob said. "But where was she?"

"About thirty minutes northeast," Billy said as he shifted himself, trying to get settled into the chair, still wondering why Maggie was staring at him. "She had been researching an accident she mentioned that killed someone she knew as a kid. And after she asked about the accident that killed my parents, she started looking for information on it."

"A few weeks ago, she asked about the accident that killed her friend," Bob said casually. "It had always bothered her, and I was surprised she listened as well as she did when we told her what we knew. But what happened? Lori said she'd been shot."

"Yes, she was," Billy said. "It's a bit of a long, twisted story. My parents were actually murdered. They died in an arranged accident, and Billy started researching everything she could think of that might help us find evidence that I could use against the man who caused it." He leaned forward, trying to keep his voice low. "Billie figured out what must've happened, and last night, without telling anyone what she was doing, she borrowed Lori's car and went out by herself, looking at places she thought evidence might be hidden away. Evidently, she found what she was looking for, in a tool shed, and got shot when she did."

Bob looked at him. "When Billie told us about you, she mentioned your parents had died in a car accident."

Billy nodded.

"Billie said you work at the Streetcar Diner," Maggie said, finally speaking and glancing at Bob.

"I do," Billy said. "Billie and I met there fifteen years ago and then again a few months ago."

"She also said," Bob added, "you look after a number of less-fortunate families. She told us about you moving a group into a subsidized apartment complex, or something like that."

"Yes, we got a group of twenty moved into housing." Billy smiled. "The first home many of them have had in many years. Some, their first home. They just needed someone to give them a chance, to be there for them."

"I'm glad Billie had someone too," Bob said. "Especially someone that knew where to find her when she needed help."

Maggie sighed heavily, revealing her unspoken fears and worries, finally resigning herself to having to wait on the surgeon. She changed the subject. "Did you have any trouble with admitting when you got here? Do we need to do anything?"

"No," Billy said, and shook his head. "I think everything is done that needs to be. Billie's insurance will cover everything. I hope you don't mind, but I put myself down as her emergency contact and gave them the Streetcar's number." He looked at them and then continued. "I hope that was all right? Since she's been living on her own and supporting herself, I assumed that would be okay with you."

"Yes, yes. That's all right. I wasn't sure if Billie had any insurance," Bob said. "I'm glad she's doing well enough in the design firm to have insurance already."

"I guess she hasn't mentioned it, but she isn't working right now," Billy said, and held up his wrist. "She was fired for having the mate to this tat." He tapped the design on his wrist. "As for the insurance, that must have been set up independently. A long time ago, I'm guessing."

Billy forced a smile when Bob and Maggie frowned at his news that Billie had been fired.

"I think Carl Boster and Robert Lange truly liked her and her work," Billy added, an attempt to help relieve their concerns over her work.

They continued their visiting and Cathy joined them, claiming that talking some might help keep her awake.

"Bob, Maggie," Billy said as Cathy sat down. "This is Cathy and that's Todd"—he gestured to Todd, still sleeping in his chair—"over in the corner. They are very close friends of Billie's and mine. They went with us last night to find Billie."

They kept their conversation light and general, mostly focusing on Billie and her years growing up. About dawn, the surgeon pushed the double doors open, walked to the waiting room, and found them. Billy introduced Maggie and Bob, and with them huddled close to hear what he had to say, the surgeon discussed Billie's condition.

"The surgery went very well," the surgeon said. "We found two wounds—one in her left shoulder and one lower in her left side, just above her waist. Both entered from behind. We had to repair a couple of ribs in her shoulder area and her scapula, and quite a bit of pectoral and infraspinatus muscle damage. Sorry, the front and back shoulder muscles. She will have some temporary loss in the range of motion in her arm until the muscles heal, but with a little physical therapy and controlled exercise, she should regain all of the movement. The muscle may never be as strong as it was and she will likely have some recurring spasmodic pain in that shoulder due to the muscle damage, maybe for a number of years. But it should heal properly and not be of real concern.

"The bullet in her shoulder missed her subclavian artery and vein so her arm should be fine, but a broken rib punctured her lung. We reset the rib and repaired the lung and they should heal without causing her any lasting pain or discomfort. She may occasionally have some shortness of breath until it heals.

"The bullet in her side missed her ribs and passed through without causing very much damage, luckily missing the critical organs in that area. I used internal stitches that will dissolve and glued the skin together. That wound will heal quickly with little to no scarring. In her shoulder, though, I also used external stitches due the amount of stretching the skin will be exposed to as she begins to move her arm.

"She lost a lot of blood so I've supplemented her IV. She's in good health otherwise and appears to have kept herself in good physical condition. Right now, she just needs rest. I'll check on her early mornings, and in the evenings or late afternoons. Please let the nurses know if you need to talk to me about anything and I can usually meet with you when I make my rounds late in the day."

"Thank you," Bob said, and squeezed Maggie's shoulders.

"She's in recovery and should be in her room in about an hour. The nurse will have a room number for you when she's transferred. She'll still be groggy and sleepy, but you'll be able to see her then."

The surgeon left and Bob and Maggie sat down, talking to each other. Billy told Lori, Becky, Cathy, and Todd what the surgeon had said, and then he settled into a chair slightly away from everyone, put his head back against the wall, and closed his eyes.

Sixty-Two

Billy woke with a start. He blinked and looked around the waiting room, remembering where he was, wondering what had startled him. Then he realized the room was filling up. Maggie was sitting next to him and nearly all of the chairs had someone waiting in them.

"Good, you're awake," Maggie said in a much calmer manner, seeing him move and look around the room. "Your friends Cathy and Todd left about a half an hour ago and said they'd stop by later, probably after work."

"That's good," he said, and stretched without getting up. "They'll tell the rest of our friends what happened and how Billie's doing."

"Lori and Becky just left," she continued. "Lori said they'd get Becky's car and bring Billie's back before they go change and go to work. Lori explained what she knows about you and Billie." She hesitated and looked at him. "It helps. Sorry if I put you off by the way I was acting."

"That's okay, Maggie," Billy said. "This had to scare you a lot. Any word?"

"Oh, yes," Maggie said, trying to sound more pleasant. "The nurse just told me they have assigned Billie a room and that we can wait for her there. I just sat down to tell you and that must've woke you up."

Billy stood up and followed Maggie to the nurse's station to get directions.

"Where's Bob?" Billy asked as they waited for the elevator.

"We called Sandy when Lori called us at home, and then again when we got here and found out how Billie was doing. She was able to get a seat on an early flight and"—she looked at her watch—"landed about twenty minutes ago. Bob went to pick her up."

"I must've really been out of it," Billy said. "I never sleep very soundly."

When they stepped into the elevator and the door slid shut, Maggie looked up at Billy. "I think it might be relief, Billy. If Lori has half of what she told us right, you've worried about a lot of people for a long time, and last night had to be terrible for you with worry. But now, things are better and the people you care about are safe."

Billy wanted to ask what Lori had said, but decided against it.

The door slid open and Maggie stepped out. Together, after a little searching, they found Billie's private room.

-¤-

A nurse and two male orderlies wheeled the recovery room gurney down the long hall and into the room where Billy and Maggie waited. The orderlies asked them to wait outside while they transferred Billie onto her bed, tucked her covers over her, hooked up the tubes and monitors, and then wheeled the gurney out. The nurse was checking her vitals, scanning a long strip of paper coming out of the monitor, when they came back in.

She told Maggie her name was Ryan and wrote it on a whiteboard hung on the wall across from the foot of the bed. "I'll be back in about fifteen minutes to check on Wilhelmina—"

"She does not like to be called that," Maggie said quickly. "She prefers 'Billie.' I don't know how she is now that she's grown, but when she was young and living at home, she'd throw things or start a fight with anyone that called her that. We made a big mistake when we named her."

Billy laughed. "She's calmed down a little since then. She still gets mad and has been known to punch whoever calls her that." He looked at the nurse, rubbing his chest, and smiled. "Just call her Billie, please."

"I'll make a note of that," Nurse Ryan said. "We certainly don't want our patients to be mad, or punching anyone, especially while they're trying to recover." She looked at the clock over the bed. "Do you know when she last ate?"

"She's probably only had a bottle of water since lunch yesterday," Billy said. "We missed dinner last night."

"I'll have them send up some gelatin and a mild juice when she's awake," the nurse said, and then looked at Billy. "Does she have a preference for either of those?"

Billy smiled. "Actually, cherry or grape gelatin. Reds, I know, and mango or apple juice and hot tea with a small amount of honey. Nothing too sweet."

Maggie smiled and watched Billy as he pulled a chair up beside the left side of Billie's bed after the nurse left. He gently took Billie's right hand as he sat down.

"You seem to know a lot about my daughter," Maggie said, moving the other chair closer.

"Yes, I do," he smiled, "and yet, not that much. I've enjoyed learning her likes and dislikes, the secrets she's willing to share, and seeing her interest in learning mine. I did finally get her to stop wearing red boots and red accessories."

"Really? I've tried to do that forever."

"She still surprises me, though," he said without looking away from her. "Almost every day she'll do something or tell me something I wasn't expecting." He chuckled. "Most of the time, I even like it."

"Well, there has to be some mystery, Billy. Otherwise life with someone would be very boring."

"Billie's certainly not boring," he said as Bob and their older daughter walked in.

"This place is worse than a maze," Bob said softly as he stopped beside Maggie. "Billy, do you remember Sandy?"

Billy half rose from his chair and reached out to her without surrendering his grip on Billie's hand. She came around the bed and took his extended hand in greeting.

"I remember the Sandy I saw fifteen years ago"—he smiled—"but not this beautiful woman. Hello, Sandy. It's a pleasure to see you again."

"Thanks," she said as she slipped her light travel jacket off and laid it on the back of the overstuffed chair in the corner of the room. "Billie said we'd met back then, but I'm sorry I don't remember."

"That's okay," he said, and turned back to watch Billie. "I'm easy to forget."

"How's she doing? Has she been awake?" Sandy asked.

"She's doing well and she was awake in recovery, but not since they moved her in here," Billy said. "The nurse said she'd sleep a lot this morning."

"Well," Bob said as he looked around the room, "I think I'll find a couple more chairs." He turned and left for the nurse's station, returning in minutes carrying a straight-backed chair and followed by an orderly carrying a second.

After a bit, Billie began to stir, rolling her head slowly from side to side, whispering. Billy leaned close.

"Keeper? Where are you?" she asked softly. "Keeper?"

Her voice became louder, more insistent.

Hearing the urgency in her voice, Billy quickly answered, "I'm here, Tiger," he said. "Tiger, I'm here." He gently squeezed her hand, rubbed her palm, and watched her tossing abate a little. "I'm here, Tiger. Open your eyes. I'm here."

Slowly her head stopped rolling, faced his voice, and her eyelids twitched.

"That's it, Tiger. I'm here. You're safe now."

She slowly opened her eyes and saw him smiling, his face close, watching her. She smiled. "Keeper. I couldn't find you," she said softly, then smiled and her eyes blinked drowsily. She squeezed his hand.

"I'm here, Tiger. You won't lose me again. I'm staying right here," he said, soothing her concerns, watching her as she relaxed and her eyes closed again.

Her smile seemed content to him as he looked up and realized Bob, Maggie, and Sandy had been quietly watching them.

"Sorry," he said. "I should have told her you were here."

"Don't be," Maggie said, a smile creeping across her face. "I'm surprised, but it's obvious who she wanted to see and talk to."

Sixty-Three

Friday, May 20

Detective Nolan found Billy holding Billie's hand, dozing in the chair beside her bed. Billie was awake and saw him.

"Detective," she said softly, and Billy stirred.

"Hello, Tiger," Nolan said. "You look a little perkier than when I saw you yesterday morning. How are you feeling?"

"Fine, unless I move or laugh," she said, and chuckled softly. "Really though, there's not much pain. I think they've turned me into a druggie and now I won't be able to go back to city center."

Nolan laughed and nodded to Billy. "Tiger? Do you mind if I borrow Keeper for a few minutes? I need to talk to him and I don't want to bother you."

"Is it something you don't want me to hear?" she asked.

"No," he said, surprised. "It's not that."

"Then please sit down," Billie said. "I'd like to know what's happened."

"Okay." Nolan pulled a chair closer to Billie. He sat down and noticed Billy was wearing a clean shirt and jeans. "Did you leave and change on your own, or did Tiger have to threaten you to make you go and clean up?"

"She threatened me," Billy admitted, and smiled at her. "Actually, Sid brought me a change of clothes from the diner. I don't know why, but she had some foolish notion my blood-stained shirt and pants would keep her visitors away."

She nodded and added softly, "He acted like I was going to jump up and run away the minute he looked the other way."

Nolan chuckled, looking from one to the other. "I think you're going to be okay, Tiger."

"About the shed?" Billie asked again.

"First, we've been able to get an arrest warrant for Mike Hammersmith on hiring Leonard the Knife to kill you, Keeper, and for being the instrument that caused Pink's death. When we went back to lock up his place yesterday morning, we found a voice message he had left telling Herb, the one that took you to the river, where he was, but he was gone when we got there." He sobered his smile and looked at Billie. "He's still at large, Tiger. And of course we'll add charges of attempted murder by one of his instruments, the one named Herb, for shooting you and trying to dump you in the river."

She inhaled deeply and slowly let her breath out. "I'm sorry, but I had to stop him. I couldn't let him dump me or drown me."

"I know, Tiger," Nolan said, and smiled. "You had to defend yourself. The records show self-defense and no charges are being raised. I am amazed how well you did, considering the pain you must have been feeling. I am truly surprised you were able to handle him and survive."

"Thank you," she said, and smiled as Billy squeezed her hand. "I've had the best trainers. But what did you find in the shed?"

"Well, that's the best part," Nolan said, and smiled again. "But first we found your phone where you hid it. Thanks. I was able to record everything the men said after they got to you." Nolan handed Billy her phone. "I cleaned it up some, but it needs charging. Inside the shed, we found just what you said we'd find. A pair of high-intensity lamps mounted on a metal framework—"

"I was thinking," Billie interrupted, "they were mounted on the front of a car or truck and used to look like oncoming traffic. Billy said he remembered it was a pickup."

"Yes, I suppose they could have been. Then we found eight-inch wide rolls of a flat finished gray tape—"

"I thought that might have been used to cover up the new shoulder stripes that were added that summer."

"Yes, possibly," Nolan said, and stared at her. "And would you care to tell me what you think the long boards were used for?"

"I think those reflective boards were put down to make it look like the road kept going straight," she said. "I told Billy, the car had to go straight. If it swerved to miss something, it would have probably gone into the trees. I think it was important to Mr. Hammersmith's plan that it looked like they fell asleep or something and just missed the turn."

"I see," Nolan said, then rubbed his chin and slowly smiled at her. "I had our lab look at the lights, and they said the intensity was about double that of a normal bright headlight. That would be consistent with your hypothesis that they thought the lights were oncoming traffic and they had to follow the shoulder stripe. The lab also found traces of fingerprints all over the lights and are trying to lift them. If they're Hammersmith's, we'll have positive proof that he handled them—maybe even made them, since I hear he was a backyard mechanic in his earlier days and still dabbled on his off days."

Billie was about to say something more when her dad stepped in. Seeing they had company, he knocked on the open door. "Are we interrupting? Thought we'd join you two for lunch."

Detective Nolan turned and shook Bob's extended hand and introduced himself.

"I'm Bob, Billie's dad," he explained, and then introduced Maggie and Sandy. "Please continue," he said as they settled into the remaining chairs.

"Detective," Billie started again. "Maybe Mace can tell you what—"

"I already have a statement from Mace, Tiger," Nolan said. "You know he and Keeper talked to me after we found the man dead in the alley. He still had most of the money he'd received in an envelope in a waist pouch. When he died, we had no other choice but to wait until we got another clue or found some other evidence. As it turned out, we had to wait for you." He looked from her to Billy and then back to her. "You know, there's always an opening for a good investigative mind like yours. If you ever think about doing any police work, give me a call."

"Thank you," Billie said, and looked at Billy. "But I think Keeper has other plans for us. Maybe trying to build up another group of homeless people, maybe improving the soup kitchens, or maybe providing shelters for those that need or want it. I think I'm going to be very busy trying to keep up with Keeper."

"We still have an 'all points' out for Westman," Nolan said with a nod. "He'll surface sooner or later."

"I don't think Westman is the bad guy," Billie said. "I think Hammersmith had something on him and kept making him do his dirty work. I don't mean like killing people, but like pulling underhanded deals and things like that."

"And why would you say that?" Nolan asked.

"From their conversation in the office. The day he told Hammersmith he wouldn't do any more work for him, I did some checking. His place here is very austere, nothing like a successful contractor should have. I also looked for information on his divorce and then on his ex-wife. She came from a family with money and didn't take anything from him in the divorce, but he set up trusts for their daughter. Maybe he set one up for his ex-wife, but if he did, I haven't discovered that one yet. I think he sent everything he made to the trust and to his ex-wife for his daughter's support in Michigan. I think whatever Hammersmith made him do caused his divorce. I might be wrong, but it seems to me he's caught in the middle of something."

Nolan shook his head. "All right, Tiger. I'll check it out. We still need to talk to Westman, and like I said…" He stood up. "If you ever decide to go into police work, call me."

Billie smiled. "Thanks."

Detective Nolan nodded at her, said his goodbyes to the rest of them, and then left.

"He must be the detective on this case," Bob said, and looked at both of them.

Billy nodded.

"I called him after I got shot," Billie said.

"Billie?" Sandy asked. "I understand nicknames, but why do Billy and the detective call you Tiger?"

Billie chuckled and glanced at Billy's nod.

"It's my street name, Sandy. I bought well-worn clothes and Billy showed me what I needed to do, how I needed to act, and I started helping him when he volunteers at a soup kitchen in a 'not-so-good' part of town. We had a confrontation with a local drug dealer" —Billy chuckled at that—"and I backed Billy up."

"Her dance classes really gave her an edge," Billy commented.

"Yeah. Modern dance with a knife in one hand and an apple in the other." She coughed when she tried to laugh at the thought and saw their blank stares. "Anyway, Lynx—sorry, Cathy told me I became part of their family that night. It's a street family, but I am pleased to be considered part of it. For what I did that night, Billy named me Tiger, and everyone started calling me that. Since then, Billy and the rest have been teaching me how to defend myself."

"Street fighting? Is that what it's called?" Maggie asked softly. "And even the police know you and call you Tiger."

"Yes, Mom." Billie smiled. "Billy has known and been friends with Detective Nolan for a very long time, so it's natural that he would know me too."

Sixty-Four

"I'm sorry I left your car out there," Billie said. "But I was there and it was the last place I needed to look. I had to try—"

"We know," Lori said, and patted Billie's leg. "Billy gave me the key they found when they prepped you for surgery and that detective—Nolan, I think his name is—said they found my car all locked up where you left it. Becky's going to take me out tomorrow to get it. Bet you didn't have time to put gas in it, did you?"

Billie smiled. "I did, after I left the drugstore, but obviously not again. I was going to refill it before I brought it back to you."

Billy squeezed Billie's hand and stood up from his usual place beside her bed. "I need to take a walk down the hall. Can I bring either of you a coffee, tea, or a drink when I come back?"

"Nothing for me," Becky said. "Thanks."

"I'm fine, Billy," Lori said, and smiled at Billy as he stepped out and turned down the hall. She looked back at Billie. "I'm still not sure you're making the right decision about getting married, but I will say he does care about you."

"Why do you say that?" Billie asked, looking at her, then to Becky and back to Lori.

"That friend of yours, Cathy," Lori continued, "said he noticed you had taken your other clothes out of your closet and came to her place looking for you. He told her it was unusual for you to have taken them. I guess he'd also checked with his boss to see if you'd left any messages."

"When Lori told him you said you had found what you were looking for, your choice number one," Becky added, "right after she got your call, he became very determined. We went back to your place and he gathered up your printouts. Nolan showed up in the lobby and Billy sort of took charge, telling Nolan where you were, to get an ambulance started, and then he put us all in your SUV and started out to look for you."

"I didn't know Billy could drive," Billie said absently.

"He was almost beside himself," Lori admitted. "We used my phone to figure out where you might be, and Billy drove. When we found you, he sat down, cradled you in his lap, and cried quietly until the ambulance got there. I don't think I've ever seen a man cry before."

"Your friend Cathy, her man—husband or whatever, and Billy's boss went with us," Becky said. "I was surprised at how many were concerned and how quickly they all showed up, wanting to help find you."

"Cathy, Todd, and Sid?"

"Yeah," Lori chuckled. "They all stayed here until we knew you were going to be okay. And Cathy said Billy paced the halls outside surgery until your folks arrived."

Billie smiled. "I know I scared him. I didn't mean to, but I did. He told me he ought to wring my neck for going out there and snooping around, and especially for going alone. And I think I scared both of you, too."

Lori sighed. "I may not like everything you're doing, but I have to admit you found a man that really, really cares about you. I'm happy about that."

"Thanks," Billie said, and looked up, hearing Billy's footsteps coming back up the hall.

¤-¤-¤-¤-¤

Joey drove slowly down the street in front of his rundown apartment building, four one-bedroom closets stacked in pairs and passed off as living spaces in a less-desirable part of the upper east side of the city. He surveyed the building, the neighboring houses and the cars parked along the street, but everything looked normal, nothing obviously out of place. He did not see Herb's pickup.

Joey knew he was running on nerves, never before having seen anyone shoot someone for simply being there. Herb had always bothered him, the calculating way he did everything from eating his food to analyzing everyone when he met them. Herb was a different sort of critter, to say the least.

As he pulled around to the back of his building, he wondered if Herb had been successful in disposing of the woman's body. She was young and pretty and he could not get her face out of his mind. He shook his head, trying to stop the recurring memories as he hurried up to his flat and went in.

Quickly checking the kitchen area and the bedroom, he was pleased, if one could be pleased in such a place. His bed was as he had left it, made up with his laundry still stacked on its corner. The kitchen dishes were still stacked in the sink and nothing appeared to be disturbed. He grabbed a beer from the fridge and looked at his answering machine's blinking light.

Joey settled on the sofa beside the phone and took a long pull on the bottle. He knew the message was either from Hammersmith or Herb, and he was not sure he wanted to hear either. He pushed the replay button.

"It's Hammersmith," the voice started abruptly. "Find out who is replacing Pink. Bring Herb and meet me at my place by the airport, Sunday night after eleven. Don't be followed!"

Joey finished his beer and tossed the bottle on top of the overflowing trash beside his kitchen counter.

"How in hell am I supposed to find Herb?" he asked himself as he stepped out and started walking to the soup kitchen on Crescent. "I really don't like him and I sure don't want to hear the details of what he did to that woman."

He was so deep in thought, wondering where Herb was and what Hammersmith wanted, that he walked past the telephone service repair truck parked at the end of the block without noticing it.

241

¤-¤-¤-¤-¤

Detective Nolan sat at his desk in his office with the pale gray walls and peeling paint, eating a cold cut sandwich with a single-serving-sized bag of barbeque potato chips. He sipped on a lukewarm can of lemon-lime soda and was studying the daily reports when he heard a phone ring in one of the other offices. After a moment, the woman from the front counter stepped into his and the lieutenant's office and asked if either of them knew a Nancy Westman.

Nolan instantly raised his hand and washed his bite of sandwich down. "I'll take it," he said, and grabbed the handset.

"Line two," she said, and went back down the hall to her counter.

"Hello, Detective Nolan speaking. How can I help you, Mrs. Westman?"

"Hello, Detective," Nancy's voice replied. "I'm Frederick Westman's ex-wife."

"Yes, ma'am. I remember," Nolan said. "What can I do for you?"

"I need to talk to you about Mr. Mike Hammersmith. Do you have a few minutes?"

"Yes, ma'am. Do you mind if I record this conversation?"

¤-¤-¤-¤-¤

"Hey, how are you doing?" Max said as he stopped in the doorway to Billie's hospital room and rapped lightly on the doorjamb. A nurse picked up Billie's tray of dirty dishes and slipped past him.

Billy looked up and Billie brightened, smiling when she saw Max and Mindy come in.

"Good to see you guys," Billie said. "Please pull up a chair. What's been going on with you two?"

"Did we interrupt your dinner?" Mindy asked, and gestured to the door and the nurse.

"No," Billy said, and extended his hand. "Billie just had a snack while Lori and Becky visited. They left a few minutes ago, so your timing's good."

"So? What's been happening, outside?" Billie asked again, trying to not sound too eager or too tired. "I feel so cut off from everyone."

"Working and watching Abby." Mindy smiled and settled into the chair Max pushed close to Billie.

"Watching Abby? Has Cathy been busy?" Billie asked.

"Just normal stuff," Mindy said, but Billie caught something in her look. "We've been taking turns watching the blocks, and I still watch Abby when it's Cathy and Todd's turn."

Billie looked at Billy and thought he saw the same hint in Mindy's look.

"Tell us, Cat," Billy said. "What's up?"

Mindy looked at Max.

"We've had a couple of new snoopers, Keeper," Max admitted softly. "Nothing we can't handle, but we wanted you to know. We really came tonight to see Tiger and let her know we miss her. I know it's only been a couple of days since she was... hurt and all..."

"We want you to hurry up and get well so you can get back out on the streets with us," Mindy said, more matter-of-fact.

Billie chuckled. "I'll do that just as fast as I can. The doc says I will need physical therapy and exercise, so I figure I'll need to keep my training up—"

"Exercise maybe," Billy said sharply, "but not training. Not for a while."

She looked at him, and even though she was smiling, her glare was obvious.

Are you going to listen to him for once?

Probably not.

How long do you think he'll keep putting up with your—

Hush!

"Call it exercise if you want, but I'll exercise at my own pace," she insisted. "I'm still strong and just need to get my shoulder and side back up to strength."

"We'll discuss this later, Tiger," he said, and she saw the unchanged, stern look in his eyes. He was more serious than she had seen him.

Well, maybe I'll listen a little.

Mindy started laughing. "You two! You'll work it out, and Billy, if she works too hard, is it your shoulder? That shoulder will tell her when she's trying to do too much."

"But Cat," Billy looked at her with a sly smile, "that means I'll be up all night rubbing her with ointments and salves to keep her complaining quiet so she won't wake the neighbors."

Mindy blinked and Max chuckled.

"If that's a promise, Keeper," Billie said, "I'll work extra hard to get back up to strength."

They visited in comfortable companionship, friends catching up on things they had taken for granted and reminiscing about things they had shared. Billie watched and noticed that Billy slowly relaxed as the visit progressed, and she wondered if she was rebelling too much.

Yes.

It was well past visiting hours when the nurse finally came in and told everyone they would have to leave and let the patient get some sleep.

-¤-

"I'll be right back," Billy said to Billie. "I'll stay with you until you go to sleep or they kick me out." He kissed her and went out into the hallway to walk Max and Mindy out.

At the elevator, they stopped and Billy asked, "Who are the new snoopers?"

"Pink's old rival, Copper," Max said. "He didn't take the news about Pink as true and has been trying to walk the blocks since Tuesday night."

"Three nights?" Billy thought out loud. "You think he'll be there tonight?"

"Undoubtedly," Mindy said. "He isn't listening very well. Last night Max and Todd confronted him. No knives, but it was close."

Billy looked at the clock over the nurse's vacant desk at the end of the corridor.

"They'll push me out in about a half an hour. It'll take me another twenty minutes to get to the block." He stopped and thought a moment. "I can be there around eleven and we can see if Copper wants to push this."

Sixty-Five

Saturday, May 21

"All right, Billy. What happened?" Billie asked. "I've let you sit here all morning without bringing it up and you haven't said a word about it. You're driving me crazy. You know that, don't you?"

He squeezed her hand and looked at her. "Happened? Nothing happened."

"I know you went and waited on the new snoopers last night, and then snuck back in here to spend the night," Billie said, looking exasperated. "I know you too, Billy."

He smiled. "Yes, you do know me, and I'm glad you do. Nothing really happened. I met Stretch and Hammer about eleven and we waited in the alley just below Baker. Copper and one crony showed up a little later and I met them. I was leaning against the corner of the building, just in the shadows, peeling my apple and"—Billie chuckled at the image—"I asked what they were looking for. We had a nice conversation and I explained that he couldn't bring his drugs into the city center area."

"And what did he say about that?"

"Well, at first he didn't like the idea, and was going to push the issue. I continued slicing off pieces of the apple and waited on his next move."

"And? For heaven's sake, Billy, tell me," she said, lowering her voice and stressing her last two words.

"Okay, okay. I had chosen where I stood so when he looked around, checking his quarters to be sure he wasn't hemmed in, he noticed the rather large bloodstain on the pavement. He saw it and I causally mentioned that was where Knife stood when he killed Pink after I got my knife in him, and the bloodstain was where my Tiger cut the Knife's hand off for pointing a gun at us."

She chuckled softly and waited.

"I told him you didn't like anyone pointing guns at us, or trying to use a knife against us or bringing their drugs into our hood." He smiled at her. "And yes, he heard what I said, and decided to go away and think about it."

"Sounds too easy," she said, still smiling.

"It was." He turned more somber. "He'll be back to try again. He has drugs to sell and he needs buyers. He doesn't know there are no buyers there, but I think some of Hammersmith's money makes him think he can find some."

"I didn't know you stuck Pink," she said, and squeezed his hand. "I wish—"

"Yeah, I did."

"I wish that night could've been different." She could not keep the depression out of her voice.

"I know how you feel. But you'll feel better once you're back helping, and in the meantime, the rest of the family is helping like they always have. We're just one short right now, and everyone's willing to take up the slack until you're back."

He smiled and held her eyes for a long moment. They both looked to the door when they heard footsteps coming down the hall.

-¤-

"Thank you, Billy," Maggie said as she entered the room with Bob and Sandy close behind, "for letting us use Billie's apartment."

"You're very welcome," Billy said. "I hope everything was okay. Billie cleaned a little before her escapade, but I didn't take the time to do anything."

"It was fine," Maggie said. "I was actually surprised at how well Billie does keep her place, especially after knowing how she kept her room at home."

"Thanks, Mom," Billie said in a flat voice, and slowly shook her head.

"If you decide you want to stay another night," Billy said, "you're welcome to use the apartment again. And Sandy, if you want something better than the sofa, you certainly can use my apartment. It isn't quite as straightened up or as nice as Billie's, but it's clean and comfortable."

Billie stared at him, then smiled at Sandy and said, "If I could get my hand free, I'd clout him and pretend to be offended for him inviting 'another' woman to come and stay with him, but he's right. You're all welcome to stay longer. Even in Billy's apartment."

"That's very nice of you," Maggie said, "but we couldn't put you out any more. We'll go out to the ranch and comeback in Monday morning. I was worried sick when we came, but I think you're doing well and I think you're in good hands."

"We stopped by the Streetcar and saw Mary and Sid," Bob added as he set a paper sack on the ledge in front of the window. "They send their best wishes. Angie and Niles said they'd stop by after work and Sid made sandwiches for all of us for lunch."

Sandy opened the bag and handed Billy a sandwich. "Sorry, sis. They won't let you have one yet."

"I know," Billie said, and closed her eyes and smiled. "But when I do, I'm going to have one of Sid's famous onion burgers. You'll have to try one. He does magic with the meat and what he puts in it, makes his own sauce with herbs and cheeses, and serves it on a toasted onion roll with all the trimmings and a complementing dipping sauce for his breaded fries. I'll think of that while I eat whatever bland food I'm getting today."

Sandy laughed. "I think she's improving. Fast."

"I'll get drinks," Bob said, and took orders. "The vending machine is just down the hall."

The orderly brought Billie's lunch tray and was just leaving when Bob returned.

"Mom, Dad," Billie said after they settled down to eat. "You know about our wrist tats and that they mean we've been engaged for a little while, but you should know Billy asked me to pick a date." She waited, watching their reaction. "We were going to come out to the ranch and tell you this weekend. I guess that's today."

Bob smiled at her, Sandy nodded, and Maggie relaxed and said, "We expected it wouldn't be very long. I think you've been in love with him since you were seven or eight," Maggie said.

Billie's mouth dropped open. "You know who—?" She looked at Billy.

Billy was staring at Maggie. "How...?"

Sandy was also staring at her mother and then looked at Billy. "William? Little Willum?"

"It's obvious to me, William," Maggie said, and smiled. "Billie told us you were Billy Carson, and last week Bob came across an old sheet of paper your dad and he scribbled notes on years ago. The letterhead had your dad's name on it: William Carson Hawke II. Then he got the old investment agreement out of the files to confirm your father's full name, and we put the pieces together and knew. I know you must have your reasons for keeping your full name secret, so we won't tell anyone."

-ۼ-

"You didn't tell me Mom knew," Billie said, her expression sad as she looked away from Maggie to Billy.

"I didn't know," he said, and raised his shoulders in a shrug. "I didn't tell them. I sidestepped that part when I explained what you were doing and why you got shot."

"I can't believe you figured it out," Billie said, looking back at her mom and forcing herself to smile. "Billy just admitted it to me this past week. I think I must've known, but I hadn't fully realized it until he explained the details." She sighed and her smile widened. "I'm glad you know, but it has to stay a secret for now. But wait! You said you visited with Sid and Mary. You know them too?"

"Of course, Billie," Maggie explained. "I knew Mary and Dotty in college and we stayed friends and saw each other often until Dotty and Bill died. Then it was hard to stay in touch, you know?"

"Oh wow. Yeah, I can see that," Billie said, and glanced at Billy. "Did you know all of that?"

Billy shook his head slowly. "I didn't know for sure, but I knew there was some connection between your mom and mine and I couldn't very well ask Mom or Dad." He smiled at Maggie and then looked at Billie. "When I started working in the diner, I made Mary and Sid swear to not tell anyone that I was alive. I didn't want Mom and Dad's killer to know I survived and was looking for him. Of course, I found out it was Hammersmith but couldn't prove it. I saw your mom come in to talk to Mary a couple of times, but I was too focused on my own problems and just figured they came in to eat like everyone else did. Mary never let my secret slip and she never told me what you talked about"—he smiled at Maggie—"so I just stayed hidden and waited. I asked Mary once, many years ago, how she knew you, and she only said she'd known you for a long time."

"Sid explained part of your secrecy when we visited this time," Bob said. "He only broke his word because he knew it was you, Billie, that had been hurt. He confirmed what we figured out last week and asked us to also keep who you really are a secret."

"I'm glad you know," Billy said softly. "But Mike's still out there. He hasn't been picked up and we still need to keep the secret."

"We won't say anything," Maggie said, and smiled at Billy.

"Thanks." Billy smiled a tight smile and glanced at Billie. "Okay, you were starting to explain about—"

"Okay, yeah, back to the wedding," Billie said, and squeezed Billy's hand. "Billy and I have been talking, and he's okay with my wish to have our wedding out at the ranch. We want to have it on the bank of the lake where we first met each other. There's an old pier there that we can use as a backdrop."

"I think that would be wonderful," Maggie said. "Do you remember which lake it was, north or south?"

"I think it was the south one, not too far from the house," Billie said, and looked at her dad. "But I can't be sure. There's a pier on both lakes."

"I can check it out," Bob said.

"Have you decided when?" Sandy asked.

"If I'm getting around okay, we chose the Summer Solstice weekend," Billie said, and smiled at Billy, "with an outdoor reception lunch and party afterwards. I know this is the first wedding either of your daughters has asked for, but you have to promise me, Mom, it will be low key—not too large and not formal."

"What do you mean, not formal?" Maggie asked, and squared her shoulders as she turned to face Billie.

"Nice, but casual. Horseback rides for kids we know. Fishing in the lake if they want. You know, *not* formal. Billy and I have a short guest list that is mostly our close friends, including nineteen from the apartments where Billy lives. They're wonderful, normal people who have had to work hard for what they have and I don't put on any airs with them. You won't either. Then there's Lori, Becky, and Stacy and her boyfriend if they're still together then, Mary and Sid, and of course Billy's co-workers from the Streetcar." She looked at Billy. "And I want to ask Cathy's daughter Abby to be my flower girl."

"I think Abby will be ecstatic," Billy said.

"Other than those and maybe a few more of Billy's friends, Mom, you can invite whoever you'd like," Billie continued. "Even Jack and Katie and the Markins."

Maggie smiled and looked at Sandy. "That'll be great." She dug around in her large handbag and retrieved a small spiral notepad and a pen. "Here we go. I thought I had something to write on," she said, and began jotting things down.

"Sounds like you two have been talking a lot about this," Bob said, and Billie smiled. "This gives us about a month to get the ranch spruced up for a celebration. You just need to get better and get back on your feet."

"They started making me walk yesterday," Billie said. "And my arm works," She raised her left arm and bent her elbow. "And with the drugs I'm on, it doesn't hurt. My side either. Shoulder's stiff, but I guess it should be."

Sandy shook her head and laughed. "You're not supposed to be doing that."

¤-¤-¤-¤-¤

"I was just wondering," Joey said as he held the paper in front of him, acting like he was reading it. "Why you thought you could just walk into the city center and no one would notice."

Copper sat at the far end of the bench and stretched out as if he were just relaxing and enjoying the sunshine on a quiet afternoon in the park near the eastside kitchen.

"Went three nights before Keeper showed up," Copper said.

"But you were told each of those nights to move on and not come back," Joey reiterated. "After what happened to Pink, and he had Knife to protect him and press his case, I'm surprised you wanted to tick Keeper off."

"He didn't sound ticked off," Copper said, and glanced at Joey.

"I'm told Keeper doesn't lose his temper. He's always very calm and doesn't shout or argue, but he's very keen with a knife, and that companion of his, Tiger, is not one to mess with. She doesn't lose her temper either."

"How d'you know all this?"

"I listen. Pink was told to go elsewhere, just like you. But

253

then he went back again and then again. The last time he went with Knife and three others. Now he's dead, Knife got his hand cut off, and him and his three pals are all being cared for by the state and county." Joey sighed. "Probably for a very long time. Copper, you're going to have to get a better game plan. Keeper has control. He has for over fifteen years, I'm told, and I think he might have an in with the cops."

"You think he's one of them?"

"Nah," Joey said, and shook his head. "Keeper does too many things a cop couldn't get away with. Not if they wanted things to stand up in court. Of course, Pink don't need no court."

"So you think going into the city center is not a good idea."

"Let me ask you, how many customers you think you'll get there? Two, three, a dozen?" Joey asked, and stared at the paper. "You don't see anyone livin' in the alleys, so where do they live? And how many street fighters do you think Keeper has with him? You're a smart man, Copper. You do the math. If you think you can make a profit after you hire enough people to break Keeper, go for it. But I might think twice, myself. A live dealer working in another part of town might be better than another dead one in the vacant city center."

"Yeah," Copper said, fingering the arm of the bench and then slapping it, "but Mr. H paid me to remove Keeper! It's either Keeper or it's Copper. One or t'other gets removed, and I say it's Keeper. He won't 'spect a dealer comin' after him. And Mr. H can do what he wants after that."

Keeper and His Tiger continues in

Book 3, *The trap.*

Glossary

Characters:

-A-

Abby — Daughter of Cathy (Lynx). Seven years old.

-B-

Bennett, Dave — Owner of a well-known and respected paving company located in a Chesterfield suburb, Briar's Green.

Bennett, Tom — Son of Dave Bennett. Stacy's latest boyfriend.

Betty — Mike Hammersmith's secretary at Boster, Lange and Hammersmith Designs.

Billie Mattis — See, Mattis, Billie.

Billy Carson — See Carson, Billy.

Boster, Carl — Partner in Boster, Lange and Hammersmith Renovation and Design Consulting Company.

Butch — An undercover cop helping in the City Center.

Butler, Sid — Owner of The Streetcar Diner.

Butler, Mary — Sid Butler's mother. Sister of Dorothy Hawke.

-C-

Carson, Billy — 31 year old homeless man. Has worked as a dishwasher and scullery man at The Streetcar Diner for seventeen years.

Copper — Streetwise drug dealer. Competitor of Pink's. Tries to sell drugs in the city center after Pink died.

-D-

Davis, Lori	26 year old, blonde woman, Accountant for Swaggard's Drugstore at Main and Branch Water Street. Long-time friend of Billie Mattis.
Diner Staff, Streetcar	Sid Butler – Owner and Head Cook
	Billy – General Scullery duties – Sid's background assistant
	Angie – Dining Room Manager and Head Waitress
	Julie – Waitress and Counter Attendant
	Carole – Waitress
	Melony – Order Organizer
	Niles – Assistant Cook
	Kevin – Assistant Cook
	Ned – Assistant Dishwasher
Donna	Frederick Westman's secretary at Westman Associates.

-F-

Filton, Grier	An Executive officer at the First State Bank and Trust. Billy's financial advisor.
Fowler, Gilbert	Sandy's college boyfriend. Medical Grad School student studying Neurological Medicine.

-G-

George, Rebecca	25 year old, brunette woman, the Assistant Curator at the City's Arts and Culture Museum. Friend of Billie Mattis. Aka, Becky or Beck.
Gibson, Walter	Attorney specializing in Business Law. Billy's personal Legal Council.

GC — General Contractor. The lead contractor on a construction job. Often referred to as the General.

-H-

Hammersmith, Mike — Principal partner and founder of Boster, Lange and Hammersmith Renovation and Design Consulting Company.

Hawke, William Carson III — Son of W. C. Hawke II and Dorothy (Dottie) Hawke (both mudered).

Herb — One of Mike Hammersmith's henchmen. A mean sort.

Homeless People — Department Store 'Street People' & their '(Street name)'

Billy (Keeper)

Max (Stretch) and Mindy (Cat)

Todd (Hammer)

Cathy** (Lynx), daughter Abby

Russell (Mace) and Barbara (Pigeon), son Ernest

Paul (Ferret*) and Donna (Mouse*), son Richard

Buddy (Falcon) and Jane (Sparrow*), son Rusty

Curt (Cutter) and Judy (Owl)

Josh (Red)

Randal (Spear)

Junior (Ditto)

* have a talent for hearing what's happening on the streets.

** Cathy's maiden name was Nikleson, married to and abandoned by Clark Jefferson.

-J-

Joey	One of Mike Hammersmith's henchmen.
June	Contracts Administrator at Westman Associates.

-K-

Keeper	The street name of a homeless man that has protected a number of blocks and properties in the City Center. Tiger's squeeze.
Kelly, Chase	32 year old owner of a Medical Supply business. Volunteers at the Crescent Street soup kitchen.

-L-

Lange, Robert	Partner in Boster, Lange and Hammersmith Renovation and Design Consulting Company.
Lawrence, Blake	Billie's recent ex-boyfriend. A con artist with a bad temper.
Leonard, The Knife	Street-wise, self-proclaimed 'exterminator' known for removing two-legged problems for a price.
Lori Davis	See Davis, Lori

-M-

Majors, Stacy	26 year old brunette woman. Works as a sales clerk and stocker at Pages Bookstore. Friend of Billie Mattis. Dating Tom Bennett.
Markins, Jack	Son of Billie's parent's long-time friends. Fiancé of Katie Biggens

Mattis, Billie	Wilhelmina Georgiana Mattis, a red haired woman, 27 year old daughter of Bob and Maggie Mattis. Works for Boster, Lange and Hammersmith Real Estate Developers and Renovations Consultants. Graduate with Master's degree in Business and Business Law (non-Barred). One older sister, Sandra, living away.
Mattis, Sandy	aka Sandra Mattis. The 30 year old daughter of Bob and Maggie Mattis; Billie's sister. Studying to become a Doctor in Pediatrics.
Mattis, Bob and Maggie	Robert (Bob) and Margaret (Maggs, Maggie), parents of Sandy and Billie. Owners and operators of a viable horse ranching business.
Maxie	Street vendor selling flowers on the north side of St. Charles Street, across from the park nick-named "The Forest."
Mitchell	Frederick Westman's 'go for' person.
-N-	
Nolan, Detective	A Chesterfield city police detective. A friend of Billy Carson.
-P-	
Pink	Street-wise drug dealer with his eye on the Chesterfield's City Center to expand his area of business.
-Q-	
Quinn, Hannah	A local socialite woman, once engaged to Mike Hammersmith in his younger days.

-R-

Rebecca (Becky), George	See George, Rebecca

-S-

Simmy	Street vendor that has a newsstand business near the west side of City Center.
Stacy Majors	See Majors, Stacy

-T-

Tiger	Keeper's squeeze.

-W-

Westman, Collin	Daughter of Nancy and Frederick Westman. No siblings. Student at Michigan State University, East Lansing, Michigan, studying to become a veterinarian.
Westman, Frederick	Real Estate Developer. Daughter Collin. Ex-wife Nancy, divorced sixteen years.
Westman, Nancy	Frederick Westman's ex-wife.

Places and Things:

-B-

Baily	A small farm town NE of Chesterfield. Mike Hammersmith's sister lives there.

-C-

Chesterfield	A middle sized, sprawling mid-west city in the United States. The city had an eighteen block City Center core with high rise buildings, the tallest being fourteen stories. The city is serviced by a regional airport and local and interstate bus services.
CR Associates	Circular Reference, Subsidiary of Pastoric Group – General Manager: John Collier.

Custer's	An eating and drinking establishment located in a strip-mall on the NE corner of Lakota and Fourth Street East.

-D-

Daisy's	A Wine Bar, NW of City Center located at Emmit and Fifth Street West.
Danny's Steakhouse	Distinguished Steak and Beverage Restaurant on Calvin and Duberry. Owned by Danny Willis and his three daughters, Lydia the youngest, Monica in the middle and Nikki (Nicole) the oldest.
Duckard's Department Store	Deserted department store building in a shared block in City Center. Situated at the corner of Second and Baker St

-F-

Forest, The	A city park in west Chesterfield bordered by St. Charles Street on the north, St. Anne on the south, and by Fifth and Sixth Street West on the east and west sides.

-K-

Kelly and Lloyd Architects	Chicago based Architectural Firm specializing in large commercial renovation projects. Owner: Jim Donaldson
	Site review architects: Bob Dawson, Joseph, Jane, Lucy

-M-

Marquee Cocktail Lounge	A modern downtown cocktail lounge on the NW corner of Main Street and St. Anne.

-O-

Olive and Onion	A Martini Bar at David and Twelfth Street West.

-P-

Pages Book Store	Book store on Main between St. Anne and Arapaho. Stacy works here.
Pastoric Group	Investment group holding and protecting W. C. Hawke's assets. Controlled by W. C. Hawke III and daily operations managed by Gregory (Greg) Madison.

-S-

Streetcar Diner, The	A shiny, metal-look diner on the west side of City Center. Owner: Sid Butler.
Swaggard's Drug Store	Drug store on Kiowa and 7th Street West. Lori works as an accountant and general clerk / stocker here.

-T-

Tri-Funds	Subsidiary of Pastoric Group.

-W-

Westman Associates	A land development and construction company owned by Frederick Westman.
Whiskey's Bar and Grille	A rustic casual dining bar and grille on the NE corner of Blackfoot and Sixth Street, two blocks south of "The Forest."

Books by Aidan Red:

Keeper and His Tiger
(After living homeless to find his parents murderer...)
Book 1: An Unexpected Complication
Book 2: Deadly Undercurrents
Book 3: The Trap

Paladin Shadows Series
Terran Assignment
Book 1: Things Are Not As They Seem
Book 2: When Luck Is Not Enough
Book 3: Fate Has A Different Idea
Terran Recruits
Book 4: In the Wake of Chaos
Book 5: Terran Talents Join Forces
Book 6: New Rules of Engagement
Operation Retribution
Book 7: The Training Phase
Book 8: Taking the Fight Off-World
Book 9: Luring the Prince Into the Open
Garda Nua
Book 10: The Proliferation of Talent
Book 11: When A Planet Is Stolen
Book 12: Right Does Not Ask Permission
Assignment: Casha-Six
Book 13: No Warning
Book 14: The Best Laid Plans
Book 15: A Change of Heart?

Fearin' the Banshee

More Books by Aidan Red

Eight's Warning
A West's Ghost Ranch Trilogy
(A tale in the world of high octane aviation fuel and restored warbirds)
Book 1: The Past Hunts
Book 2: The Past Attacks
Book 3: The Price of Escape

About the Author

Aidan Red's passion for aviation and aircraft design, engineering, and a deep interest in space and space travel go back many years. An avid reader from an early age, Aidan, with great trepidation, ventured into the world of writing during college. With real world experience in business aviation, Aidan's creative side led him to create an alternate world where the beautiful Riggs Valley was born and Shara's life became chronicled in his epic science fiction series, Paladin Shadows.

Paladin Shadows consists of the five triptychs (three-part works), *Terran Assignment, Terran Recruits, Operation Retribution, Garda Nua* and *Assignment: Casha-Six*. In between the Paladin triptychs, Aidan has penned two, three book series, *Keeper and his Tiger,* and *Eight's Warning,* a West's Ghost Ranch Trilogy, and a novel, *Fearin' the Banshee.*

The unpublished books in his various series are scheduled for release on a regular basis in the coming months.

You can visit

www.RedsInkandQuill.com or

www.AidanRedBooks.com

for more information on books published by Aidan Red books and where to purchase them.